MW00893449

It Could Be Worse

Also by Lester Wertheimer

AT SEA

Being an Eccentric Voyage of Discovery
In the Company of Misfits, Rogues, and Vagabonds

It Could Be Worse

Or How I Barely Survived My Youth

A NOVEL

Lester Wertheimer

iUniverse, Inc.
New York Bloomington

It Could Be Worse

Or How I Barely Survived My Youth

Copyright © 2009 by Lester Wertheimer

All rights reserved. No part of this book may be used or reproduced by any means, graphic, electronic, or mechanical, including photocopying, recording, taping or by any information storage retrieval system without the written permission of the publisher except in the case of brief quotations embodied in critical articles and reviews.

iUniverse books may be ordered through booksellers or by contacting:

iUniverse
1663 Liberty Drive
Bloomington, IN 47403
www.iuniverse.com
1-800-Authors (1-800-288-4677)

This is a work of fiction. All of the characters, names, incidents, organizations, and dialogue in this novel are either the products of the author's imagination or are used fictitiously.

Because of the dynamic nature of the Internet, any Web addresses or links contained in this book may have changed since publication and may no longer be valid. The views expressed in this work are solely those of the author and do not necessarily refl ect the views of the publisher, and the publisher hereby disclaims any responsibility for them.

ISBN: 978-0-595-49785-0 (pbk)
ISBN: 978-0-595-61245-1 (cloth)
ISBN: 978-0-595-49820-8 (ebk)

Printed in the United States of America

In loving memory of the original
Sam and Jenny

Contents

CHAPTER ONE

In The Beginning

The first time I felt a girl's breast was shortly before my fifteenth birthday. I was sitting in the balcony of the Fox Wilshire Theater on a summery Saturday afternoon, and the small breast beneath my right hand belonged to Anita Kornfeld, who, at that moment, appeared oblivious to the sexual attention being paid. Anita and I were school friends, and this was not the first time such an attempt was made. Two weeks earlier, while sitting in the same balcony, I carefully put my right arm behind Anita, and slowly worked my hand down along her right side. Eureka! I struck what I believed was pay dirt. However, after fifteen minutes or so I realized, to my utter consternation, I was fondling Anita's right elbow. I felt both disappointment and relief; disappointment that I missed the object of my carefully contrived maneuver, but relief in realizing that breasts didn't have sharp, elbow-like bones.

When, on this second attempt, I actually scored a hit, I completely lost interest in the Betty Grable musical we were watching. I could not have told you who was in love with whom or which suitor Miss Grable would end up with. When my hand found its target, and my advance to second base was confirmed, I felt a rapturous thrill—not unlike an electric shock—travel through my entire body. Anita, on the other hand, seemed completely unaware that she was providing me with an unforgettable thrill I would remember for the rest of my life.

1

During this entire episode, and not before the movie ended, was there a word between us. At that point I asked, "Would you like to go to Curry's and get a milk shake? My treat."

I don't know why I said that; I didn't particularly want to spend more time with Anita—unless, of course, it was in a darkened theater. Okay, I know that sounds selfish and uncaring; but let's face it, Anita and I weren't actually involved romantically. We'd never even kissed. I would characterize our activity as youthful exploration; or, to use a phrase of the day, fooling around. As far as I knew, if you were just fooling around, normal relationship rules didn't apply. But, no question about it, my invitation was motivated by guilt.

"Sure, I'd like that," she answered.

There was an awkward, self-conscious silence while we sipped our drinks. And then it was time to go home.

"Thanks for the milk shake," she said. "Maybe we can do this again some time." And then she gave me a peck on the cheek, turned quickly, and walked home.

As I headed in the opposite direction I wondered what was going on. Were we boyfriend and girlfriend now? I mean, I liked Anita, she was nice enough, but I didn't really want the responsibility of a girlfriend. I didn't want the obligation of regular phone calls, passing mushy notes, or having to walk anybody home from school. What I wanted was more of that incredible excitement I'd just experienced in the balcony. But what did Anita want? Was she as excited as I to be fooling around? Did girls even feel the same sort of thrill? I had no idea. But what I did know was this: Anita liked me. I mean, you got to admit, she let me get to second base, and I hadn't even rounded first.

One week later, same scene, different movie, but this time Anita wore a blouse that was low-cut in front. Now I didn't know what to think. Was this an invitation? I couldn't be sure. I felt like someone who missed the first few lectures in Basic Relationship 101. Why wasn't there a handbook I could consult? I put my arm around Anita, and a half hour later my hand was inside the blouse. I could not believe my luck; Anita was not wearing a bra! As my hand covered her breast, I kept thinking, what a wondrous thrill! Here I am with my hand on Anita Kornfeld's bare breast! Everything before was child's play; this was the real deal, and I hoped it would never end. But when an usher with a flashlight approached, it did end.

"Darn usher," exclaimed Anita.

Aha! She did know what was going on. And then we shared a nervous laugh.

But why am I telling you this? What makes me think you would care about something that happened so long ago? Well, this is intended to be a factual story, and I don't think anything should be held back. I intend to reveal every detail of my earliest experiences and convey the truth, as I remember it, no matter how shocking or embarrassing. Anita Kornfeld's breast, if you'll forgive the allusion, was just the tip of the iceberg.

While on the subject of truth, I'd like to correct a misunderstanding that existed for years. It has to do with my place of birth. One day, while in a facetious mood, I claimed I was born in a log cabin in the Midwest. I'm not sure what I was thinking, but I suppose in some odd way I was trying to elicit compassion. You know, if you're from a humble background, a Lincolnesque sort of fellow, folks will think you've overcome tremendous odds to get where you are today.

"Wow, imagine that, born a log cabin; and just look at you now. What a guy!"

Sorry to say, the log cabin story was totally fabricated. My background may have been modest, but a log cabin was not a part of it. I was, however, born in Chicago, which *is* in the Midwest. To be exact, it was at the Norwegian American Hospital. It's not because we were Norwegian; that just happened to be the name of the hospital. In fact, my mother came from Poland, and my father was born in a part of Austria-Hungary that later became Czechoslovakia—but more about them later.

I was born at the respectable hour of nine o'clock one Thursday evening in September and weighed in at about nine-and-a-half pounds, which was pretty hefty, according to Dr. Flugelman, the attending physician. Despite my bulky size, my mother always claimed that I was "an easy birth". I have no idea what she meant by that. I once picked up a nine-pound watermelon in the market and wondered how on earth something that size could pass through a human body. I figured my mother had no recollection of the discomfort she suffered or, possibly, was so completely anesthetized she could have expelled a baby rhinoceros and not known it.

I was named Peter, after a distant, dead cousin much admired by my family. What the original Peter did to generate such admiration remains a mystery to this day, but I assume he was important enough to have his name perpetuated. I've always liked the name Peter, and I feel that among the credits due my parents was choosing a name that went well with the family name, Newman. Now, for the sake of accuracy, you should know that Newman was not the family name in the old country. Actually, the name was—and this is no joke—Schwartzenvogelmacher; but that was changed within hours of my father's arrival in New York. The officer at Ellis Island had considerable difficulty with that lengthy name—and that wasn't his only problem. He was unable to distinguish that my widowed grandmother was a woman. If you saw a photo of her, you would appreciate his confusion.

My paternal grandmother, Bertha by name, was a large woman with a deep voice and hair cut short, in the manner of Gertrude Stein. She wore mannish clothes, including hiking boots, and generally appeared in public wearing an Alpine hat topped off with a peacock feather. In addition, she had the faintest hint of a moustache just above her upper lip. As she strode through the cavernous halls of Ellis Island, wrapped in a full-length wool cape and carrying a walking stick, she could easily have passed for an eccentric burgomaster from a mountain village in Austria. If ever there was a matriarch that could be easily mistaken for a patriarch, she was it.

So, as the story goes, the Ellis Island officer said to my grandmother, who understood very little English, "You're making a new life in this country, so how about starting off with a new name? After all, you'll be a new man, so I suggest 'New-man'. Get it?"

She didn't quite get it, but why not, she thought; Schwartzenvogelmacher had always been a mouthful, whereas Newman contained a concise two syllables. In addition, it had a nice ring to it and sounded, to her immigrant ears, very Yankee Doodle Dandy. So, she concluded, why not? It could be worse. From that moment on, the Schwartzenvogelmachers were history, and the family proudly entered their new country as the All-American Newmans. An old-world family friend settled in Chicago and wrote glowing letters about her experience. That's all the incentive the Newman clan needed to follow in her footsteps. Thus, my recently widowed grandmother and her six children proceeded by rail to Chicago.

The Newman children, consisting of two girls and four boys, were between the ages of one and fourteen. My father, Samuel Alexander Newman, was nearly three years old at the time and next to the youngest in age. He did not speak a word of English, but then again, he rarely spoke any language. Some family members assumed Sam was retarded, but, as they would later learn, he was perfectly capable of speaking but chose to remain silent. Eventually, when there was a need to express himself, fully formed sentences flowed from his mouth, and, thereafter, it was difficult to shut him up.

The Newman family rented an apartment on the northwest side of the city, and, at the appropriate age, each child was enrolled in the local public elementary school. My father and his siblings received the finest public education offered, and his graduation from the eighth grade occurred exactly two months after his bar mitzvah. Both events marked the end of my father's formal education.

"It's time to go to work now," said his mother. "Dave, Arthur, and Julia already have jobs—and we're counting on your help to support the family."

Young Sam Newman held a series of odd jobs as he continued to search for a profitable lifelong path. He delivered newspapers, worked in a tobacco shop, was apprenticed to a furrier, a jeweler, and a photographer, and was employed in at least a half-dozen other occupations. None of these pursuits, however, offered much satisfaction. There was, in addition, a serious obstacle to success that would plague Sam throughout his life; and that was a persistent sense of insecurity. Sam could not escape the irrational fear that he didn't quite have what it takes to be successful. Although he was capable and generally exhibited a façade of self-confidence, beneath that image was, essentially, a frightened young man.

At some point during his early years, Sam determined that if he couldn't be the boldest or the brightest, he could certainly strive to be the best liked. Having the approval of others not only allayed his feelings of anxiety, but as his popularity grew he developed a more positive self-image. Thus, being well liked became Sam's ultimate aspiration. Clearly, he believed, one's self-worth was based on other people's perceptions.

Being well liked was a commendable goal, but it often made Sam a target of those who would exploit this superficial need. He knew when advantage of him was being taken, but he figured, what the hell, why make a fuss? I don't need any more enemies. Thus, he generally avoided controversy, rarely defended his true beliefs, and most often, internalized hostile feelings. On the other hand, almost without exception, everybody thought that young Sam Newman was one hell of a swell guy.

Early on, Sam discovered that having a sense of humor was indispensable to being popular. He possessed a natural wit, as did most of his imme diate family. Without a sense of humor how could they have survived the pogroms in the old country, that interminable steerage-class odyssey that brought them here, and their new life that was more bewildering than anything they had ever faced before?

Sam acquired a few one-liners from vaudeville, and with no embarrassment whatever, he would say something like, "I got this dog for my girlfriend. In my opinion it was a great trade." Or perhaps, "You want four suits for a dollar? Buy a deck of cards."

I know, I know—these ancient jokes were unbelievably hackneyed; but even more amazing was the *chutzpah* it took to use them at virtually the drop of a hat.

"Lose the one-liners," suggested his brother Art. "They make you sound like a nitwit."

"But they get laughs," said Sam. "You know, the other day some people at the office asked why I missed work last week. I said, 'I was in bed with 102'. Then I paused and said, 'Boy, was it crowded!' Well, they just about fell off their chairs laughing. They think I'm a riot."

"You *are* clever," said his brother, "but relax—you're trying too hard."

Little did Sam know then how his future would unfold, or how valuable and comforting a sense of humor would be. He was about to embark on a series of questionable ventures, and his survival depended on his ability to laugh through the misfortunes that lay ahead.

CHAPTER TWO

The Majestic

As a young adult, Sam Newman realized that success in business required specific skills that his eighth-grade education failed to provide. Thus, he enrolled in night school classes at the Myron Liebowitz School of Business Practices. He learned typing, shorthand, basic finance, and the principles of accounting. He completed his studies after a few months and received a Certificate of Competence signed and personally presented to him by Myron Liebowitz.

"You're ready to conquer the world," said Liebowitz. "I have nothing more to teach you. Go forth with confidence, and never forget: the Myron Liebowitz School of Business Practices is behind you one-hundred percent." Whatever *that* meant.

With his Certificate and a pat on the back, Sam entered the world of business. His first job turned out to be a plum. He was hired by the H. J. Weissberger Real Estate Company, where he became, within a matter of months, H. J.'s personal secretary. The job was prestigious, the salary was more than adequate, and after a short while, Sam was basking in the admiration and respect of his superiors and fellow workers.

But prestige, money, and respect, were apparently not enough for Sam. Even if he worked for John D. Rockefeller and earned double his current salary he would not have been satisfied. Sam believed that working for others was a dead end; he had much grander ideas. His dream was to be his own boss, an entrepreneur, and he wanted to work within the realm of entertainment. Sam, quite simply, was enamored with show business. Hardly a week went by without his attending some play, musical performance, or vaudeville show. He had no pretensions about becoming a performer, but he knew that somewhere along the periphery of the entertainment world was a place he longed to hang his hat.

It was the Jazz Age, the early part of the Roaring Twenties, and silent movies were all the rage. Sam saw them all—from Harold Lloyd and Buster Keaton comedies to dramas with vamps like Pola Negri and Clara Bow. He could think of no greater pleasure than to sit in a darkened theater and be magically transported to another time and place. One day, a daring idea struck him like a lightning bolt. *That's it, he thought—why not? Why the hell not? I'll buy a theater of my own and watch movies any time I want.* His bright idea was not particularly rational or, for that matter, even well thought out. But Sam was a dreamer, not a man anchored by the shackles of reality.

He discussed his business plan with his siblings, and once they realized he was serious, they were unanimous in their opposition.

"What kind of lunatic scheme is that?" asked his brother, Dave. "This is crazy talk."

"Look," said his sister Julia, "you're acting like a *nudnick.* If you want to throw away your money, that's your business. But why take such a foolish gamble?"

Even his normally quiet brother, Arthur had a comment. "You realize, of course, you don't actually have to own a theater to see a movie. You want to go to a movie? Great, here's twenty-five cents. Now stop already with the nonsense."

Sam Newman was undaunted by his family's criticism. He had a dream that would not die, and he pursued it like a man possessed. He had a small nest egg and figured he could go into debt for the rest of the necessary funds. He had left his job with the Weissberger Real Estate Company nearly a year earlier, but he remained on good terms with his former employer, whose advice he now sought.

"H. J.," he began, "I'm planning to go into the movie business, and I thought you might help me locate a theater. What do you think?"

"I think it's a lousy idea; you'd have to be crazy to own a theater. The business is too risky; forget it. If you need a change in your life, come back and work for me. Things haven't been the same since you left."

"No thanks, H. J., I've got this dream to own a theater, and I've got to see it through."

"I'll see what I can do," answered his former boss, "but I think you're making a big mistake. Movies could be here today and gone tomorrow, but real estate is forever."

The coming Great Depression would soon prove him wrong on both counts.

Three weeks later Weissberger located a small legitimate playhouse that was for sale on Halsted Street. He also introduced Sam to a banker who was willing to provide a loan for its purchase. Within two months Samuel Alexander Newman, together with the First National Bank of Chicago, were proud owners of the seventy-five-seat Majestic Theater. The building was anything but majestic, but it had possibilities. With hard work and some minor remodeling, it became a functional and reasonably attractive silent movie theater. By now, Sam was up to his eyeballs in debt, but for the first time in his life, he was a deliriously happy entrepreneur.

Sam was now twenty-four years old and still lived at home, which was not unusual in those days. Most young people continued to live with their families until they were married or the last of their relatives was dead. Nevertheless, Sam had a full social life. He saw friends, attended theater performances, and dated a variety of young women. Sam was reasonably popular with women, but he could not imagine living the rest of his life with any of those he dated. Then along came Jenny.

Three months after purchasing the Majestic, Sam was introduced to an attractive flapper named Jenny Kramarsky. He was struck dumb by her beauty and wit, and he knew at once this was the woman for him. Jenny typified the modern young woman of the twenties. She was slender, fashionable, and wore her dark hair bobbed, as was the current style. Jenny knew she was clever and attractive, and thus, she radiated great poise and self-assurance. She was, in fact, so popular and desirable Sam feared he might be reaching beyond his grasp. The familiar self-doubts reappeared. Why would a girl like Jenny, who could have anyone she wanted, go for a guy like him? But he was driven by desire and felt the risk of rejection was worth the reward.

"How about having dinner with me some evening?" suggested Sam.

"I'm pretty busy most evenings," answered Jenny.

"Is lunch better?"

"I usually skip lunch."

"Breakfast?"

"My—you're persistent, aren't you?"

"We don't have to eat at all," said Sam. "How about going to the theater with me? Or a movie, or a museum, or a walk along the lake?"

"You're not going to give up, are you?"

"Not until you say yes."

Jenny was fascinated by Sam's determination. Three days later they finally had dinner together. The next evening they went to the theater, and on the third night they dropped by the Majestic and laughed through a few Charlie Chaplin films.

Sam might have been surprised to learn that, from the start, Jenny really liked him. He had a slender build, attractive features, and a full head of black hair that was brushed straight back and parted precisely down the middle, in the manner of Rudolph Valentino. Jenny thought he was sweet and caring, and she was charmed by his delightful sense of humor. But— and this was a big "but"—he was *so* short.

"I don't know how to say this," began Jenny. "I like you, I like you a lot, but I also love dancing. I go dancing three or four times a week; it's a huge part of my life. My partners are never shorter than five-foot seven or eight. But you're about five-foot-three. And, forgive me for saying so, but you're also a bit of a *klutz* on the dance floor. I know this sounds trivial and a bit callous, but for me, these are serious problems."

"What do you want me to do?" asked Sam. "I am what I am. Maybe I could learn to dance better, but I don't know how I can learn to be taller."

Sadly, a few inches of height kept this otherwise compatible couple apart for nearly three months. In an act of desperation, Sam consulted a shoe expert, who prescribed lifts for his shoes. He was suddenly elevated to a respectable, if not perfect height of five-foot-six. He also took a few dance lessons, unbeknown to the object of his affection. When the suddenly towering Sam showed up for a date one night, the delight radiated from Jenny's eyes.

"Well, hello, big boy," she said. "You remind me of someone I once dated, but you're a lot taller. Tell me, can you dance?"

They danced all that night, and the newly tutored Sam proceeded to whirl Jenny around the floor with extraordinary elegance. By the end of the evening all resistance evaporated. Jenny realized how superficial her objections had been. Finally and unquestionably, she knew that Samuel Alexander Newman, five-foot three though he may have been, was the man for her.

There was a bit more to it, of course, but Jenny was only vaguely aware that her genuine attraction to Sam was based on reasons deep in her psyche. Jenny's mother was the third wife of old Mr. Kramarsky, my grandfather, who outlived two previous wives. This prolific man produced twenty-four children among his three partners. Kramarsky was nearly sixty years old when Jenny was born, and he was approaching senility. Thus, Jenny grew up without the comfort and guidance of a dependable man. She recognized in Sam the qualities she yearned for, and she found little reason to look further. Two months later, they eloped to Iron River, Michigan. They honeymooned for two full days, and then returned to an apartment in Chicago they had rented a week earlier.

From the beginning of their involvement Sam felt that his love for Jenny was greater than her love for him. Most marriages were that way, he figured, and most other relationships were as well. If anything happened to him, he thought, Jenny would be sad, but he had little doubt she would get on with her life. On the other hand, he was convinced that life without Jenny would not be worth living. He might just as well throw himself under a streetcar. Jenny sensed these feelings in Sam and so did everything possible to reassure him. She loved him, she declared, and there was no way she would ever leave him. But all the assurances in the world did not entirely allay Sam's neurotic fears. He would forever go through life with the low-grade, nagging feeling that he just didn't deserve such a wonderful woman.

Jenny was the perfect wife for Sam. She cooked and baked and kept their apartment scrupulously clean. Far more important to Sam, however, was that Jenny developed into the perfect ticket seller, theater usher, and record keeper of the day's receipts. She became an indispensable partner in the ownership and management of the Majestic

Theater. Not only that, Jenny had an uncanny ability to anticipate what movies would have the greatest success, and she was rarely wrong. One of their early disagreements concerned two competing westerns.

"I'm certain of this: *Riders of the Purple Sage* is going to be far more successful than *Tumbleweeds*. William S. Hart is getting too old for this sort of thing, and Tom Mix has far more ability and charm; audiences are crazy about him."

"Hart has been a star for years," answered Sam. "Do you really believe his popularity is an accident? The guy's fans are as loyal as they come."

"His time is passed," persisted Jenny. "Trust me, Tom Mix is going to make us big money."

As it turned out—once again—Jenny's assessment was right on target.

Life for the Newmans was comfortable. There was never quite enough money, of course, but no one they knew had much more. They could afford the essentials, and entertainment was available, for free, any evening of the week and twice a day on Saturdays and Sundays. Then, quite suddenly, everything changed. It was 1927, and the first, feature-length talking picture, *The Jazz Singer*, made its debut. It was an astonishing box-office sensation.

Al Jolson, an immensely popular singing star from vaudeville, appeared in *The Jazz Singer* as Jakie Rabinowitz, son of a fourth-generation Cantor. The father is grooming his son to take his place in the synagogue, but Jakie prefers modern music. Jakie Rabinowitz turns into the jazz singer Jack Robin, and, at the film's climax, he is forced to choose between devotion to his family and an opening night opportunity on Broadway. What a dilemma! By the end of the film there is not a dry eye in the house—nor is there a dry eye among silent movie house owners. *The Jazz Singer*, single-handedly, signaled the end of silent films.

The Majestic Theater had no sound system. Sam never thought it was necessary, and there wasn't enough money to purchase and install one, even if he had wanted to. Within months, the SS Majestic began to sink and all hands aboard seemed destined to go down with the ship. Jenny, however, refused to be a victim.

"Look," she said, "the Majestic is dying, and if we don't do something, we're going to die along with it. We've got to face reality."

"What do you want me to do? We still owe the bank a fortune."

"Sell the place. Let's get what we can and move on. We're going to need a new plan and a new job, especially now that I'm pregnant."

"What?" exclaimed Sam. "You're having a baby?"

She put her arms around him and said softly, "No, sweetheart, *we're* having a baby."

And that's how Jenny let Sam know that my older brother Alan was about to make his appearance and change their lives forever.

The next day Sam contacted his ex-employer, H. J. Weissberger, who originally found the Majestic, and told him he was considering selling the place.

"I may be able to help you," said H. J. "A guy was in here the other day looking for just that kind of investment. What'll you take for it?"

"Have the guy make an offer," said Sam. "I'll work with him." He already knew he would probably accept whatever price the buyer offered. He would not disappoint Jenny.

Two days later a nicely dressed gentleman by the name of Gunter Hermann Schmitz appeared to inspect his prospective investment. Schmitz was somber, a bit grim, and he had a nervous tic that affected his left eye. He said little during the inspection tour, until he asked to view the boiler and other mechanical equipment.

"They're located in the basement," said Sam, "and access is down a wooden ladder."

"Not a problem," said Schmitz. "Let's go."

The two men climbed down the ladder to the small basement, and that's when Schmitz suddenly pulled a small revolver out of his coat pocket.

"What the hell?" asked a confused Sam. "What's going on?"

"So you thought you'd screw me, you dirty kike. Thought you'd give me a real going over, didn't you? Isn't that just like you penny-pinching Jews?" The tic in Schmitz's left eye suddenly began to flutter like a trapped bird.

"What do you mean, you crazy maniac? We haven't even talked money yet."

Sam instantly had an irrational thought: *what the hell am I saying? That kind of name-calling is liable to make this guy mad.* But Schmitz needed no further incentive; he seemed to be on a fanatical mission.

"Let's talk this over," pleaded Sam. "And for Christ's sake, stop pointing that gun at me!" He was terrified beyond belief, but now he was angry as well. How dare this idiotic anti-Semite threaten him? If I only had a baseball bat, Sam thought, I'd give this guy a *klop* on his *kop* he'd never forget. On the other hand—maybe I should just make a run for it. Fight or flight, that ancient, deep-rooted dilemma suddenly made its appearance. But for a peace-loving man like Sam Newman, it was no dilemma at all; fight never stood a chance.

Schmitz seemed oblivious, as if in a dream. With a crazed expression on his face he suddenly fired a shot that missed Sam by inches. The echo resounded in the small basement like a kettledrum gone mad. The shot pierced a steam pipe, and Sam used the diversion of the escaping steam to race up the ladder with the speed of an Olympian. Before reaching the floor above, he felt a burning sensation in the calf of his left leg. Without stopping, Sam limped, bleeding, to the drugstore adjacent to the Majestic, and then he passed out.

When the police arrived at the Majestic Theater, they found Gunter Hermann Schmitz sitting up against the concrete basement wall with a bullet through his temple. Jenny rushed to the hospital where Sam's leg was being bandaged.

"Oh Sam," she said, hugging him tightly. "What a terrible thing to happen."

"You're a pretty lucky guy," said the doctor. "The bullet hit nothing but flesh, and it made a clean exit. I figure you should be walking again in a week or two."

"Yeah," said Sam, "bad luck. But I suppose it could be worse." And then stating the obvious, "I guess the sale to Schmitz is pretty much out of the question."

An article on page nineteen of the Chicago Tribune two days later reported the following:

THEATER OWNER SHOT BY SUSPECTED ANARCHIST

Samuel A. Newman, owner of the Majestic Theater on Halsted Street, was shot last Tuesday and seriously wounded by suspected anarchist, Gunter Hermann Schmitz. Indicating an interest in purchasing the theater, Schmitz was in the process of inspecting the mechanical room, when he pulled out a gun and shot the owner. Police arrived thirty minutes later and discovered that Schmitz had taken his own life. A spokesman for the Presbyterian Hospital advises that Mr. Newman will make a complete recovery.

Exactly six weeks after the shooting incident, the Majestic Theater was sold to a small investment company. After the loan and outstanding bills were paid, the Newmans had a profit of nearly two hundred dollars. The day the deal became final an elated Sam and his three-month pregnant wife put on their dancing shoes and went out on the town.

CHAPTER THREE

The Little Florist Shop

One door closes and another one opens. As an unintended victim of modern times, Sam was now finished with show business. After a week or two, he characterized the sale of the Majestic as a blessing in disguise. Though he still enjoyed movies, he began to suspect that motion pictures might be a passing fancy. Thus, he rationalized the sale as "getting out while the getting was good". Didn't he have the two hundred bucks to prove it?

The next two years were difficult. Sam and Jenny were now parents, and between the noisy newcomer and Sam's continuous search for a career path, there were numerous sleepless nights in the Newman house. Sam worked at several odd jobs, and for a time, even returned to the H. J. Weissberger Real Estate Company. But the Great Depression was now descending over the country like a black cloud, and real estate activity was dwindling to a standstill. Buyers were scarce, and sellers were reluctant to let properties go at a substantial loss. Despite the bleak economic situation, Sam made a decision about his next venture that was as questionable as his judgment about the future of movies. With little forethought and no hint whatever to his patient wife, Sam bought a flower shop on Clark Street. The country was now mired in a serious economic struggle, and money was tighter than ever. Owning a flower shop during a depression seemed unrealistic at best and reckless at worst.

"How could you do this?" asked Jenny. "I thought we were a

partnership. Why didn't you at least say something so I could talk you out of this harebrained scheme? Tell me, Mister-Flower-Shop-Owner, who do you think is going to buy your flowers, when most people today don't have money to pay their rent?"

"I know this might seem like a crazy idea," Sam answered, "but trust me. I've always loved flowers, I'm good at working with them, and I know we're going to be okay."

The fact was, Sam did love flowers, and he had a creative side that yearned to be expressed. But Jenny's point was well taken; who needed flowers during a depression? The answer came soon after the official grand opening of the *Little Florist Shop on Clark Street*. Early one morning, a large man with a dark complexion entered the shop wearing a well-tailored black suit with white pinstripes, accented neatly by a black fedora and gray spats.

"What can I do for you, sir?" asked Sam.

The man looked around the shop apprehensively and then responded in a low voice.

"One of my close associates had an unexpected accident, and we're having a funeral this afternoon. Think ya can whip up a funeral wreath on such short notice?"

"Service is our specialty," said the congenial shop owner. "I can have the wreath ready by noon. Where do you want it delivered?"

At one o'clock that afternoon Sam carried the elaborate floral wreath into the chapel at Angelo's Family Mortuary on the city's west side. The wreath had the words "Ice Man" spelled out in white flowers, and this was placed next to an open casket containing the now inanimate body of Mario "Ice Man" Marini. Sam knew who it was immediately. He also noticed, sitting in the front row of the chapel, a veritable who's who of Chicago's criminal elite. If you walked into any post office in the city you would see these same faces staring back

IT COULD BE WORSE

at you from the "Wanted" posters on the wall. There was Johnny "Big Lips" Locasio, Tony "Gas Pipe" Scala, Al "The Executioner" Milano, and Salvatore "Fat Sally" Corallo. And these were just the ones Sam recognized. There were at least two dozen others in the chapel whose identities were a mystery, but whose line of work was obvious. Sam was sensible enough to avoid any sign of recognition or panic, but inside he was dying. What was he getting into, he wondered? That scene in the basement of the Majestic Theater abruptly came to mind, and Sam wondered if he should make a run for the exit. The wound inflicted by that madman Schmitz suddenly began to throb.

At this point, the man who came to the shop earlier that morning approached Sam and thanked him for providing such a spectacular wreath.

"Ya did a great job, Sammy, and the boss wants me to thank ya." And with that he pulled out a wad of bills, peeled off a fifty-dollar bill and handed it to Sam, who was prepared to charge his customary fee of three dollars.

"Sorry," said Sam, "I can't change a fifty."

"Forget it, Sammy-boy, keep the change. And if we need your services again, we'll be seein' ya. Count on it."

When Sam got home that night and told Jenny what happened and then showed her the fifty-dollar bill, she burst into tears. This was more money than Sam had ever earned in an entire week.

"Oh Sam," she said, "You are such a wonderful man. I love you."

During the next year or so, Sam and the Little Florist Shop on Clark Street somewhat reluctantly became the official flower shop of Chicago's most renowned gangsters. Nervous though he remained, Sam found consolation by sharing in the profits extorted by the thugs, bootleggers, and killers who constituted the lion's share of his clientele. But as Sam was quickly learning, when everything appears too good to be true, it invariably is. The Newmans' comfortable life was about to be disrupted again.

The St. Valentine's Day Massacre, which came to symbolize the violence of the Prohibition Era, had a profound effect on gangland activity in Chicago. On that memorable day devoted to love, seven members of Bugs Moran's gang were lined up against a brick wall in a warehouse and brutally machine-gunned to death. By coincidence, the warehouse was located just up the block from the Little Florist Shop on Clark Street. The likely culprit was a bootleg competitor of Moran by the name of Al Capone, but Capone was in Miami at the time and was never charged.

By this time there was considerable pressure on the Chicago Police Department. Crime had run rampant for years, and the public demanded change. A crackdown began with the intent of putting out of business several powerful gangs who ran the gambling tables, bootleg liquor clubs, and prostitution rings throughout Chicago. Some gangs picked up and moved to other cities, some went into hiding, and others disbanded. The devastating result for the Newmans was a sudden loss of their core business. Sales withered like week-old daffodils, and so, too, did their income.

"What are we going to do?" asked his anxious wife.

"I don't know," answered Sam. "I guess we've got to hang in there. We'll find a way. I know there'll be other customers."

But there were no other customers, except for the occasional youngster buying a corsage for his prom date. Just like the movie business before, nobody wanted what Sam was selling, and he soon became detached and despondent. He spent his days like Ferdinand the Bull, who in the popular story sat around most days just smelling the flowers; and the Little Florist Shop on Clark Street began to resemble a funeral parlor.

Several difficult months passed, and the Newmans' savings were about gone. They now had two small mouths to feed—I was born two years after Alan—and Jenny was seriously concerned about the family's future. Something had to be done.

"Sam," Jenny said one day, "my brothers are starting a new cellophane business. They need a salesman, and they thought you'd be perfect for the job. I think you should consider selling the florist shop and join them."

"But I love the flower shop; I'd really miss the place."

"The flower shop is dying. Last month It took in less than thirty dollars."

"Things will change. You've got to be patient. And anyway, what do I know about peddling cellophane?"

"What did you know about movies or the flower business? You're bright and charming and people love you. I'm sure you could sell an ice box to an Eskimo."

"I'll think about it," conceded Sam. But in his heart he knew Jenny was right. He was drowning and his brothers-in-law were throwing him a life ring. Still, it was painful to admit failure, and it was even more painful to see the disappointment in Jenny's face.

The Kramarsky brothers, Nathan and Daniel, adored their sister, and there was nothing they would not do for her. When she discussed the financial troubles she and Sam were having, they immediately agreed to offer Sam a job in their new Transparent Materials Company.

"But be careful," she advised, "Sam is depressed about giving up the flower shop, and he's particularly vulnerable these days. And whatever you do, don't mention this conversation. I don't want him to know I had anything to do with this."

A despondent Sam accepted the disappointment of his second failed business, and the flower shop was put up for sale. The Depression was well into its third year, and the mood of the country was deeply depressed as well. Bank failures, unemployment lines, and soup kitchens were widespread, and just about the last thing on anyone's wish list was having a flower shop of their very own.

There was a Depression-era song, *Melancholy Baby* that proclaimed that, *every cloud must have a silver lining*; and much to everyone's surprise, that phenomenon appeared a few months later. Sam's savior turned out to be the United States Government, whose need for a new post office sub-station coincided with the small brick building that housed the Little Florist Shop on Clark Street. The last time Sam had any contact with the government was during the Great War, when he was unceremoniously rejected for military service and, because of his place of birth, classified as an enemy alien. Now his adopted country needed something from him, and they were willing and able to pay a generous price for a piece of property that no one else in the entire world seemed to want.

"What a stroke of luck," said Jenny hugging Sam and giving him a big kiss. "And it's my luck I'm married to *you*."

"Didn't I tell you everything would be all right?"

But Sam breathed an exhausted sigh of relief, realizing he had just dodged another bullet. It was not the same as facing Schmitz's revolver, but it might have been just as deadly.

After a lengthy number of meetings, endless governmental red tape, and reviewing the small print in dozens of documents, the deal was consummated. Sam and Jenny paid off the loan and went to the bank together to deposit their small profit. Then, engaging in their preferred means of celebration, for the first time in months they went dancing.

CHAPTER FOUR

Cellophane

My Uncle Nathan and Uncle Daniel, like most of the Kramarsky siblings, were confident, witty, and had good heads for business. I liked them both very much. Whenever our families were together, there were jokes, laughter, and plenty of good food. The brothers had a stream of comic stories, and my Uncle Nathan's impersonation of Charlie Chaplin would leave us giggling helplessly on the floor. Every so often, after a visit, Alan and I would reach into our pockets and find a shiny quarter that had not been there before. They were fun, they were generous, and they were my father's new bosses.

Uncle Nathan was married and had three children. He was personable, handsome, and remarkably stylish with his full head of black hair and carefully trimmed moustache. His suits were custom tailored, his shoes came from England, and he favored colorful bow ties. He had the appearance of a successful young professor, though his formal education ended at the eighth grade. Nathan drove around in the latest, elegant automobile—currently a Packard sedan—and those who didn't know better were convinced he was a wealthy man. The family knew, however, that most of what they saw was an illusion; Nathan often spent more than he earned to create an image of affluence and sophistication. Not surprisingly, his profligate ways were a perpetual irritation to his otherwise loyal and subservient wife, my Aunt Gracie.

If Nathan was the flamboyant entrepreneur, his brother was the introspective intellectual. Daniel was unmarried, but he had an active

social life and was much involved in family affairs. My mother was
Daniel's favorite sister, and, since he was single, he had dinner with us
at least once a week. He was always cheerful and always good company.
Many years later we learned that it was Daniel who originated the
Gentlemen's Club that so enchanted us in those early years. The
Gentlemen's Club included Alan, me, and our cousin Alfie; but at the
time, we believed it was a huge national organization rivaling Little
Orphan Annie's Club. We received periodic letters from the Club
president, J. Jones, who mysteriously knew when any of us were guilty
of inappropriate behavior. The letters encouraged us to mend our
ways, respect our parents, and—most importantly— always behave
like gentlemen. The reprimands were gentle, and the letters often
contained gifts, like automatic pencils with our names engraved.

Daniel was creative, charming, and more concerned with substance
than style. His dress was beyond casual, often consisting of crumpled
suits, scuffed shoes, and occasionally, a gravy-stained tie. He also
owned an unwashed Chevrolet sedan, although he generally preferred
walking. Daniel spent considerable time and money on intellectual
pursuits, such as art shows, concerts, and the theater. Nathan thought
his brother wasted too much time on "artsy-fartsy" pursuits, as he
called them, while Daniel thought that Nathan's life was shallow
and superficial. Nevertheless, the dissimilar brothers were successful
partners whose business thrived from the moment they opened their
door.

Nathan established Transparent Materials Company shortly after
my father became a florist. Having read an article about cellophane,
Nathan decided the material had great potential. His plan was to
distribute cellophane to small businesses in the Chicago area, and to
enlist Daniel's good business sense and financial support to achieve
that goal.

"What makes you think anybody *needs* cellophane?" asked Daniel. "We've lived without it all our lives. What's suddenly changed?"

Actually, Daniel believed Nathan's business proposal had merit, but the purpose of his question was to test the extent of his brother's convictions.

"Cellophane is one of the truly great twentieth century inventions," began Nathan. "It's right up there with windshield wipers, pop-up toasters, and zeppelins! At first, people didn't think they needed those things either. But now we can't live without them."

Zeppelins, thought Daniel? *What the hell does Nathan know about zeppelins?*

"I predict," continued Nathan from his figurative soap box, "someday cellophane will replace paper as the wrapping material of choice, and it may eventually be used for windows in houses and for articles of clothing. We are heading for a clearer world, a more modern world, where people will live their lives freely and transparently."

Cellophane windows? Cellophane clothing? Now he sounds a bit wacky, thought Daniel.

Nathan wrote a letter to the DuPont Company, the only manufacturer in the country that produced cellophane, and he outlined a vague business proposal. Much to everyone's astonishment, the DuPont people agreed to see him. One week later Nathan traveled by train to their headquarters in Wilmington, Delaware.

"I want to become your distributor in the Chicago area," said Nathan with bold self-assurance. "I'm familiar with your product, I believe in it, and I think we would have great success working together."

The officials with whom Nathan spoke reviewed his sketchy business plan, inquired about his experience and capitalization, and in less than twenty minutes rejected his proposal. The senior official explained.

"We're impressed with your enthusiasm and dedication, but, quite frankly, we feel you lack the proper experience and necessary funds. Furthermore, your letter failed to state your desire to become a regional distributor. Had you mentioned that, we could have saved you a trip. You may not be aware, but we already have a distributor in Detroit who adequately serves the Chicago area. We thought perhaps you wanted to distribute converted material."

"And by that you mean?" asked Nathan, trying to conceal his utter confusion.

"A distributor of converted material," explained the official, "buys material from the regional distributor and provides custom-sized pieces to small businesses. For example, a candy company needs very small pieces to wrap individual chocolates. A distributor of converted material would cut those pieces from large rolls. Get it?"

"Of course I get it!" declared Nathan in a commanding voice. "That is precisely what I had in mind!"

The DuPont executives were a bit confused, but now Nathan had their full attention.

"Perhaps I failed to make myself clear, but my intention has always been to become a distributor of converted material. You must forgive my ignorance of these technical terms."

He then laid out an elaborate plan of how he intended to become a material distributor, which was a business he first learned about exactly three minutes earlier.

Nathan's linguistic performance was a brilliant display of fancy footwork that would have made Nijinsky proud. From the image of an ill-prepared dolt, he was suddenly transformed into a smooth and experienced businessman. By the time the meeting adjourned the DuPont executives were convinced that Nathan Kramarsky was indeed a brilliant entrepreneur. They also believed if they ignored his request, it would rank right up there among the major business blunders of all times. Nathan left Wilmington Delaware with DuPont's assurance of a successful future relationship, their best wishes, and a pat on the back.

When he returned to Chicago, Nathan presented the good news to his brother Daniel. They shook hands on the deal, and within a few months the fraternal partnership began operation. Though they were equal partners, Nathan always felt he was the boss. After all, the cellophane business was his idea; besides, he was eight years older than Daniel and an inch-and-a-half taller as well.

Sam liked his brothers-in-law, but with this new business association, he wasn't sure how to behave toward them. Except for his inferior position in the firm's hierarchy, Sam felt they were more or less equals, but now there was a new relationship, one of employer and employee. Sam recalled his earlier work experiences and remembered how averse he was to working for others. The period of adjustment took some time, and there were evenings when Sam would complain to Jenny about her "thickheaded, narrow-minded, insensitive brothers". But mostly, their good sense helped overcome otherwise challenging situations.

Despite the failures of the theater and flower shop, Sam felt he knew something about running a business; and—let's not forget—both previous businesses were sold at a profit. He often let his employers know that his opinion counted for something, and, much to their credit, they considered and respected his judgment.

The Transparent Materials Company sold cellophane; a product invented twenty years before, but in popular use for only the last ten years. Almost immediately, the Kramarsky brothers saw its possibilities as a new and exciting packaging material. It was perfect for protecting food and other commodities. It was moisture proof, sanitary, and, most importantly, it allowed consumers to see what they were buying. It was a natural for wrapping cheeses, candies, nuts, flowers, and dozens of other products. The Kramarskys' excitement about the new material was contagious, and Sam quickly became part of the enthusiastic team.

As time went on, business prospered, largely because Sam discovered that he had a real talent for selling. Despite inner doubts, he rarely took no for an answer; and if there was the slightest chance of booking an order, he would not rest until he succeeded. His motivation was twofold; first, after two major business failures, he feared disappointing Jenny again. Secondly, he wanted the Kramarsky boys to know that a Newman was every bit their equal. Also, not incidentally, the Depression was becoming a nightmare without end, and Sam realized he could not afford to bungle what he perceived to be his last opportunity.

At this point, you may ask, what was going on with the Newman children? When our father went into the cellophane business, my brother Alan and I were about nine and seven years old respectively. Our world was far removed from the trials and vicissitudes of our parents. If someone asked, "How are you making out during this agonizing depression?" we would have answered, "What's a depression?" We had the simplistic idea that life was pretty nice, thank you. Hardship? What was that? Money may have been tight, but we never missed a meal and were always neatly dressed, though most of my clothes were Alan's cast-offs. Our activities were conventional and affordable. During the summers we swam in Lake Michigan, and during the winters we went sledding in Lincoln Park. And nearly year-round we played baseball in the street. We were not even aware that summers were brutally hot and humid and winters were excruciatingly cold. Things were the way they were, and if we thought about it at all, we probably believed that's the way it's supposed to be. After all, we weren't philosophers; we were just little kids.

During several summers we escaped the seasonal heat by spending a week or two at a rented cottage, usually along some lake in Michigan, Indiana, or Wisconsin. We frequently shared the cottages with other relatives, so there were always congenial playmates among our dozens of cousins. Sometimes the cottages had no electricity or plumbing, and we used kerosene lamps, outhouses, and pumped our own water. We viewed these primitive facilities as exciting departures from our usual routine. All in all, we had to admit, life was pretty good.

If I had the power to change anything at all, I definitively would have been an only child. Early on, my brother became my chief tormentor, and this was a role he continued to play for the next twenty years or so. It began with, "Let me hug the baby," during which the baby turned blue, and progressed to, "Oops, I didn't mean to sit on your model airplane."

Alan and I could not have been more different. He was better than I at physical activities, but I was smarter. While he would taunt me with a pinch or a poke, I would counter with mind games, like pretending he didn't exist for hours, or sometimes, for days. That usually drove him crazy. Our parents labeled him a tease and me intolerant; which in my parents' minds, made us equally guilty. My most common complaint during those years was, "It's just not fair," and I truly believed I was the victim of profound injustice.

It certainly didn't help that we always shared a room. Such an arrangement often brought siblings closer, but it had the opposite effect on us. We both resented sharing a room, and I was constantly occupied keeping my brother away from my things. I learned to be distrustful and never lend or share anything that had meaning, because very likely I would never see it again. Clearly, I was the good one and Alan was the bad one. I followed the rules; my brother found ways to subvert them. I got good grades in school; he was a mediocre student. And I was careful and considerate, while Alan wove a path of destruction wherever he went. Like I said, we could not have been more different.

One more thing: Alan was left-handed, which might explain a few things. First of all, he had difficulty learning to write and tie his shoes. I also once read that left-handers were more likely than right-handed people to get into accidents, be committed to insane asylums, and serve time in jail. Perhaps I should have pitied his left-handedness, but I was generally too busy pretending he didn't exist.

A few years earlier, Alan said to me, "You know, don't you, we're not really brothers."

"What are you talking about?" I asked.

"Mom and Dad bought you at F. W. Woolworth's five-and-dime store. If you don't believe me, go ask them. Your real parents left you there because you were such a pain in the ass."

I didn't really believe Alan, but as I thought more about it, I figured that might possibly explain our extreme differences.

Growing up distrustful and cynical was certainly not ideal, but my parents must share the blame. I think I see now what was going on. I'm sure my parents loved us both, but I'm also certain my parents *liked* me more than they liked Alan. And why not? He was the one carving initials in the furniture, breaking windows, and telling so many lies his nose should have been longer than Pinocchio's. He was nothing but trouble, and as I've pointed out, I was the good one. Who in his right mind wouldn't like me better? Since our parents felt they had to be rigorously impartial, they were obliged to treat us equally to avoid any sign of favoritism. Thus, when punishment was doled out after a fight, the number of whacks to my bottom precisely equaled those applied to my brother's bottom.

I suppose I hated Alan, from time to time; but, to tell the truth, there was something about him I admired. He was charming, resourceful, and genuinely good-looking. Also, I greatly admired his ability to flout the rules and march through life to the beat of his own defiant drummer.

As I look back on those early years, I would characterize Alan as an imperfection in my life, much like a humpback or clubfoot. I could hardly ignore him, he was always there; but I resented that I was born with such an obvious and annoying defect. Very soon, however, Alan would become the least of my worries. My life was about to be transformed in a most dramatic way.

CHAPTER FIVE

Father Drops A Bomb

Shortly after I turned nine, my father came home from the office one evening, and with no prior hint of what was to come, announced to my brother and me that we were moving. We were not moving to another apartment in our neighborhood, to a house on the other side of town, or even to a place in the country outside of Chicago. We were moving to California! At first I thought it was a joke, and I waited for the punch line, but this was no joke. Of course I had heard of California, the *Golden State* they called it. But I knew nothing about this strange place, except that it was a long way away. As far as I was concerned, California might just as well be located on another planet in another solar system.

"Why?" I asked, "Why are we moving at all, and why *there*?"

"Your Uncle Nathan and are I are opening a west coast branch of Transparent Materials Company. It's a terrific opportunity and you're going to love it."

"I'm not going to love it," I said. "I love it here. My school is here, my friends are here, and everything I want is already here. Why do we have to start all over again someplace else?"

"Peter," interrupted my mother, "did you know it never snows in Southern California?"

What kind of goofy argument was that, I wondered? I loved playing in the snow.

My brother Alan's reaction to this bombshell was the opposite of mine. He thought moving to an entirely new state was a wonderful idea. I guess he assumed the move would bring new opportunities for mischief-making in a place where he was completely unknown. In Chicago, he was pretty much a marked man; the neighbors, shop owners, and schoolteachers all knew that Alan was trouble. It was doubtful, however, that his wicked reputation was common knowledge in an entirely different state.

It was now two weeks before Thanksgiving, and the target date of our move was mid-January. The plan was to form a modern-day wagon train consisting of three cars rolling down Route 66 like the pioneers who settled this great land more than a hundred years before. My Uncle Nathan, his wife Gracie, and their two daughters would drive to Southern California in their new Buick; and my seventeen-year-old cousin, their son Gary, would drive his own car, a convertible Ford. My father and our family would drive in our 1936 Chevrolet. It sounded like a great adventure, but I wanted none of it.

"I've decided to stay here," I announced the following morning. "If the rest of you want to drive to California, it's okay with me. But I think I'll skip it."

"Where do you plan to live?" my mother wanted to know.

"Gee, Mom, we've got about a zillion relatives, and any one of them would be happy to take me in. I'm the good one—remember? My preference is Aunt Sarah or Uncle Daniel."

"I'm afraid that's not an option for you," said my mother. "We're a family, and we stick together. We're all driving to California. Get used to the idea."

When I look back at this moment in history, it appears incredible to me that neither of my parents, nor in fact, anyone, except my Uncle Nathan, had ever *been* to California. And my uncle was only in Los Angeles on a one-day stopover, and that was two years earlier. We were giving up our home and school and leaving friends and relatives to live in a place about which we knew absolutely nothing. How incredibly foolhardy I thought. We weren't pioneers or trailblazers, we weren't homesteaders, and we sure as hell weren't explorers. I was convinced my entire family had gone crazy and finally lost what was left of their minds.

"Mom," I asked a few days later, "don't you think moving to California is kind of risky? I mean, what if we get lost somewhere, and we never get found? What if Indians attack us? And even if we do get there, what if we don't like the place? What do we do then?"

"Now calm down," my mother answered. "First of all, we have road maps, so getting lost is very unlikely. Secondly, there are no longer any hostile Indian tribes, so there's absolutely no chance of being attacked. I think you've been watching too many western movies. And as far as liking California, I'm sure we're going to love it. After all, the sun shines there nearly every day, there are flowers all year long, and there'll be no more freezing weather and shoveling snow. It's an absolute paradise and we're lucky to have this opportunity."

"Yeah, but Mom, what if you're wrong?"

"Peter, I know the idea of moving upsets you, and I'm sorry about that; but we're moving to California, and that's that. This discussion is over!"

What my mother failed to mention was that she had a similar conversation with my father a couple of weeks earlier.

"Are you sure this is a good idea? I hate the thought of leaving our friends and family and everything familiar. We've never lived anywhere else, and California is so far away from here."

"I know you're worried," replied my father, "but your brothers and I have thought a lot about this move, and we don't see any other way out. The fact that California is far away is an important reason for this move."

"What are you talking about?" asked my mother. "What's going on?"

My father was quiet for a long time, and then he began to speak very softly.

"I'm not supposed to mention this—I told them I wouldn't—but I think you should know; Nathan has gotten himself into some serious trouble."

"Trouble? What kind of trouble?"

"He borrowed a lot of money from some shady characters, and he can't pay it back."

"Can't we help him out, or couldn't he borrow what he needs from the business?'

"I'm afraid we're talking about more money than all of us, including the business, have. He's in very deep, and the lenders have threatened that, if he doesn't pay up, they'll break his leg or some other body part. I know that sounds melodramatic, but the situation is serious."

"This is like a bad movie," said my mother. "This kind of thing isn't supposed to happen to people like us."

"Well," answered my father, "Nathan isn't *like* us. He spends and spends, and when he runs out of money he borrows more money and spends that, too. Your brother is out of control."

"So we're just going to run away from all this and hope nobody follows us?"

"Yeah, that's pretty much what we're doing. But we really don't think we'll be followed. Like you said, California is a long way from here, and it's probably the last place they'd look for Nathan. Anyway, having a branch office there *is* a good idea, and we all think it's a great opportunity."

"My God, what a nightmare! Does anyone else know about this?"

"Just me, Daniel, and now you. But no one knows that *you* know."

"I don't understand all this," said my mother. "I'm going to have to think about it."

I, for one, didn't have to think about it; I knew from the start that moving to California was a really bad idea. And I said so repeatedly to anyone who would listen. My father tried to be reassuring, but I sensed his optimism was based more on hope than reality.

"I understand how you feel, Peter, but I assure you, no one ever knows how things will work out." And then he launched into one of his many heartfelt sermons on the philosophy of life.

"Now pay attention," he began; "this is one piece of advice you should never forget. No matter how bad things turn out, no matter how down in the dumps you may be, no matter how hopeless the future appears— believe me—it could be worse. It can always be worse. And sometimes it can be worse than that; there's no limit to how bad things can get."

"Is this supposed to make me feel better?" I asked.

"Just let me finish," my father answered. "Do you remember the Titanic and the Hindenburg? How about the Great Chicago Fire and the San Francisco Earthquake? Well here's an interesting fact: some people survived those horrible events! That's right—every one of those miserable disasters had survivors. So remember, no matter how bad it gets, look on the bright side, there's always a chance you'll survive. And one day you'll look back and say, well, what do you know, here I am, alive and still kicking. I guess the old man knew what he was talking about. It sure as hell *could* be worse."

Instead of reassuring me, my father's words set off an internal alarm. If there was any chance our trip to California could end up being a legendary disaster, I figured I had a lot more worrying to do.

When Thanksgiving arrived two weeks later I was still in a low-grade depression. I figured that, for the first time in my short life, I had absolutely nothing to be thankful for. Even having more food than the starving Armenians, of which my mother constantly reminded me, brought little satisfaction. I enjoyed my life in Chicago; it was familiar and comfortable. And the only thing I didn't like about it was going to be sitting next to me in the back seat of a car for ten days in January. If I understood the concept of irony, I would have said, "Boy, is this ironic!"

In the next several weeks both my parents engaged in a campaign to make Southern California sound like it was Heaven on Earth, the Garden of Eden, and Cloud Nine, rolled into one. We heard about the beautiful Pacific Ocean, the waving palm trees, the endless beaches, the orange groves, the constant sunshine, and not least of all, the movie stars with whom we were about to rub elbows. One evening my father showed up with a couple of picture books about California, to further promote the brainwashing process. But still, I had serious doubts.

My mother had doubts, too, but she only discussed them with my father.

"After we leave, what's to stop Nathan's lenders from putting pressure on Daniel? They don't exactly sound like reputable business people. What if they decide to break Daniel's leg instead?"

"We've discussed that," answered my father. "Daniel's attitude will be one of shock and ignorance. He'll claim that Nathan stole company funds, disappeared, and no one has the faintest idea where he is. Daniel's a good actor, and he thinks they'll believe his story. And it's unlikely these shady guys will go to the cops for help. Since most of them are wanted for one crime or another, the cops would probably lock them up."

By the time the holiday season passed, I was led to believe that the trip to California would be the greatest adventure of my young life. We were leaving in about two weeks, and I began saying goodbye to my friends. A few classmates were as unhappy as I about my leaving Avondale School. Avondale was a classic, rusticated stone building from the 1880s. It was the place I learned to read, write, multiply and divide. It was also there—on the frozen playground pond—that I learned to ice skate. I remembered the summer picnics, the Halloween bonfires, and the first time I played spin-the-bottle. I was miserable beyond belief.

By modern day standards, Avondale didn't have much to recommend it; there was no library, no nurse's office, no cafeteria, and not even a comfortable place to sit when eating your homemade lunch. And the mechanical amenities were strictly nineteenth century. There was a single bare light bulb that illuminated our classroom, a coal-fueled furnace in the basement that provided minimal heat, and always, it seemed to me, too few toilets. But all that seemed unimportant now. Of greater significance to me was that Avondale was familiar, comfortable, and the place from which I was being exiled. Why, I kept wondering, why is this happening to me?

On the last Friday before we left Chicago, my teacher, Miss Rosengarten, threw a small going-away party for me. She finished the geography lesson twenty minutes early and then brought out a cake she had baked the night before.

"Boys and girls," she addressed the eighteen others in our class, "Peter Newman is leaving us today. His family is going to California next week, and we all want to wish him a happy trip and great success."

Most of my close friends already knew about the move, but to some others, this was startling news. A cute classmate by the name of Anna Polanski uttered a gasp and said, "Oh no." What did she mean by that? I didn't even know she was aware of me. Did this mean she cared? I'd always had a secret crush on Anna, but I figured she was the last one to whom news of my departure would matter. What a time to discover my unrequited affection was, in fact, requited. I seemed to be drowning in terrible luck.

Miss Rosengarten cut the cake and each classmate participated in the tribute to my departure. Among those who later spoke to me was Anna, who confirmed the significance of her involuntary gasp.

"I'll miss you, Peter," she said. "Maybe you'll send me a postcard from Los Angeles, maybe a picture of the Hollywood Bowl."

"Sure I will. Let me have your address." At that moment I was prepared to send her a postcard every day we were apart. Regrets overwhelmed me—if only I knew about Anna sooner.

Miss Rosengarten approached me and said, "I will especially miss you, Peter. You've been a joy to have in this class, and I know you'll do well in California." And then she gave me a hug.

That's all I needed to start the tears flowing, and I turned away to hide the embarrassment. Lately, it seems, I'd been doing an awful lot of crying. I hadn't even left town, and here I was experiencing the most profound grief I had ever known.

When I got home, my mother asked about my last day at Avondale.

"Pretty much like any other day," I responded. I was depressed and unhappy, and I just couldn't talk about it.

CHAPTER SIX

Get Your Kicks

On the morning we left Chicago the weather matched my mood—dreary and depressing. It snowed the previous night and our familiar neighborhood wore a fresh white blanket. I loved new snow; it was clean and soft and I regretted I would not see it again for a long time. We had packed our bags the night before, and little remained in our apartment. Much of the furniture, clothes, and household items were shipped to Los Angeles the previous week. As the car warmed up, I stood in the new snow and looked up at the red brick apartment house for the last time. What a poignant moment; it was the only home I had ever known. All the memories came flooding back—the neighbor kids with whom we played street games; the familiar horse-drawn wagons driven by the milkman, vegetable dealer, and junk peddler; and the candy store on the corner, where a penny bought you a world of sweetness.

I even recalled the unhappier moments, like when the Polish hooligans chased us home from school. "You killed our Christ," they yelled; and I had no idea what they were talking about. But, in my nostalgic frame of mind, I even felt wistful about the anti-Semitic Polacks. All these memories were just too much; I started to cry again.

Little did I know that, in other parts of the world, at that very moment, other children my age were also crying. They, too, were being uprooted; and they faced frightening and uncertain futures. In those days I knew little about Hitler and the Nazis, and I had no idea

43

that Fascists in Europe were persecuting Jewish families like ours. The children being displaced were running for their lives. It was hardly the same for us; but on that snowy morning in January, I thought no one could feel more devastated than I. I figured I'd make one last-ditch try.

"What if I stay here until the end of the semester and then meet you in Los Angeles?"

"That's the best idea I've heard all day," said my brother Alan.

"The answer is no," said my mother. "We've been through this before, and the matter is settled. Whether you like it or not, we're all traveling together. Now get into the car."

My father put the car in gear, and we headed towards my Uncle Nathan's house. Our modern-day wagon train would begin the journey to California from there. My aunt, uncle, and cousins were waiting for us and ready to go.

"Why so gloomy, Peter?" my cousin Gary wanted to know.

"I'm not very happy about moving," I answered, "and I'd rather not be here."

"Hey, this going to be fun," he said. "And if your folks don't mind, maybe you can ride with me part of the way."

Wow! What a great idea! Finally, this would be a way to escape my brother. My spirits suddenly soared.

"Why don't I just hop in your car right now?"

"Well," he answered, "maybe you better ride with your folks today. Being that it's our first day, they probably want the family to be together. There'll be plenty of time to switch around later."

The three cars started up, and my uncle led the way, as he would continue to do for the entire journey. Not only did he plan our route and have a complete collection of Automobile Club road maps, but also, he was the boss and simply playing his part. Gary followed in his Ford convertible, and the Newman Chevrolet brought up the rear. Finally we were off, and there was no turning back. For about the hundredth time my mother asked, "Now, are you sure you haven't forgotten anything?" And for about the hundredth time I checked every pocket to be sure I had my automatic pencil, package of chewing gum, and forty-two cents in coins. I also had my rabbit's foot, although in recent days I had about as much luck with it as the rabbit that originally owned it.

We were heading for Route 66, and we would follow it about twenty-five hundred miles, until we practically fell into the Pacific Ocean. We would travel through eight of the forty-eight states, seven of which none of us had ever seen before.

The new snow slowed our travel, and it took nearly forty minutes to reach Buckingham Fountain, the official starting point of Route 66. We all stopped there so my Uncle Nathan could consult with the other drivers.

"The map seems to indicate going north from here," he said, "but California should be in a generally southwest direction." Oh, no, I thought, we were still in the middle of Chicago and already lost. My worst fears were confirmed.

"I think we go north for several blocks," said Gary, "and then we begin to head south."

"Maybe we should have studied the map before leaving home," suggested my father.

"Now, let's not start with the criticism, Sam. We're doing our best here." My father quietly walked back to our car and said to my mother, "Your brother's an idiot."

"I knew it," I said, "we're lost. No one has any idea where California is, and even if we find the right road, Indians will probably get us. You promised, Mom, you promised we wouldn't get lost, and that we wouldn't be attacked. Now, how can I believe anything you say?"

"Calm down, Peter, we'll find the right road, and there won't be any Indian attacks."

What made me more nervous was that Alan was suspiciously quiet. I sensed he was even more frightened than I. This was not a good sign.

The cars started up again, we followed Gary's suggestion, and within ten minutes we found the well-marked Route 66. After an hour of driving, we were out of the city and deep into the farmland surrounding my now former hometown. We motored at a steady thirty miles an hour along the icy, two-lane road running southwest towards Springfield. It snowed most of the day, which made it difficult to go very fast or see much of anything along the way. It was probably an omen, I thought; the God of Transcontinental Travel was probably punishing us for even attempting this stupid trip. After two hours of driving I was bored beyond belief. I wondered how I could possibly last another nine days. This was like serving time in a maximum-security prison. I once read that prisoners on death row, probably the most boring situation conceivable, generally slept sixteen hours a day. Maybe that would be my solution—I'd sleep through this trip.

If you've heard the song, *Get Your Kicks on Route 66*, you probably know more about our itinerary than I did that first day. A piano player named Bobby Troup, who was with the Tommy Dorsey band, made the same trip a few years after we did, and he wrote a song about it. It was recorded by Nat King Cole and was a huge hit. If you check out the lyrics, you'll have a good idea what we experienced. The only difference, as far as I was concerned, is that, so far, I wasn't getting much of a kick out of Route 66. Of course, we had just begun and were heading for St. *Louie*. Next up was Joplin, Missouri, and Oklahoma City, which, he advised, was mighty pretty. After that, we would see Amarillo and Gallop, New Mexico; Flagstaff, Arizona, (don't forget Winona), Kingman, Barstow, and San Bernardino. There were dozens of other towns we would pass through, but those were the ones mentioned in the famous song.

The route we followed was dedicated in 1926, but at that time, more than half of it was gravel or graded dirt. It wasn't completely paved until 1938, the year of our journey. The road was created when the federal government decided to provide an all-year paved highway to the West Coast for the use of truckers. They wanted to avoid the worst of the Rocky Mountains, so the route was located southerly, in a more geographically accessible area. A short time after the route was dedicated, service stations, motor courts, and cafés were established along its length.

The Bobby Troup song was far more romantic than the actual road, but I think it represented more than just a cross-country, two-lane asphalt strip. For most of the people who originally used it, Route 66 was the embodiment of a dream for a better life. In his famous book, *Grapes of Wrath*, John Steinbeck named it the *Mother Road*, and it became a highway of opportunity for the migrants escaping the poverty and despair of the Dust Bowl. We could not realize it at the time, but our trip was practically an historic event; few had made this journey on a paved road, *winding from Chicago to L.A.*, before we did. So as I look back now, I think maybe we *were* modern-day pioneers. But I certainly didn't feel like one that morning.

In the first couple of hours, there was a lot of chatter between my parents, indicating their excitement mixed with what I guessed was some apprehension.

"Isn't this a great adventure?" asked my father. Then referring to the snowstorm we were driving through, "And aren't we lucky we won't have to face this kind of awful weather much longer? What do you think, boys?"

Alan responded with an enthusiastic, "You betcha!"

"What about you, Peter?"

Everyone on earth knew I hated leaving Chicago, and driving several hours through a blinding snowstorm wasn't doing much to change my mind *or* my mood. I had been told I was negative, critical, and unappreciative. I even heard Uncle Nathan remark that I was becoming a "pain in the neck". It was difficult to think of myself as anything other than the wettest blanket who ever lived. But instead of repeating my usual mantra, "This trip is stupid and I'll probably resent it until the day I die," I said, "No complaints from me."

By the end of the first day, just as the last, gray light faded, we arrived in Springfield, the capital of Illinois. We had driven less than two hundred miles, which—considering the weather—was not too bad. We found a small motel outside the city, had some dinner in a nearby café, and then turned in. That night, for the first time in years, I wet my bed.

"What happened?" my mother wanted to know.

"I don't know," I answered. And I really didn't. It was embarrassing and disturbing, and I hated for my brother to know about this. There was definitely something wrong, but neither my parents nor I had any idea what it could be. After breakfast that morning, my Uncle Nathan had a private word with me.

"Peter," he said, "tonight when you go to bed, be sure your feet are elevated well above the level of your head. Use some extra pillows under your feet, if you have to."

Why, I wondered, did my parents have to discuss this awkward subject with everybody in the whole world? And what kind of practical advice was that? I couldn't believe that my 'accident' had anything to do with the level of my feet.

Before lunch that day, we crossed the mighty Mississippi River, and I stared in wonder at this giant body of water. We studied the Mississippi in school, but nothing I ever read or heard mentioned that it was just a huge, dirty brown river of mud. Somewhat later we stopped to eat outside of St. Louis. My mother took me aside and broached the uncomfortable subject.

"I've been thinking about this, and here's what I believe happened last night. I know you're unhappy leaving Chicago, and I think you're mad at the whole family for forcing you to go to California. And you're so upset with everybody, you want to pee all over everything, just to show us how angry you are. That's what I think. Now, what do you think?"

I sat there a long time and thought about what my mother said. I was angry, all right; there wasn't much question about that. But I didn't pee on purpose; I was fast asleep when that happened. How could I possibly control peeing when I was unconscious?

"I don't know, Mom, maybe that could be it, but I'm really confused."

"That's okay," she said. "I just want you to know that wherever we live—Chicago, Los Angeles, or Timbuktu—you're a very important part of this family and we'll always love you. And then I began to cry; not puny little tears, but huge torrents of water, like a human Niagara Falls. All my anger, confusion, and embarrassment came gushing out, and it took more than twenty minutes for me to regain my composure. As I was still drying my eyes, my brother Alan came by and said, "C'mon you fruity little kid, we gotta get going."

"Alan," I said, "why don't you just shove it!"

CHAPTER SEVEN

More Kicks

By the time we reached the other Springfield—the one in Missouri—
the snow stopped falling, and we saw sunshine for the first time. I was
now riding with my cousin Gary and acting, once again, as if Alan
didn't exist. Earlier in the day, when leaving Springfield, Alan said,
"I heard that crack about shoving it, you little creep. Now take that
back."

"Too late, Alan; you can't take back things that've already been
said."

"Take it back, you jerk, or I'll give you a knuckle sandwich."

"Yeah? You and what army?"

At this point our father frowned into the rear view mirror and said,
"That's enough now! This is going to be a long trip and you two better
learn to get along. Now I don't want to hear any more arguing from
either of you."

Before the echo of my father's words faded, Alan wound up and
punched me in the ribs.

"Ow!" I cried. "Alan just punched me! I think he broke
something."

Our father was now in a predicament. Normally, he would pull
over, stop the car, and give us each a whack on the behind. But if
he followed that routine, the others in our procession might be in
Oklahoma by the time the squabble was resolved. What to do? The
three drivers had previously agreed on an alarm strategy that employed

their horns. Three toots was the pre-arranged signal for: Everybody Stop! However, it was only to be used in emergencies. Well, thought my father, if this isn't an emergency, it's close enough. He hit the horn three times, then Gary in front of us gave three toots, and finally my uncle's car began to slow and pull over. At least the system worked, I thought; that's a comfort. But now what?

The three cars stopped at the side of the road, and the drivers got out to confer.

"I'm afraid we have to separate the boys," said my father. "They've been sniping and bickering all morning, and they're about ready to kill each other."

"Peter can ride with me," suggested Gary. "I could use some company; it's been kind of boring driving alone."

"Well," said my Uncle Nathan, "if everyone's agreed, let's make the switch and hope things work out. By the way, Sam, I trust this kind of thing isn't going to be a habit; we've got a schedule to maintain, and it doesn't include reprimanding your kids. Seems to me, the boys could use a bit more discipline."

My father didn't respond, but everyone could see he was infuriated by my uncle's unsolicited advice. Who did this pompous ass think he was? He may be the boss, Sam thought, but that didn't give him the right to tell him how to raise his kids. This was none of his brother-in-law's damn business!

Nevertheless, the decision was made; I would ride with Gary, and my brother would remain in solitary confinement in the back seat of the Newman sedan. I was delighted; finally I would be rid of Alan, even if only temporarily. I enjoyed riding with Gary, we got along well, and now I wouldn't even care if Alan set fire to the back seat upholstery. Things were definitely looking up.

We stopped that evening outside of Joplin at the Sleep Haven

Motel. Attached to the motel was a Chinese restaurant named Ding Dong. No kidding, I'm not making this up; that's what it was called. It combined the names of the two partners who settled there several years before. Now if you're wondering why two cooks would come all the way from China just to open a restaurant outside of Joplin, Missouri, your guess is as good as mine. But I will say it was the best chop suey I ever had. Not that I was an expert in such things, but when we lived in Chicago we often ate Chinese on Sunday nights, and I always ordered chop suey. We had kind of a routine; Saturday afternoons we went to the movies, and Sundays we ate Chinese. Just thinking about all that made me homesick again.

If I hadn't spilled my tea, the dinner would have been perfect. But when reaching for my water glass, I knocked over my teacup and its contents stained the white tablecloth.

"Better cover that up," warned my Uncle Nathan. "If the waiter sees that mess, there's no telling what he might do." Little did I realize this was one of my uncle's sadistic jokes.

I covered the large spot with my napkin, but some of the stain still showed. When the waiter returned to clear the dishes, both of my outstretched palms covered as much of the tea stain as possible. It looked as though I was about to play a make-believe piano. The waiter frowned but said nothing, and I quickly got up and walked out. Boy, that was a close call, I thought.

The next day we spent about twenty minutes driving through the state of Kansas. For some odd reason Route 66 just nicked the southeast corner of the state for a length of exactly thirteen miles. If you sneezed you could have missed the entire Kansas experience, which wouldn't have been a great tragedy. Kansas didn't seem all that different from Missouri, where we came from, or Oklahoma, where we now found ourselves. Almost this entire area consisted of farms, small towns, and a lot of empty, flat country. It was really, really boring, and I said so.

"Stop complaining," said my father. "It could be worse."

So I stopped complaining, and it did get worse—it started to rain! Then the thunder and lightning began, and the rain came down in buckets. It was the most excitement we had in days.

By this time we were running out of ideas of how to pass the time. Two days earlier, just after leaving Chicago, we played a few word games, like Twenty Questions and the Country Game. The Country Game is played this way: One person names a country and the next person has to name another country that begins with the last letter of that name. For example, if I said France, you would say something like England, since the last letter of France is the beginning letter of England. Get it? Well, my mother began by saying, "Iceland", and then I said, "Denmark". Alan was next, and he thought about this, for what seemed like half the day. Then he said, "Canada".

I said, "Denmark ends with a 'k,' you moron, not a 'c.' How can we play a spelling game if you don't even know how to spell?"

"I'm not playing this stupid game," said an embarrassed Alan. "Just play without me."

"Come on, Alan," said my mother, "this is the way you learn to spell. Let's try again. And this time, Peter, no comments, please."

Alan sat quietly for a few minutes, and then he said, "Kansas."

"Oh no," I said. "He's hopeless."

"Alan," my mother calmly advised, "Kansas is a state, as a matter of fact, the state we just drove through. We're looking for an entire country that begins with 'K.' Try it again."

My brother's an imbecile, I thought. I'm sure he'll end up digging ditches for a living.

Then Alan said, "Korea—that's a country."

"Brilliant!" I said.

"Peter," my father warned, "don't be sarcastic. Alan gave a perfectly good answer."

Now that I think about it, the punch in the ribs Alan gave me that morning probably had something to do with the Country Game we played two days earlier. Since Alan was the older brother, he always felt he should be the best at everything. But unfortunately for him, he was absent the day the brains were passed out.

After we used up all the good countries, everyone got tired of the Country Game. There was a long period of silence, and all we heard for the next hour or so was the hum of the motor. Then my father suggested we play Guess the Number Game. In this game someone chooses a number between one and one hundred, and the others take turns narrowing down the guess. There are only five questions allowed, and each has a turn asking a question. My father said he was thinking of the number, and I asked, "Is it more than fifty?" It was.

Then my mother asked, "Is it between fifty and seventy-five?" It was.

Next it was Alan's turn, and with little patience and no common sense whatever, he asked, "Is the number sixty-three?"

"Oh for crying out loud," I said. "Use your noodle. We're trying to narrow down the answer, and now that you've wasted a guess, we've only got two guesses left."

"Well, you won't need any more guesses," said my father, "Alan got it right; the number *was* sixty-three."

"That's impossible," I said. "Do you expect us to believe that Alan just randomly picked a single number out of twenty-five possibilities and got it right? That's ridiculous."

"Not if you know what you're doing," said Alan. "I guess you don't know everything, smarty-pants." Then he stuck out his tongue, which showed how really dumb he was.

I was sure my father set it up so that Alan would win and not feel like such a dimwit. But when I asked him about it two days later, he said, "You ought to give your brother more credit; he could be a lot smarter that you think." I wasn't convinced. I figured, if anything, he could be a lot dumber than I thought.

Riding with Gary was great fun; he was cheerful, funny, and had a million stories. He was nearly eighteen years old and had just graduated high school. Gary was tall and slender, blond and blue-eyed, and had the build of an athlete. He loved baseball and had played on his high school team the past two years. If Gary had followed his dream, he would be trying out with the Chicago Cubs right now. But like me, he was a hostage being hijacked to Los Angeles; and once there, he was destined to work for the Transparent Materials Company. Gary's older sister, Shelley, was also going to work in the family business, which was fast becoming the classic model of nepotism.

Whenever we stopped for lunch or to get gas, Gary would say, "Okay, Pretzel," which was the funny name he called me, "let's play a little catch." He carried some bats, a few mitts, and several baseballs in the back of his car. We would stand by the side of the road and throw the ball back and forth. Sometimes he threw the ball high, like a pop-up, and I would run around trying to figure out where it would fall. It was practically the only exercise we got during the trip, and it felt good to get the blood pumping and work up a sweat. Every so often Alan would join in, and although he was a good athlete, he was typically annoying. He often threw the ball so that you had to stretch one way or the other to barely reach it. I would complain, "Come on, Alan, throw the ball *to* me." Then he would burn it in at top speed, so it would sting my hand, even through the mitt.

Shelley never played with us and rarely even spoke to us. She was twenty-one years old, not particularly attractive, and considerably overweight. Okay, let's be honest—Shelley was fat. I had no idea why she acted so stuck-up. As far as I could see, she had absolutely nothing to be stuck-up about. I once heard my parents talking about her, and the big family concern was that Shelley would never find a man. Gary's sixteen-year-old sister, Kay, however, was another story; she was cute, vivacious, and loaded with sex appeal. The family worry about her was how to keep the boys *away*. Everybody loved Kay, and every guy over the age of twelve wanted to date her. She had a great figure and always wore tight sweaters; so whenever she played ball with us, she practically stopped traffic along Route 66.

I once asked Kay, "Why is Shelley so unfriendly? She practically never talks to me. She acts like she doesn't like me."

"You have to ignore Shelley," answered Kay. "She's unhappy and she doesn't like anybody, including herself. She's a real sourpuss, and it has nothing to do with you. I mean, how could anybody dislike an adorable kid like you?"

So you can understand why I was crazy about Kay. I often wished I could trade in Alan for a sister like her. I even thought that, someday, when I'm ready to settle down and was looking for a perfect companion, I'd like to find a girl just like Kay. In my book she was O-Kay, which was an expression my cousin Gary originated, but it expressed my sentiments perfectly.

We reached Tulsa before noon, and since there was such a large choice of restaurants and everybody was hungry, we stopped there for lunch. I don't know why sitting in a car for hours doing nothing should make anyone hungry, but we began talking about food a couple of hours after each meal. As a matter of fact, food was one of our favorite subjects. Tulsa was known as the Oil Capital of the Nation, since an immense oil field had been discovered there thirty years earlier. We saw endless oil derricks and storage tanks, and the whole town, it seemed, smelled of crude oil.

"Well, folks, where to?" asked my Uncle Nathan. "We've got the Crude Café over there and the Barrel Inn down the street."

"How about that one across the street?" asked my mother. "It's called the Oil Pit."

Apparently, every restaurant in town suggested the oil business.

"None of them sounds very appetizing," said my father, "so I don't think it matters."

We ate at the Oil Pit, and the food was surprisingly good. Thankfully, nothing we ordered had anything to do with oil. An hour later, we were fed, gassed up, and back on the road. Within minutes we were out in the country, staring at cattle, sheep, and oil wells, and heading straight for Oklahoma City, which, as the song promised, was sure to be mighty pretty.

CHAPTER EIGHT

Still More Kicks

When the composer of *Get Your Kicks on Route 66* said that Oklahoma City is '*mighty pretty,*' I figure he used the word 'pretty' because it rhymed with 'City'. In my opinion Oklahoma City was not only *not* pretty, it wasn't even attractive. We passed through it quickly and began to look for a place to spend the night. A few miles from the Texas border we found a motel called the Thunderbird Tourist Villa. A strange combination of words, I thought. There *were* colorful Indian thunderbirds painted on the door of each unit, but we saw few tourists, and it could hardly be considered a villa. Actually, it was more like a shack. We traveled nearly three hundred miles that day, and we were exhausted. My Aunt Gracie and her two daughters decided to go straight to bed, and my Uncle Nathan and Gary joined the Newman clan for dinner.

The only place nearby was a café called the Trading Post, and it was run by a group of real Seminole Indians. At least they looked authentic. The waiters were dressed in their tribal finest, as though they were preparing to hold a powwow or maybe scalp a few customers. I'd never seen an actual Indian before; all I knew about them came from books and the dozens of westerns I sat through on those Saturday afternoons at the movies. Except for people like Hiawatha and Tonto, the Lone Ranger's pal, most were portrayed as threatening characters, who galloped around covered wagons shooting flaming arrows and generally causing a lot of death and destruction. Those in the Trading

Post didn't seem like that at all, but I was apprehensive nonetheless.

A solemn-looking waiter approached our table. He had dark braids, an eagle's feather in his headband, and was dressed in buckskins and leather moccasins. He raised his arm and said, "How!" Jeez, I thought, this guy's the real McCoy.

"What you have?" he asked in a deep bass voice. There was a large wooden plank hanging on the wall, and the menu items were spelled out in letters that were applied with a wood burning set. Most dishes were the same as could be found in any café anywhere, and I was disappointed. I figured this would be a great opportunity to sample some authentic Indian food, whatever that was.

"Excuse me," I said, "do you serve any real Indian dishes?"

"We have some," he answered, "but most white folk don't like Indian food."

"Well, like what have you got?" I persisted. He paused for a moment before answering.

"We have roast desert turtle, braised bison heart, barbecued doves, and I think maybe there still some simmered dog brains left. So, what sound good to you?" There was a long, awkward silence.

"Actually," I said, "I think I'll have a hamburger."

My innocent order set off a burst of laughter from both Gary and my brother Alan. "What a close call," said Gary. "I thought for sure you were going to fall for the roasted turtle." And then they started to laugh again. I still don't know what they found so funny.

The others ordered conventional dishes from the menu on the wall, and the waiter left.

"I think Old Chief Sourpuss was having a little fun with you," said my father. "Maybe you should call his bluff and order the dog brains."

"Oh yeah," said Alan, "I'd love to see what those look like."

"Okay," I said, "I'll do it—but only if Alan takes the first bite. What do you say, Alan?"

My brother didn't answer, but the look on his face said he would rather be trampled by a herd of buffaloes.

The next day we drove across the Texas panhandle, which was shaped like a handle only if you considered the rest of Texas a pan. By this time we were seeing dozens of Okies—as Gary called them—displaced farmers from Arkansas, Oklahoma, and Texas who were driving to California. This area had experienced a terrible drought over the last few years, and the land had turned into the now famous Dust Bowl. The result was no crops, no income, and crushing poverty for thousands of destitute farmers. Most were packed into cars, the tops of which were stacked high with everything they owned. It was depressing to witness all that poverty, but it suddenly made us realize how lucky we were. All of us traveling down this highway were going to California for a second chance in life, but that's where the coincidence ended. While we looked forward to establishing the branch of a going business, the desperate farmers had nothing to look forward to but uncertainty.

We spent the next two days traveling through New Mexico. The longest part of Route 66, almost four hundred and fifty miles of it, cut right through the middle of the state. Finally, the landscape began to change. Missouri, Kansas, Oklahoma, and Texas were not only flat as a pancake, but, without doubt, more boring than anything I'd ever experienced. After leaving Texas, however, we found ourselves in the foothills; and now, we were driving through the first real mountains I had ever seen. A few peaks near the town of Tucumcari were over five thousand feet high; and as we traveled further west, some rose more than ten thousand feet. None of us had ever seen anything like the Rocky Mountains, and we were glued to the window staring at that incredible sight.

Before reaching Gallup, New Mexico, we crossed the Continental Divide, which I learned was the crest of the mountain chain that ran from Canada to Mexico. On the east side of the divide, water flowed towards the Gulf of Mexico, and on the west side, water flowed towards the Pacific Ocean. I didn't understand why the Continental Divide was such a big deal, but there was a large sign proclaiming the precise location of this prominent line. It felt like we were crossing something as important as the equator or the International Date Line.

Although this part of the country was more interesting than the flat lands of the Midwest, driving for an entire day was still incredibly boring. There was little to do but read my comic books, stare at the scenery, or make small talk with my relatives, who I still blamed for messing up my previously comfortable life.

To escape reality, I often fell into a semi-conscious state and engaged in fantasies inspired by the exciting serials I watched on Saturday afternoons. There I was, for example, the legendary frontiersman, Peter Trailblazer Newman, making my way through uncharted territory that looked a lot like the land around the Continental Divide.

I was surrounded by hostile tribes and in constant risk of being captured. One day, my horse stumbled, I hit a rock as I fell and was knocked unconscious. When I came to, I was a prisoner in the enemy camp. The Chief wanted to know where the Army troops were. "No dice, Chief, I'm sworn to secrecy. Torture me if you must, but you'll get nothing out of me." The chief's daughter, Winona, who looked like my cousin Kay, pleaded with her father for my life. "Let him go, he means us no harm, and besides, I'm in love with him." The Chief said, "If he can defeat our bravest warrior, Sakima, he can go free. Otherwise he faces torture and death." The fight lasted less than a minute. As Sakima came at me with a tomahawk, I deftly stepped aside and caught him with a ferocious blow to the head. He was out like a light. "I'll be going now," I said, "and Winona's coming with me." We disappeared over the hill and rode away into the setting sun.

My fantasies always had a happy ending, and they did wonders to help pass the interminable time.

The frequent Burma Shave signs were another diversion. These were a series of five, individual signs spaced about fifty yards apart along the edge of the highway. They were four-line jingles that always ended with a fifth sign that simply said *Burma Shave*. The Burma Shave Company created these to advertise their product, brushless shaving cream; and they generally offered driving advice, a moral message, or were related to shaving. The signs were comical or witty and we loved reading them out loud as we drove by. Some of my favorites were these:

Do not pass—On curves or hill—If cops don't catch you—Morticians will

Ben met Anna—Made a hit—Neglected beard—Ben-Anna split

On curves ahead—Remember, Sonny—That rabbit's foot—Didn't save the Bunny

We all had our favorites, and just thinking about them made us laugh. My mother particularly liked this one:

To kiss a mug—That's like a cactus—Takes more nerve—Than it does practice

And my father thought this was the wittiest:

Her chariot raced—At eighty per—They hauled away—What had Ben Hur

It was pretty corny stuff, I'll admit, but you have to remember we were driving through the vast, empty expanse of our country, and the entertainment options were about as limited as those on a desert island.

Shortly after leaving the state of New Mexico, a tire on my Uncle Nathan's Buick had a spectacular blowout. Our Chevy was bringing up the rear, as usual, perhaps fifty yards behind my uncle's car, and the explosion was deafening. I thought at first the entire Buick had blown up, but it turned out to be only a tire. We all pulled off the road and the driver's gathered to survey the damage. Strips of rubber were lying all over the place, and the car's right rear wheel was sitting on the gravel shoulder. Nothing was left of the inner tube or tire, except the mess of shredded rubber lying on the pavement.

My distraught Aunt Gracie was standing on the shoulder of the road next to the car, and her daughters were hovering around, consoling her. The explosion had practically given her a heart attack, and she was sobbing and shaking and directing a lot of her remarks to God, who, I was pretty sure, had nothing to do with the blowout. My cousin Shelley wasn't in much better shape; she was also crying, but she seemed more angry than frightened. Cousin Kay, unlike the rest of her family, was doing her best to suppress her laughter. She obviously thought having a massive blowout was the funniest thing that happened to us since leaving Chicago.

My mother rushed over to my aunt and said, "It's okay, Gracie, no one is hurt, and all we've lost is a tire and a little time."

"Easy for you to say, Jenny; you weren't in our car when the explosion went off. I thought we were all dead and that we'd never even get to *see* California"

My father, Uncle Nathan, and Gary surveyed the situation and concluded that there was no damage, other than the loss of the tire. They got out the jack and spare tire and began to jack up the car. When the new tire was in place and secured, Gary let the car down slowly until the tire rested on the ground. That's when we discovered the spare tire had no air, none at all. It was as flat as a pancake, and we let out a communal groan.

"Anyone got a pump?" asked my uncle.

"What?" responded my father, "Doesn't this fancy new Buick come with a tire pump?"

My mother pulled my father aside and said, "Now look, don't get started. We're in a bit of trouble here, and we've got to get through this. So stop already with the sarcasm."

"Okay," said my father, "but your pompous, know-it-all brother has been bugging me since this trip began. He's acting like a real *putz*, and I'm just giving a little bit back to him."

"Well take it easy," replied my mother. "He's your boss and your brother-in-law, and we've all got to get along. Now try to be more understanding."

My father was still annoyed, but he knew my mother was right. He hollered to my uncle, "Sure, Nathan, I've got a pump; it's in the trunk."

The three men took turns pumping up the spare tire, and within thirty minutes we were back on the road and rolling along through the state of Arizona.

Meanwhile, in the Kramarsky Buick—as we later learned—Nathan asked his wife, "Did you hear what Sam said? I don't think that crack was about my car: that was meant for me."

"Don't be so sensitive, dear; we've all had a terrible shock. I'm sure Sam was just feeling upset, like the rest of us."

"I'm not upset," spoke up Kay. "I think the exploding tire was just about the most exciting thing that's happened since we left Chicago."

"Well aren't you the brave one," said Shelley. "Maybe we should all give you a medal."

"Oh relax," replied her sister. "Have you completely lost your sense of humor?"

"Well maybe I don't find you very funny."

"You don't find *anything* funny. Seems like you just can't wait to be an old maid."

"Now that's enough," said Uncle Nathan. "Let's stop this bickering. In a few days this trip will be over. Until then, try to remain civil and be nice to one another."

We had been on the road for a week now, and clearly, the strain was beginning to show. It felt as though we were all stuck in a small rowboat in the middle of some vast ocean. There was no escape; we slept together, we ate all our meals together, and being together every day was our only companionship. But being together had become a challenge. We needed some time off, we needed a little separation, and most of all, we needed for this trip to end.

CHAPTER NINE

The Promised Land

"You know the best part about being in Arizona?" asked my father.

We were coming down the western slope of the Rocky Mountains and were now some sixty miles south of Grand Canyon National Park.

"Yeah," answered my indifferent brother Alan, "we're not in Oklahoma, Texas, or New Mexico."

"You're right, of course, but that isn't what I had in mind. The best part about being in Arizona," and here his voice began to rise, "is that in twenty-four hours we'll be in California!" And then he began to sing *California Here I Come*, which, incidentally, was not the first time he did that. It had practically become the family theme song. My father's voice wasn't particularly good, but he more than made up for it with his unrestrained enthusiasm. There was little doubt my father believed California was the Promised Land, and not just in a manner of speaking. He truly believed it in the larger, biblical sense.

I remember from Sunday school that the original Promised Land was Canaan, the land God promised to Abraham and his descendants. According to the story in Genesis, God ordered Abraham to *go forth to a land flowing with milk and honey;* and it was there, God assured him, the ancient tribe would find ultimate happiness. My parents were convinced that California was our Promised Land, and if we didn't actually drown in milk and honey, we'd certainly find more happiness there than we had known in Chicago. None of this made much sense to me. I was happy living in Chicago, and I believed that going through this ordeal was too great a risk for the chance I'd be even happier in California. I mean, how happy is a guy supposed to be? I also thought my folks were unrealistically optimistic. What made them think they would find more happiness in one place than the other? As far as I was concerned, the jury was still out on that one.

I had serious questions about this move, and they caused me plenty of anxiety. My parents discussed these concerns with Alan and me, and they tried to be reassuring. But how could they possibly know anything when neither of them had ever been to California? For me, it remained one great big question mark. I asked the questions, and their answers kept ringing in my head.

Where would we live?

An old friend, who now lives in Los Angeles, rented an apartment for us.

What's it like—will I have my own room?

It's very nice, and no, you'll continue to share a room with Alan.

What about my new school; is their fourth grade the same as at Avondale?

It's probably better than Avondale.

Will I make any new friends?

Are you serious? A great kid like you? The Californians will love you.

And what about the really good friends I left in Chicago, (including Anna Polanski, who might have been the new love of my life), would they all forget about me?

Don't be silly, how could anyone forget about a wonderful kid like you?

Most frustrating of all, why did I have to go through all this; was it some kind of punishment? And if so, what had I done to deserve it?

No answer to that one.

I was suddenly miserable and angry and depressed all over again.

By lunchtime we were near Flagstaff, where we found a restaurant that specialized in western-style barbeque. A large sign announced: BRONCO BOB'S BIG-TIME B-B-Q. The day was bright and sunny and warm enough to eat outside; so all nine of us sat around a large, picnic table under a big umbrella.

"Imagine that," said my Aunt Gracie, "eating outside in the middle of January. Oh, how I wish my bridge club could see me now! I know it's an unkind thought, but I kind of hope that, at this very moment, they're freezing their little behinds off in Chicago."

"If I remember correctly," said my Uncle Nathan, "no one in your bridge club *has* a little behind." Even Aunt Gracie had to laugh at that one.

After we finished lunch, my father suggested, "Since we're so close to the Grand Canyon, what do you think about taking a detour and having a look at it?"

"Great idea," said Gary, "I've always wanted to see the Grand Canyon."

Before any discussion could take place, my Uncle Nathan said, "I think it's too far out of the way. It would take us an hour and a half each way, at least another hour to see the place, and by the time we got back on the road, it would be getting dark. No, I think we should skip it."

"Well," said my father, "maybe we should talk about it and get everybody's opinion."

"I'm not sure this is something we should be voting on," answered my uncle. "There are a number of practical considerations here. You know, we're not exactly on vacation. We're supposed to be in Los Angeles in another couple of days."

"Oh come on, Dad," chimed in my cousin Kay, "What difference will a few hours make? It would be exciting to visit the Grand Canyon. You know it's one of the Seven Natural Wonders of the World, and I've never seen a single one of them."

"Well, despite that awful deprivation," chimed in Shelley, "you seem to have survived." Her sarcastic remark was intended to strengthen her father's position while antagonizing her sister.

"Oh be quiet," answered Kay. "I just thought it might be interesting for us to see a natural wonder that's bigger than your enormous butt."

"Hey, nice shot," said Gary. "Got her square in the behind." Then everyone within earshot burst out laughing, except for Shelley, who looked close to tears as she stormed off in anger.

"Hey, hold on," said my father. "I didn't mean to start a civil war; I just thought it'd be a good idea to break up the trip and for all of us to visit a great national monument."

My mother, the peacemaker, attempted to mollify the group. "You know, dear, I think we'd all like to visit the Grand Canyon, but Nathan has a point. We're on our way to California to start a new business, and that's where our focus should be. If we're half as successful as I think we'll be, we can return to Arizona one day and spend as much time as we want seeing all the sights. For now, I think we should get to Los Angeles as quickly as we can."

That pretty much settled the matter; no one felt like opposing the powerful Kramarsky team of Nathan and Jenny. My father was obviously annoyed, and Kay looked disappointed, but the rest of us were too tired and too indifferent. We climbed back into our respective cars and headed west.

We stopped that night outside of Kingman, Arizona, at a place named Green Acres Motel. It was an odd name, I thought, because we were in the middle of a desert, and although there were plenty of acres, the only thing green was the neon sign on the motel roof. We saw nothing but the distant hills and lots of scrub brush. It looked so desolate I figured even cactus would have a tough time surviving in that environment. At precisely nine-o'clock the following morning we crossed the Colorado River and entered the Promised Land. Unfortunately, it looked a lot like the barren desert on the other side of the river. Nevertheless, the sign said WELCOME—YOU ARE NOW ENTERING CALIFORNIA, so I figured it had to be true. When he saw the sign, my father began to sing again. To the same tune that regularly drove us crazy he sang, "*Cal-i-fornia here we are, lead me to the nearest bar …*"

Suddenly, in the middle of my father's performance, we saw my uncle's car stop abruptly. The other cars pulled over as well.

"What's up?" asked my father.

"Gracie wants to take a picture of us in front of the sign," said my uncle.

"Aren't you afraid that might make us late to Los Angeles?" asked my father. My mother gave him a dirty look, and Nathan pretended he didn't hear the sarcastic remark. But all of us knew what the derisive comment was all about; family relationships were deteriorating faster than the leftover snacks on the back seat of our car.

We spent most of that day traveling through the Mojave Desert, which was more desolate and far more boring than any previous part of this boring trip. Signs of life were few and far between; and when we did reach a town, we were just as happy to keep driving right through it. There was nothing of interest to see, and literally nothing to do. The usual activities—the word games, the comic books, the conversations— all that had grown tiresome. I would even have welcomed a little teasing by Alan, but he seemed lost in a zombie-like trance. The trip was wearing us down, and it felt like a black cloud was hanging over our gloomy caravan. Even the place names sounded unfriendly—Needles,

Daggett, Chambles, and, believe it or not, Siberia. Time to get lost in another fantasy, I thought.

There I was, Space Cadet Peter Newman, alone on a strange planet, and the hostile terrain looked a lot like the Mojave Desert.

My spaceship had crash-landed, and I was searching for help. I heard a sound from behind a pile of rocks, and suddenly there emerged three fantastic creatures. They had lizard-like heads, webbed hands at the end of their arms, and dinosaur-like tails. "I come in peace," I said. Instead of answering, they opened their mouths and long flames shot towards me. Holy smokes! I thought, I've got to get out of here. I turned and ran back towards my ship, but the creatures began to follow. "Okay, boys, you asked for it!" I drew my ray gun and gave them a short blast. "That ought to hold you," I said. But no—they kept coming; my ray gun had no effect on their lizard-like skin. I reached my ship, slammed shut the hatch, and aimed my super ray cannon at my aggressive pursuers. "Don't say I didn't warn you," I said, as I gave them a lethal blast. That did it; they evaporated in a cloud of steam. I cranked up my engine, and, much to my surprise, it started. I blasted off and headed back to earth, where the only place you found lizard heads were on real lizards.

My uncle decided we should arrive in Los Angeles early in the day, so we stopped that evening in Azusa, some forty miles from our final destination. We stayed at another crummy motel, which was indistinguishable from the other crummy motels we had stayed in since leaving home. But the good news turned out to be the place next door. It was called Freddy Pfefferman's Famous Foot-long Kosher Weiner Factory. None of us had even heard of a foot-long hot dog before, and here they were—twelve inches of deliciously spiced pink meat served on a twelve-inch-long bun and generously slathered with mustard, onions, and pickle relish. This was a nine-year-old's fantasy come true. In the time it took me to savor every delicious bite, my cousin Gary downed two of them, washed down with two large root beers. The sighs of satisfaction were exceeded in magnitude only by the belching that followed.

I slept fitfully that night, and it wasn't the twelve inches of undigested hot dog lying in the bottom of my stomach. I knew that tomorrow our trip would be over. For the past nine days I had been in limbo, but finally, I would have to face the uncertainties surrounding my new life.

CHAPTER TEN

Beverly Hills

"Beverly Hills? Beverly Hills? You rented us a place in Beverly Hills? Sylvia, what were you thinking? We can't afford to live in Beverly Hills!"

My mother was shouting in a phone booth somewhere near downtown Los Angeles. The party on the other end of the line, Sylvia Garbo (née Garbrotzky) was the family friend who had rented a new apartment for us. My mother called Sylvia to let her know we just arrived in Los Angeles, and, by the way, where exactly *was* our new apartment?

"Calm down, Jenny, and I'll tell you everything," answered Sylvia. "First of all, there's something you should know about Beverly Hills. It's not all fancy-schmancy movie star mansions. Not by a long shot. There are lots of people just like you and me living in Beverly Hills. Your new place is on the eastern edge of the city; and—get this—the rent is twenty-eight dollars a month. Tell me, Jenny, how you gonna beat that? But there *is* a problem, and I'm sorry to be the one to tell you. Your furniture hasn't arrived yet, so you'll have to stay in a hotel for a couple of days. There's a small place two doors away from me, and it's just a block from your new apartment."

None of us heard what Sylvia said, but we clearly heard my mother use one of the forbidden four-letter words. My brother and I looked at each other and suddenly realized things were not going well, and the problem, we assumed, had something to do with Beverly Hills. I didn't know much about Beverly Hills, but, of course, I had heard of it. I mean, who hadn't? Anyone who ever read a movie magazine knew that's where lots of movie stars lived—people like Charlie Chaplin, Douglas Fairbanks, and Marlene Dietrich. What I didn't know, however, was that Beverly Hills was an entirely separate city lying within, and completely surrounded by, the city of Los Angeles. I always thought Beverly Hills was like Hollywood, not actually a city, but an area of Los Angeles where film studios were located.

"We can discuss everything when I see you," continued Silvia, "but right now let me give you directions to the hotel. We can talk there."

My mother scribbled down the directions, hung up the phone, and emerged from the telephone booth looking forlorn and miserable.

"What's wrong?" asked my father. "You look awful."

"Sylvia just told me our furniture hasn't arrived, and we have to spend a couple of nights in a hotel. We can't sleep in our new apartment tonight because there are no beds. In fact, there's nothing, not even an apple crate to sit on."

"That's it? We have to spend two more nights in a hotel? Of course that's disappointing, but all things considered, it could be worse."

"I just want to be settled," my mother said despondently. "I finally want to be settled. We've been traveling forever, and I want us to be in a place of our own. I'm sick and tired of living like gypsies. When will this ever end?" And then, very softly, she started to cry. My mother, the Rock of Gibraltar, was finally cracking under the accumulated stress of our cross-country journey. I had seen my mother cry a couple of times before, and it always made me anxious. Mothers weren't supposed to cry; that's what little kids did.

We returned to where the others in our caravan were waiting and gave them the news.

"Well this is it," said my father. "We're off to a hotel near our new apartment. Seems our furniture hasn't arrived yet."

"I told you not to use those cut-rate people," said my uncle. "This is exactly the kind of trouble you should have expected from a company called Good and Cheap Movers."

"Thanks for the advice, Nathan, but it's not particularly helpful right now. I'll see you at the new office tomorrow. So long, Gracie, and see you soon, kids."

My aunt, uncle, and cousins were heading to a house rented more than a month ago, which was also in Beverly Hills. For the benefit of my cousin Kay, the house was located near the high school. We were going our separate ways, and for the first time in a long time, we would be apart. I kissed my aunt and uncle, hugged my cousins, and suddenly felt sad and depressed. The long motor trip was over, and I was glad about that, but now I was forced to face the anxieties of my new life in the Promised Land.

The Beverly Hills Tower Hotel was not a tower at all; it was named after Tower Drive, the street on which it was located. It was a relatively new, two-story structure; and it looked similar to all the other buildings in the neighborhood, neat, clean, and with a manicured lawn leading to the attractive entrance. When we arrived, Sylvia had already rented a suite that we would occupy until our furniture arrived. She hugged my mother and the two women chattered on for several minutes, rarely even stopping to hear what the other was saying.

Silvia Garbo came to Los Angeles four years earlier with the express purpose of becoming a movie star. Although that ambitious goal continued to elude her, she had appeared in a half dozen minor movies, generally as a gangster's moll or showgirl type, and once as the owner of a saloon in Dodge City, Kansas. The actual number of words she spoke on camera could be counted on two hands. Sylvia was in her mid twenties, attractive in a platinum blond, Jean Harlow sort of way, and she had a full figure that attracted considerable attention from men and women alike.

"Don't tell me this cute little guy is Peter," Sylvia said, tousling my hair. "What a big boy you've become." And then looking towards my brother, "Alan, my God, another couple of years and you're gonna be a real lady-killer. What good-looking kids you have, Jenny!"

Finally she got to my father. "Sam, you gorgeous guy, come here and give me a big hello." She practically wrapped herself around my father and gave him a deep kiss square on the mouth. My father seemed embarrassed, but he didn't offer much resistance.

"You better keep this guy locked up, Jenny, or some young starlet's gonna steal him away."

"As long as it isn't you," answered my mother, who was looking more than a little annoyed by the scene just witnessed.

Sylvia ignored the comment and said, "Drop your bags, boys and girls, and let's stroll over to your new apartment."

Our new—and very empty—apartment was located a short block away on Gale Drive. As we rounded the corner, Sylvia pointed out La Cienega Park, which was situated at the end of the street.

"It's a wonderful place for the boys to play," she said. "There's a baseball diamond, swings, slides, horseshoes, and a public swimming pool that's open all summer. They're gonna love it here." I don't know how Alan felt, but for me, "love" wasn't exactly the word that came to mind.

Our new apartment building was a two-story, stuccoed structure containing four units—two on the ground floor that were mirrored images and two identical units above those. It was built a few years earlier and was undistinguished in almost every way. Our red brick apartment house in Chicago had character, but this new place had no personality whatsoever. To begin with, it was beige, probably the most boring color ever invented. And the windows and trim were dark brown. The whole thing looked like an old piece of chocolate cake. Palm trees were evenly spaced along the street, and those provided an exotic quality to the building; but our new home had an overall sense of impermanence. Our particular apartment was on the south side of the second floor, so at least it got plenty of sun. The empty rooms were scrupulously clean, the wood floors looked recently waxed, and we tried to imagine how our Chicago furniture would look there.

"Where's my room?" I wanted to know.

"I told you," answered my mother, "you and Alan are sharing a room, and I think it's at the end of the hallway."

"Oh how lucky you are!" cried Sylvia. "The rear bedroom is the largest bedroom."

"Not large enough for me," I answered. "I'll still be able to see Alan."

"Well, it's no big thrill for me either," remarked my brother.

"Now stop this," said my father. "Let's try to get along."

My mother seemed embarrassed by the dispute taking place in front of her old friend, and she shot us all a dirty look. But Sylvia barely noticed that the dysfunctional Newman boys were simply relating in their customary way.

Sylvia suggested a kosher delicatessen around the corner where we could get a modest meal, and my mother invited her to join us. We sat at a large table and Sylvia played the part of tourist guide. She advised which was the best neighborhood grocery store, bank, cleaners, service station, and even suggested where my father should go for a haircut. She sounded as authoritative as a native Californian.

"Now," she asked, "any questions?"

"I have a question," I said. "Do you know anything about my new school?"

"I sure do," Sylvia answered. "The school you're going to is called Horace Mann, and it's within walking distance. You boys are lucky to be in one of the best school districts in the entire country. The schools here are terrific; the teachers are the best, and you're going to get a fabulous education."

"How do you know all this?" asked my father.

"I dated the high school English teacher for several months," answered Sylvia. "What a great guy! He told me a lot about his job and the school system, as well as a whole lot more. You might say I got an up close and personal view of things, if you get my drift." Everyone got Sylvia's drift.

"That's great," I interrupted. "But do you know what the fourth grade arithmetic class is studying, or where they are in history or geography?"

"You got me there; I have no idea what fourth graders study, but I'm sure it isn't much different from the Chicago schools. A smart guy like you should have no problem."

No problem for Sylvia maybe, but I felt there was plenty to worry about.

The food at Morty's Kosher Delicatessen turned out to be the best we had eaten since leaving Chicago, even better than the chop suey at Ding Dong's outside of Joplin, Missouri. On the other hand, I had to admit, we had not even *seen* a delicatessen since leaving Chicago.

We left Morty's, said goodbye to Sylvia, and walked back to our temporary apartment at the Beverly Hills Tower Hotel. Another night, another hotel, and another bed. Like my mother, I, too, was getting tired of this endless nomadic existence.

I crawled into bed that night, but I wasn't very sleepy. My mind was racing across half a continent, trying to assimilate the experiences of the last ten days. We had traveled so far, seen so much, and suffered through so many long, boring stretches of our country. And for what? To make a new life, to find greater happiness, to avoid shoveling snow? I couldn't believe any of those reasons were worth the stress of the past ten days.

My mother came into our room to say goodnight.

"Well, boys, we made it. We didn't get lost, Indians didn't attack us, and here we are in California, safe and sound. Even though we're not in our own apartment yet, we will be in a couple of days. I think the worst is over. And the best part is, we don't have to drive anywhere tomorrow. Your father and I think you boys have been wonderful travelers, and we love you both."

Nice speech, but I think the endless travel must have warped my mother's brain. How could she forget the continuous battles between Alan and me, the times we had to ride in separate cars, the insults, the sarcasm, and the general hostility? Where was she when all that was going on? On the other hand, if she thought we were great travelers, who was I to argue?

"Goodnight, Mom," we said almost in unison.

The following morning my brother and I would enroll at Horace Mann elementary school. That decisive event would be the final indication we were here to stay. No more dreams of waking up in my old bedroom in Chicago, no more hopes of retuning to Avondale School, no more chance to see old friends, and, sadly, no more fantasies about Anna Polanski. Finally, it was over. I was tired and anxious and felt my life was still out of control.

I just hoped I wouldn't wet my bed again.

CHAPTER ELEVEN

Horace Mann

Horace Mann, an educational reformer from the nineteenth century, was acknowledged to be the father of American public education. He believed that every child, until the age of sixteen, should receive a basic education funded by local taxes. Because of his prominence in the history of education, hundreds of schools throughout the country were named after him. This included one of the four elementary schools in the city of Beverly Hills, where I now found myself. Of course I knew nothing of Horace Mann on that first day. The name sounded old fashioned; I mean, these days, who names a kid Horace? But I figured he must have been somebody important if they named a school after him.

My mother accompanied my brother and me to the registration office, and I was quickly assigned to the fourth grade and Alan to the sixth. The first thing I noticed about my new school is that it was a really attractive building. It was built in an Old Spanish style, with light-colored plaster walls, a red tile roof, and colorful decorative tiles. Adjacent to the sizeable, gravel-covered playground was a spacious patio bordered by colorful shrubs. The patio was shaded by large olive trees and furnished with wooden tables and benches. Compared with Avondale, which didn't have a single potted plant, Horace Mann looked like a classy country club. It was also bright and clean inside. The wide corridors had light plaster walls, and the large classroom doors were made of beautiful natural oak. What struck me about all the buildings in our new hometown was their brightness. Buildings in Chicago were mostly dark red brick, and many had a coat of soot from the constant coal-burning furnaces. But here they were light and bright and somehow looked happier.

"I'll take you to your classroom now," said the registration lady.

I kissed my mother goodbye, waved to Alan, and was suddenly reminded of my first day at Avondale, when I began kindergarten. I felt the same unease; it was all so new, and I had no idea what awaited me. My new teacher, Miss Gridley, was a cheerful, attractive young woman. She greeted me and then introduced me to the class. "This is Peter Newman, boys and girls; he's just arrived here from Chicago." Several new classmates said, "Hi Peter," but I heard one voice say, "Big deal, so what."

After being assigned a seat, I noticed something that generated such overwhelming mortification that I wanted to leap out the window. Every boy in the class was wearing long pants! I, of course, was wearing knickers. Knickers! Every kid in Chicago under the age of sixteen wore knickers— knickers and long socks—that's what we wore all winter long. In the summer we wore short pants and short socks. But at Horace Mann every kid was wearing long pants. I could not have felt more foolish, more unfashionable, or more humiliated. Why didn't somebody warn me about this? Certainly Sylvia Garbo must have noticed my knickers.

The only time in my life I ever wore long pants was when I was six years old and my cousin Florence insisted that I be ring-bearer at her wedding. Her father, my Uncle Benjamin, rented me a tuxedo, complete with black tie and cummerbund. I performed my part flawlessly, but afterwards everyone said I looked less like a ring bearer and more like a ventriloquist's dummy. But now, I would have given anything to look like a ventriloquist's dummy; a dummy with long pants was infinitely better than a yokel in knickers.

The class was studying the Missions of Early California, and Miss Gridley was describing the one in Santa Barbara. She tacked up a few photographs of the Mission, and was referring to the beautiful design of the principal entrance. She was speaking English, but her words had absolutely no meaning to me. I had never heard of a mission and had no idea what it was. And the name that kept coming up, Junipero Serra, was another mystery. Was he the builder, the guy who owned the building, or possibly the name of the donkey posing prominently in one of the old photos? If there was a quiz that morning, I was sure I'd fail it completely and probably be put back into the third grade— maybe even the second.

When the lunch bell rang, I thought: saved by the bell, but for how long? Miss Gridley approached and said, "This subject is probably a bit confusing to you, Peter. I'm sure fourth-graders in Chicago don't study California missions." Then she handed me a small book entitled *The Missions of California* and said, "Read the first two chapters of this book tonight, and you'll know as much as most of the others in this class."

As we filed out of the classroom, half the kids headed for the cafeteria and the rest went to the patio. It was a beautiful winter day, and the sun shone brightly. Many had brought their lunches from home, and thanks to my mother, I also had a bag lunch consisting of a salami sandwich (courtesy of Morty's Deli), a chocolate cookie, and an apple. She may have failed me in the pants department, but in the lunch department, she was a winner. Since Alan was nowhere to be found, I chose a seat at one of the wooden tables under the olive trees and opened my lunch.

A few moments later, someone I recognized from Miss Gridley's class approached me.

"Hello," she said. "We're in the same class; my name is Lindaberg."

"Did you say Lindbergh or Hindenburg?"

"No, no," she said laughing. "I said Linda Berg."

"Oh, sorry," I said. "I figured you were either a famous flyer or a zeppelin."

She laughed again. "That's funny. I just wanted to say you looked pretty confused in there. Was it the mission business?"

"Yeah, the mission business, as well as the Horace Mann, Beverly Hills, and California business. *Everything* is confusing; we just arrived yesterday."

"I figured," she said, "the knickers kind of gave it away. But don't worry; it gets easier. We came here from Philadelphia about two months ago, and I'm just beginning to feel at home."

"Well I hope it doesn't take *me* that long," I answered. "By the way, who's the guy who said 'big deal' when Miss Gridley introduced me?"

"That was the class clown, Stan Fishbein, a real jerk. Don't pay any attention to him; he always acts like a moron."

Linda sat down at my table, and we continued chatting throughout lunch. What a pretty girl, I thought. She was wearing a pale blue dress, a white bow in her hair, and her smile lit up the entire patio. But what is she doing here, I wondered? Nobody before had ever befriended me like this. Was it my bewilderment? Was it the knickers? It couldn't be my personality—I hadn't opened my mouth in class. Whatever the reason, I could not have been more grateful. Right then and there, I decided I really, really liked Linda.

When the bell rang again we returned to the classroom. I've made a friend, I thought, and I couldn't help feeling optimistic. Later that afternoon I felt even more encouraged when I discovered that the material being covered in arithmetic was the same as I studied several weeks earlier. They were just learning to multiply three-digit numbers, a skill I mastered at Avondale, and I was also miles ahead in the use of fractions. I raised my hand several times and always had the right answer. What a great feeling! That afternoon my classmates began to suspect that the new arrival from Chicago, despite the funny-looking pants, was an absolute genius. I thought to myself: *maybe Horace Mann won't be so bad after all.*

When classes ended, I found Alan in the schoolyard.

"How'd it go?" I asked.

"Not too bad. I wasn't quite the dumbest guy in class; they've got some real nitwits here."

"You walking home?"

"Naw, a couple of guys asked if I wanted to play some ball. Think I'll stay here."

That was Alan, maybe not the dumbest in his class, but even with his dumb-looking knickers, charismatic enough to be invited to play ball.

When I got home, my mother wanted to know every detail of my first day in school.

"Not actually horrible," I said, "but I'll tell you this, I'm through wearing knickers. Everyone here wears long pants, and they all looked at me like I was from another planet. We've got to get me some long pants, and until we do, I'm not going back to school."

"Take it easy," said my mother. "We'll get some long pants, but we can't go anywhere until your father gets home from the office. Think you can wait that long?"

"Okay," I answered, "but I'm not going outside. I don't need anyone else laughing at me."

It was late in the afternoon when my father returned from his first day at the new office.

"Let's go," I said, "the stores close in a half hour, and I've got to get some long pants!"

"What's going on?" asked my father. "And what's this about pants? I've had a tough day and I need to sit down for a minute."

"No time for that," I said. "If I don't get some long pants right now, my school days are over, and maybe my life, too."

"I agree," chimed in Alan. "For once, the midget here is right."

My mother explained the situation to my father, and we all jumped in the car and headed for the Sears Roebuck store on Pico Boulevard. In less than thirty minutes Alan and I were wearing new, and properly long, corduroy pants. His were brown, and mine were navy blue. It was my first article of clothing that wasn't a hand-me-down. Almost at once I began to feel like a Californian. All that was left to do was go home and toss the knickers into the incinerator.

Later that evening my mother asked my father about his first day at the new Transparent Materials Company office.

"Well, it could be worse. It's a great place our agent rented—big warehouse, nice front offices, and a lot of interesting commercial stores in the neighborhood. We're still getting settled, but we should start seeing customers by next week."

"And how is Nathan doing?"

"Okay I guess," answered my father, "but what a *shmendrik*! If I say the desk belongs here, he says no, it belongs there. Everything is such a *megillah* with that man. I just hope we can settle down and do some business. Otherwise, I might just as well hand him over to the Chicago lenders and let them break his leg."

"Don't talk like that—not even as a joke. Nathan's my brother; and in case you forgot, he's also your employer."

"You don't have to remind me; he lets me know that several times a day."

Stuck in a temporary hotel after a long and arduous trip did not make our transition to a new life any easier. My parents were having their serious conversation in the bedroom, I was in the living room reading *The Missions of California*, and Alan was somewhere in the neighborhood, probably exploring new ways to cause trouble and embarrass the family. Each of the Newmans would require more time and more patience. But finally, here we were, in the Promised Land, and each of us was doing his best to make the necessary adjustments.

CHAPTER TWELVE

Becoming Californian

It is surprising how quickly I forgot about my early life in Chicago. Who would have thought? What had been my entire world was now the old world. After all the emotional outbursts about my ruined life, how I would regret this move forever, how I'd never be happy again; I became, within a couple of months, a totally integrated and comfortable Californian. Ah, the resilience of youth! I was saddened to realize I could not recall the names of some old Avondale friends—friends to whom I pledged everlasting devotion. Worse yet, for the life of me, I could not conjure up an image of my first true love, Anna Polanski. I remember that she had dark hair and was pretty, but that was all. Why didn't I have a photograph of her? I wrote to her a few times and even sent her a postcard of the Hollywood Bowl, as she requested; and she always answered my letters and cards. But I never thought to ask for her picture. It was about two months since we last corresponded, and now, I feared, it was too late. Anna, like my erstwhile knickers, had become part of the old world.

My life in Beverly Hills was filled with activities, most of which centered on Horace Mann and our new neighborhood. After finally moving into our apartment on Gale Drive, we all felt more comfortable, and the bonus for me was discovering several new playmates among our neighbors. There were even three from my own class, Hobart Johnson, Lenny Strauss and Stan Fishbein—yes, *that* Stan Fishbein, the one who said, upon my arrival in class, "Big deal, so what". The same guy Linda Berg characterized as a jerk and a moron. That very same Stan Fishbein! A few months after the incident I felt I knew him well enough to speak about it.

"You remember my first day in class? When Miss Gridley introduced me, you said, 'Big deal, so what'. Maybe you said it to be funny, but that was kind of mean. It was my first day of school, and that crack didn't exactly make me feel welcome."

"No, I don't really remember that, but why are you being such a baby about it? I think it was pretty harmless, and it probably did get a laugh."

That was it? He hurt my feelings to get a laugh? Linda was right; Stan was a jerk. So plain old Stan Fishbein, my new acquaintance, became known thereafter as Stan the Jerk, which was a designation he cheerfully accepted as a badge of honor.

Stan was basically a well-meaning, fun-loving guy. He had a husky build and looked like a miniature version of Babe Ruth, but a whole lot sloppier. Stan's sense of style—even for a little kid—was appalling. It's a wonder his parents permitted him to leave home dressed the way he often did. No two articles of clothing ever matched, and his outfits often looked as though a colorblind man in a dark closet chose them. He even wore mismatched socks on several occasions, but I suspect he did that to get a laugh.

Lenny Strauss was a short, slender, brainy guy who, among other intellectual pursuits, collected stamps. He reminded me of a much younger Albert Einstein, complete with messy hairdo, tiny glasses, and a careless personal style all his own. I was also interested in stamps, and Lenny and I spent hours collecting, cataloguing, trading, and comparing recent additions to our collections. He was easy to be with and always had an interesting story about a stamp, an obscure fact from history, or the latest detail of his older sister's sex life. We were just beginning to notice girls, and Lenny's older sister was definitely worth noticing.

Unlike Stan Fishbein, who was a jerk, and Lenny Strauss, who was a brain, Hobart Johnson was a mechanical genius. He understood how everything worked and was happy to share his knowledge. Hobie, as he was called, was tall, athletic, and very good-looking. By comparison, he made my other two friends look like a couple of unemployed sideshow performers. Hobie introduced me to model airplanes and thus became one of my closest friends. I was passionate about building model airplanes; and I decided, after a short time, that when I grew up I would become an aeronautical engineer. I was not only fascinated by the idea of flight, but I loved the smell of balsa wood, model airplane glue, and even the aroma of gasoline and motor oil. I could work for hours at a time putting together dozens of carefully fitted parts; and, if I do say so myself, I was really good at building models.

I began with simple rubber band-powered planes, and quickly graduated to gas-powered engines. I flew the early models at La Cienega Park, but the gas models had to be flown at a much larger open area. Hobie's father was usually available to drive us to the huge flying field near Rosecrans Avenue, because he was always home. I assumed he didn't have a job. Both he and his wife emigrated from Bristol fifteen years earlier, and both retained British accents. He could normally be found sitting on his front porch reading the newspaper, wearing an ill-fitting undershirt, and sporting a three-day growth of beard. It was hard to believe that when this overweight, balding, coarse-looking man spoke, he sounded exactly like Cary Grant.

My model building took place in our shared bedroom, and that caused problems. I built a table out of an old hollow-core door and set it up on two wooden horses in the corner near my bed. The homemade table became my personal and private world. It was there

I built my models, worked on my stamps, read comic books, and did my homework. It was the only place in the house that was exclusively mine, and everyone was warned never to invade that space. But not everyone respected my desire to build models, or, for that matter, my need for privacy.

"When are you going to get this crap out of here?" asked my irritated brother Alan. "The place smells like a glue factory, and besides, it takes up too much space"

"What are you complaining about?" I responded. "You've got your bed, desk, and chest of drawers, and all of that stuff takes up more than half the room."

"Yeah, well, I'm older, bigger, and I need more space than you."

"That isn't how it works, Alan. Fifty-fifty—that's the deal. Think of this as a jail cell; one bunk is all you get. If you're unhappy, speak to the warden."

"Well, I am unhappy. But I'm not going to speak to the warden; I'm going to strangle you."

Just then my mother walked into our room and asked what was going on.

"Alan's about to strangle me," I said. "He doesn't like me building models here."

"There'll be no strangling in this house, Alan." She said it in the same tone she used when telling us to pick up our socks. Don't be messy and don't strangle anyone.

"Isn't there enough trouble in this world without you two constantly fighting? Would it kill either of you to get along?"

"He's a knucklehead," I said.

"And he's a *putz*," replied Alan.

"When your father gets home," remarked my mother, "we'll discuss this with him."

That's a waste of time, I thought. These days my father was completely absorbed with Transparent Materials Company. Things were not going smoothly, and my father and uncle were spending long hours each day trying to solve problems. I saw my cousin Gary a few times, and he confirmed the situation.

"You ought to be glad you're still in school," he said. "Working for a living is a real pain. You wouldn't believe the screw-ups; material doesn't arrive on time, customers complain, money is tight, and our dads are at each other's throats. My advice to you is never grow up."

I knew my father was under a lot of stress, but he rarely spoke about it. In fact, he rarely spoke to us about anything; the implied message was: stay out of my way—I've got too many things on my mind. So bringing up Alan's unhappiness about my model building didn't seem like a great idea. If Alan strangled me, however, that might change a few things.

Nine months after arriving in California my father's older brother and his family arrived in California, having made the same trip down Route 66. My Uncle Arthur was married to my mother's favorite sister, Ethel. That's right; two brothers married two sisters. Therefore, our families were always close, and their children, my cousins, were almost like siblings. Their son, Alfred, known as Alfie, was half a year younger than Alan; and their daughter, Lynn, was five years younger than I. Our families always lived in the same apartment house in Chicago, and so it felt natural when they moved into the newly vacated apartment downstairs from us on Gale Drive.

We were pleased to see them again, but Alan and I continued to wonder what they were doing here. My father later explained that the two sisters simply could not bear to be separated. My father enjoyed the company of his brother, but as far as he was concerned, he could have lived a rich, full, and happy life without ever seeing Ethel again.

He considered her an opinionated busybody with whom he rarely agreed, but they remained mostly civil for the good of the family. My father once mentioned that ancient Judaic law required a man to take into his home the widow of a deceased brother. He made it clear to my mother, "If Art ever dies, I'm changing my religion."

Arthur was nine years older than my father and, unlike my father, retained an old world accent. He was quiet, serious, and not particularly sociable. He had many of the strong facial features of the Newmans, but was completely bald. He was the last of my father's siblings to be married, and many thought he would remain a bachelor forever, Ethel was four years older than my mother, and not nearly as attractive or charming. The family was convinced she would end up an old maid. After my parent's marriage, the two single siblings began spending time together and decided that being with an imperfect partner was better than living life alone.

For many years Uncle Art ran a hardware store that never made money on Evanston Avenue in Chicago. So they figured, if we're not going to make a decent living, why not be unsuccessful in a more benign climate? The sisters were thrilled to be reunited, and they spoke continuously for what seemed like the first two weeks. Ethel greatly admired my mother and tried to emulate her in every way. She even named her first child Alfred, so that Alan and Alfred could both be called Al. As my father sarcastically noted, "Can you believe, she actually thought that was a cute idea?"

Alfie was a quirky kid with some of the same antisocial habits of my brother. But he was bright, athletic, and generally got along well with others. His sister, Lynn, was considerably younger and still in kindergarten. As far as we boys were concerned, she pretty much didn't exist. Alfie was placed in my brother's class at Horace Mann, and the sibling rivalry that began in Chicago was reignited and thrived until well past their high school days. Neither of the Als, as I called them, set a commendable record for deportment. Therefore, when I followed in their footsteps, some two years later, teachers would eye me suspiciously wondering what kind of disruption I was about to perpetrate. At every grade level I was obliged to prove that I was, indeed, the good one.

One day I asked Alfie, "When Alan does something really dumb and destructive, why do you always go along with it—like throwing stones over the swimming pool wall at the park?" That was the caper that brought a visit to our house from the Beverly Hills Police Department.

"Oh he's just looking for a little fun and excitement," answered my cousin.

"What's the fun in having a police record?"

"Take it easy, Peter. We went back the next day and cleaned things up. We picked up every stone, even those at the deep end of the pool. And we also swept up the glass from the two broken windows."

"I figured you did that to avoid jail time," I said.

When the two Als became high school students, they and six others of their infamous group formed a social club called the Cossacks. They wore green felt jackets with tan leather sleeves, and the word Cossack was embroidered across the back.

"Do you know anything about Cossacks?" I asked my brother. "They were not exactly respectable guys. They raped and pillaged, persecuted Jews, and committed endless pogroms."

"That was a long time ago," answered Alan. "Cossacks have just the image we're looking for; they were daring and heroic."

Do you ever think about what you're doing?" I asked. "Being a Cossack is the same as if you belonged to the Beverly High Nazis and wore jackets with embroidered swastikas."

"You're way too sensitive, Peter. Why don't you lighten up? Anyway, it's not like we're asking you to join—that'll never happen."

The two Als had inadvertently become an anti-Semitic Butch Cassidy and Sundance Kid; and I, for one, was embarrassed and offended.

CHAPTER THIRTEEN

A Disastrous Year

At the beginning of 1941, I was twelve years old and in the seventh grade at Horace Mann. War was raging throughout Europe, and newspapers and newsreels reported the consistently bad news. Nazis had overrun much of northern Europe, Russia, and North Africa; and the Luftwaffe was regularly bombing British cities. Some Americans went overseas to fight with the Allied Forces; but except for the surge of activity in local defense factories and the regular defense bond drives, life in Beverly Hills continued pretty much as usual. That included both the good and bad.

"In a few months," said my mother, "you'll be thirteen, and your father and I want you to begin training for your bar mitzvah. We think you should study where Alan did, at the Olympic Jewish Center."

"I hate that place," I said. "It's dark and depressing and smells of boiled cabbage."

"Don't be silly. They have very good people there, and you'll get a fine education."

"I'm already getting a fine education at Horace Mann; and besides, I don't believe in all that Jewish hocus-pocus."

"Shush!" said my mother. "You want someone to hear you. This is part of your culture, your heritage; how can you call it hocus-pocus?"

"Well I think it's baloney. I don't want to learn Hebrew, and I don't need a bar mitzvah. Anyway, Lenny Strauss isn't having a bar mitzvah, and neither is Stan the Jerk. Why can't I be like them?"

"I suppose their parents don't care about Jewish culture; we do. And as sorry as I am that you feel that way, the decision has been made. You're starting classes at the end of next month, and in September you're having a bar mitzvah."

The irony of the moment did not escape me. At twelve years of age I was being treated like a baby, but in six months, after my bar mitzvah and according to Jewish tradition, I would be a man. Something just didn't add up. Jewish law declared that a boy became entirely responsible for his actions after a bar mitzvah, provided—and this seemed to me an important escape clause—there was the appearance of no fewer than two pubic hairs. No kidding, I'm not making this up. Why two hairs? Well, I suppose a single hair could be construed as something of a loose cannon, like a rebellious outgrowth in your nose or ear. But two or more pubic hairs, that's real proof of manhood. My hope was that two hairs might appear sometime before I was twenty-one. I was currently five-foot-one, my voice was in the soprano range, and except for what was on my head, not another hair could be found anywhere else on my entire body. If in six months I proclaimed, "Today I am a Man", I figured God would strike me dead with a lightning bolt.

None of my arguments changed a thing; by March I was attending afternoon classes twice a week at the Olympic Jewish Center. At about this same time I developed a habit in which I would arise very early in the morning, quietly get dressed, and walk down to Wilshire Boulevard. I would sit on a fire hydrant there for about twenty minutes, watch the traffic go by, think my thoughts, and then return home before anyone else was up. No one seemed to know about this or even miss me, and I enjoyed having those early morning moments to myself every day. Several years and one skilled therapist later I discovered this was a feeble revolt against authority; I was figuratively running away from home every day. At least it was relatively harmless and preferable to wetting my bed, my previous favorite way of expressing resentment.

The OJC, as we called it, was every bit as awful as I anticipated, and the odor of boiled cabbage was even worse. My instructor was a disagreeable former rabbi from Poland named Mordacai Sokolofski. He had been in this country for fifteen years and was not even close to speaking understandable English. His accent was so thick, it sounded like he was speaking under water. Sokolofski was short, plump, and had an aura of darkness about him. His long *payes* and beard were black with touches of gray, and he dressed entirely in black, including a large hat that was so much a part of his image, we all assumed he wore it to bed. Six other students were in my class, and, like me, none of them was happy to be there. Sokolofski insisted that everyone call him Rabbi, though he no longer was one. What did I care? Rabbi was easier than Sokolofski.

The Rabbi carried a sixteen-inch-long wooden ruler that was sporadically used as a pointer, baton, and weapon. He used the pointer to denote certain letters or words, the baton was used when leading the chorus, and the weapon was used to punish acts of perceived misbehavior. The ruler was also used occasionally to slap a desk and make a thunderous bid for absolute attention. After the first fifteen minutes of instruction I was sure I hated Sokolofski, and I wondered how I would survive six months of his aggressive tutelage. I was also certain it wasn't worth the tuition my parents were paying.

"Why are you having such trouble learning Hebrew?" the Rabbi wanted to know.

I wanted to ask him why *he* was having such trouble learning English. But instead I said, "I don't know. I've learned the alphabet, I know the sounds, but the words have no meaning to me."

"What?" he thundered. "No meaning? This is the Torah we're talking about. It is the most sacred scroll, the most important document in all of Judaism. No meaning? You're an imbecile!"

Now, how do you deal with that? Me, I just sat quietly hoping, perhaps if there were a God, he would give our unhappy Rabbi a small heart attack. No such luck. I complained to my parents about my sadistic teacher, but they felt I was being overly critical and intolerant. Even when the Rabbi struck me across the hand with his ruler one day, my father assumed I had provoked an incident. If things continued this way until September, I would not only be a man; but very likely, I'd be an unrepentant Rabbi-killer.

It was bad enough giving up two afternoons a week and having Hebrew School homework in addition to my other schoolwork; but when summer arrived, I got no time off for good behavior. When most of my friends were at the beach, I was spending three mornings a week reading meaningless symbols and avoiding confrontations with my nemesis, Sokolofski. In addition, I worked every evening constructing a speech, to be given in English, wherein I thanked my loving parents, dedicated teachers, and honored guests. When I look back on those days, I think my lack of faith and disdain for all things religious can be traced directly to the Olympic Jewish Center.

The summer passed quickly, and, ready or not—I felt not—the date of my bar mitzvah approached. Every relative, friend, and minor acquaintance was invited to the ceremony at the temple and the reception that followed at our home. My mother had been cooking and baking for weeks, and one would have thought the event was not about my coming of age, but about eating. Two days before the big Saturday performance I spoke to my parents about my anxieties.

"I hope I don't embarrass you or myself, but I don't feel all that confident about reading from the Torah. I've pretty much memorized the sounds, but I don't understand a single word I'm saying."

"That's okay," said my pragmatic father, "that's how some actors make movies."

I had no idea what he meant, but I said, "You know it's not too late to call the whole thing off. We can cancel on a technicality—the two required pubic hairs have not yet appeared."

"We will do no such thing," said my mother. "Pubic hairs or not, the show *will* go on!"

The night before my big day, Alan asked if I was nervous. I thought it was uncharacteristically considerate of him to ask. "Sure," I said, "a little."

"Well, don't worry about it; it doesn't matter how you do. Everyone has already bought you a fountain pen or a card with cash in it. You're going to get presents anyway, even if you screw up royally. So who cares how you do?"

"I care. A bar mitzvah is about more than just presents."

"Oh you poor sap," he said. "You've got so much to learn."

I went to sleep early, because I wanted to go over my speech a few times in the morning. But the God of my forefathers had other plans. At about three-thirty in the morning I was awakened by a commotion in the hall outside my bedroom. I opened the door and through sleepy eyes saw my father standing in the hall. He was leaning against the wall and both hands covered his eyes. He was sobbing uncontrollably. I had never before seen my father cry, and the scene was bizarre and profoundly disturbing. I wondered if I was dreaming this.

"What's wrong?" I asked.

My father put his arms around me, hugged me tightly and said, "Uncle Art died."

"What? Uncle Art? When?"

"About thirty minutes ago. Ethel just came upstairs to tell us. The kids are still asleep."

"What should we do?" I asked.

"There's nothing for you to do. Your mother has made the necessary phone calls and the mortuary is sending someone right away. I'm sorry, Peter, but I'm afraid the bar mitzvah is off."

In an old joke from vaudeville a comic defines mixed emotions as watching your mother-in-law drive off a cliff in your new Cadillac sedan. There I was, having mixed emotions.

The rest of that day, which should have been devoted to celebrating my maturity, was instead dedicated to mourning my uncle. My mother called Sokolofski to tell him the news; today I would *not* become a man. He offered condolences and quickly hung up. I think he was afraid my mother would ask for a refund. It would be years before I saw Sokolofski again, and, apparently, neither of us cared. Sadly or otherwise, my moment had passed, and six months of painful preparation quietly disappeared down the drain. Notices were posted at the temple, and guests were advised that the family would receive mourners, rather than celebrants. After all, there was enough food to feed an army; so, my mother decided, "Why should it go to waste?" By noon the house was overflowing with guests. Some slipped me pre-wrapped gifts surreptitiously, as though it were somehow inappropriate or embarrassing. Others, such as Stan Fishbein's father, spoke to me about his conflicted emotions.

"I hope you understand, Peter, that under these unusual circumstances, the cash we planned to give you for your bar mitzvah should really go to your Aunt Ethel, for a widow's fund."

Of course I understood, but I also thought Mr. Fishbein was an even bigger jerk than his son.

Sylvia Garbo appeared in a very slinky, low-cut, black dress. She embraced my father and said, "Sam, darling, I was so sorry to hear about your brother." And then she wrapped him up in her arms and held him tightly. "You poor baby," she kept repeating, until my mother came over and said, "He's okay, Sylvia. He'll be just fine." Then Sylvia approached me and said, "What bad luck, Peter." She threw hers arms around me, and I found my face buried in her ample cleavage. The entire day had been so surreal, having my nose in Sylvia's bosom did not seem at all odd.

At the end of that exhausting day our two families sat in our living room and tried to put the recent events in perspective. I felt such relief at having been spared the executioner's axe that I continued feeling guilty for months afterwards. My brother showed little emotion, but I knew he was affected by our uncle's death. The fact was, he was abnormally well behaved during the entire day. My father was so quiet I figured he was worried sick about that ancient Jewish law requiring Ethel to move in with us. My aunt was devastated; she had no idea her husband was on the brink of a massive heart attack. How could she know? And how would she manage? Where would the money come from? Her brother Daniel called from Chicago and promised to provide a monthly check for her. Uncle Nathan also offered financial help and even suggested she might work part time at Transparent Materials Company. And my cousins? It still had not hit them. There would be plenty of time to deal with the grief.

Two days later, on a hot September afternoon, Uncle Art was laid to rest at Hillside Memorial Park, where Al Jolson would be buried some years later. The ceremony was brief, and tears were plentiful. It was the first time in my life I viewed a dead body, but the body looked like a copy of my Uncle Art that had been molded out of wax.

Within several weeks our lives began returning to normal. Aunt Ethel started working part time at Transparent Materials Company (Nepotism, Inc., as it was now known), and everyone was amazed at her bookkeeping proficiency. Who could have guessed that beneath that mousy exterior was an incipient accountant yearning to manipulate numbers.

My last year at Horace Mann began, and I spent most of my spare time cataloging stamps with Lenny Strauss and building model airplanes with Hobie Johnson. A major model competition was scheduled at Rosecrans Field for the beginning of December, and I intended to enter in two categories: towline gliders and small gas-engine, single-wing aircraft. I was so confident in my ability, I decided to enter planes of my own design. Those were the projects that occupied me for the next two months, and it did little to improve my relationship with Alan.

"For Christ's sake," he began, "when is this model-making bullshit going to stop?"

"Why do you care—it isn't bothering you."

"Your being here is what bothers me. The model making is just more aggravation."

"You can always leave, you know. There's a war going on in Europe; why don't you join up and use your hostility for some noble purpose."

When December arrived my two models were completed and thoroughly tested. Both planes performed beautifully, and I was convinced I had a good chance to win a cash prize. We loaded up the car and my father drove to Rosecrans Field. Alan decided to join us.

"I thought you didn't care about model airplanes," I said.

"I don't. But it's Sunday, I've got nothing to do, so I don't mind wasting some time."

We arrived just after sunrise, and the field was already crowded with model enthusiasts. I registered with the officials and began to get my planes ready. The towline glider contest was first, and I took a couple of trial glides with my plane. Everything worked perfectly. I had designed a lightweight plane with a large wingspan and an extremely low center of gravity. Towlines were limited to fifty feet in length, and the first thing the officials did was measure the lines. The idea was to run with the towline, like you were flying a kite, until the rising plane was directly overhead. At that point the towline would drop off, and the plane would make lazy circles until gravity brought it back to earth.

When the official gave the signal, I began running into the wind, and the glider climbed to its maximum height in a matter of moments. As it reached its zenith, the towline disengaged; and at that point, the official pressed his stopwatch. We would now see how long the plane would remain aloft; the longer the better, and for the flight of longest duration, first prize. My glider was making slow, concentric circles, just as planned, and I was thrilled beyond words. Even Alan was excited, though I suspect he came along to watch me fail.

After ten minutes my glider was no closer to earth than it was when the towline disengaged. The timing official said, "Ya sure ya don't have a motor in that thing?"

"No, sir, you're looking at nothing less than superior aerodynamics."

"Well, sonny, ya seem to be defying the laws of gravity."

After another ten minutes, my glider was actually higher than when it was launched. It suddenly hit me. Oh, no, I thought; I know what's happening. I'm caught in a thermal!

A thermal is a column of warm air that rises from the ground, usually when the sun appears, and its effect is to lift lightweight flying objects, like birds and model airplanes. I figured if my plane climbed high enough, the cooler air might force it to descend. But that wasn't happening.

The timing official said, "If your plane kicks free of that thermal, you've got yourself a new record and first place fer sure."

An hour later my plane was barely visible; it looked like it was heading for Pluto, or at least somewhere a long way away. In a few more moments my plane disappeared completely, and I was cursing my luck.

"Sorry to disqualify ya," said the official, "but the rules state the glider's gotta return to earth. Ya can't win a prize if there ain't no plane." Alan thought that was the funniest line he ever heard, and he repeated it several times. "Ya can't win a prize if there ain't no plane."

"Oh, shut up, Alan," I said.

Fortunately, I had taped my name and address to the fuselage, so if the plane was lost or stolen, someone could contact me. That strategy worked perfectly, but a bit late. Three weeks after my plane took flight I received a letter from a Salvador Scarpelli in Tucson, Arizona. Scarpelli found the remains of my plane in an empty field. It had flown nearly five hundred miles! I figured when the word got out, I'd get a congratulatory letter from Franklin Delano Roosevelt, or at least recognition from the Army Air Corps.

Meanwhile, back at Rosecrans Field, I was trying to get over my loss and prepare for the small gas-engine competition. When my turn came, I started my engine, set the timer for exactly twenty seconds of power flight, and launched my plane. It climbed at a steep angle for the first ten seconds and every detail of the launch appeared perfect. Then came the unanticipated disaster—my plane suddenly banked to the left and plunged awkwardly, straight to earth. It hit the ground with tremendous force and was obliterated beyond all recognition. The sound of the impact was so deafening, all eyes turned towards the idiot who, purposefully or not, had just destroyed a perfectly fine gas-powered plane. This was fast becoming the worst day of my life.

Hobie was there and said, "Tough luck, buddy, you didn't deserve that."

Even Alan was sympathetic; he turned and walked away without a word.

"Let's go," said my father. "No point waiting around to see what else can go wrong." For the first time in living memory he didn't say, "It could be worse".

I picked up my toolbox and we walked back to the car, as if in a funeral procession. We drove in silence until my father said, "Maybe some soothing music would help." He turned on the radio, but instead of music, we heard the following:

"This is Clyde Culpepper with continuing coverage from the roof of our KTU studios in Honolulu. This is what we know so far: Early this morning Pearl Harbor suffered a brutal bombing raid by enemy planes, undoubtedly Japanese. The battle has continued for several hours, and to the west the sky is filled with black smoke. Hickam Field has also been attacked. We cannot estimate the damage at this point, but it is severe. This is not a joke; this is war."

Moments ago I could not imagine how things could get any worse. Now I knew.

CHAPTER FOURTEEN

At War

That Sunday evening was an anxious time in our neighborhood. My mother heard the news about the Japanese attack before we arrived home, but she had no way of knowing about my devastating luck at Rosecrans Field. She tried to console me, but it was difficult for any of us to think about model airplanes when our minds were focused on the disheartening military reports that flowed from our radio.

"What do you think about the news?" she asked my father. "Is this bad for the Jews?"

"It's always bad for the Jews," he said, "but now it's going to be bad for the whole world."

I wandered down the block to Hobie's house, where I found the unshaven Mr. Johnson sitting on the porch in his undershirt reading the evening newspaper. He appeared more somber than ever.

"That's all we needed," he said in his clipped Cary Grant accent, "another crazy fanatic who wants to rule the world. But now, maybe the Yanks will help out with that rotten scoundrel, Hitler." He gave a long sigh and mumbled, "The goddam world's going to hell."

Hobie appeared and we went to his room.

"Terrible day," he said, "especially for you."

"Yeah," I answered, "I'm thinking of giving up model building. It's just too depressing."

I expected Hobie to talk me out of it, but he remained quiet and lost in his thoughts. After a long silence, he said, "I'm thinking of joining the Air Corps. I'll learn to fly, go over there, and bomb those sneaky bastards back to the Stone Age." I had never seen him so angry.

"What are you talking about? You're only fourteen; there's no chance they'd take you."

"Well, as soon as I can get away with it, I'm joining up, even if I have to lie about my age."

While walking home I ran into Lenny Strauss. Lenny didn't want to fight anybody.

"This is scary," he said. "I don't want to be a soldier; I'm a peaceful guy. In all my thirteen years I've never been in a fight. Besides, there's no way in the world I could shoot anybody. I wouldn't even know which end of the gun to use. All I want is to be left alone."

"Why are you worrying about that now? There's no chance you'll be drafted before you graduate high school; and that's more than four years away. You won't have to shoot anybody for years, unless, of course, the Japs decide to invade Santa Monica." On that sad Sunday evening, a good many others feared that frightening possibility.

The next morning the entire student body of Horace Mann was ushered into the school's Assembly Hall. Sitting prominently in the center of the empty stage was a large Philco console radio. We were there to hear Franklin Delano Roosevelt, the only president we ever knew, address a joint session of Congress. A voice boomed out from the radio, "Ladies and gentlemen, the President of the United States."

The familiar voice, reflecting indignation and resolve, began: *"Yesterday, December 7, 1941—a date which will live in infamy, the United States of America was suddenly and deliberately attacked by naval and air forces of the Empire of Japan. The United States was at peace with that nation, and at the solicitation of Japan, was still in conversation with its government and Emperor, looking toward the maintenance of peace in the Pacific ... "*

Not a sound, other than the President's voice, could be heard in the packed auditorium. Even the most fidgety, disinterested students realized they were witnessing an historic event.

"... *With confidence in our armed forces—with the unbounding determination of our people—we will gain the inevitable triumph—so help us God. I ask that the Congress declare that since the unprovoked and dastardly attack by Japan on Sunday, December seventh, a state of war has existed between the United States and the Japanese Empire.*"

At the conclusion of the President's speech, we heard the thunderous applause of both chambers of Congress. We sat quietly in the Assembly Hall for another several minutes, at which point our Principal, Thomas Mock, walked across the stage, turned off the radio, and said in a somber voice, "May God watch over us all. Please return to your classrooms."

That same day, Britain declared war on Japan. Three days later Germany declared war on the United States. So there we were, the uncertainty was over; our country was at war, and life, as we knew it, would never again be the same.

The first several weeks of the war was like watching a Joe Louis boxing match. It was so one-sided, the referee should have stopped it after the first round. The Allies were being pummeled with jabs, hooks, and uppercuts; and they were reeling. By the end of December Japan had invaded Thailand, Burma, the Philippines, Hong Kong, Singapore, Borneo, and dozens of smaller islands. Meanwhile, in Europe, Mussolini's Fascists joined with Germany and Japan to create the Axis Powers. The Nazis had already overrun France, Scandinavia, and the Low Countries. Now they were marching through Yugoslavia, Greece, and North Africa, while the invasion of Russia was nearing Stalingrad, and the bombing of Britain continued unabated. At this point, nobody, including the greatest military minds in our country, could predict how the conflict would end.

My father came home one evening with a large map of the world.

"If we're going to follow the war," he said, "we should have some idea where the action is." He tacked up the map and stuck in little colored pins indicating countries controlled by the Axis powers (red), those controlled by the Allies (blue), and the neutral countries (white). When he finished, it looked like a board game in which the red team was miles ahead.

During the following spring we lost our faithful gardener, Kagunori H. Takashima. The H. stood for Henry, and that's what everybody called him. Henry was the gardener at our Gale Drive apartment house long before we moved there. He was cheerful, reliable, and had a wonderful way with plants and flowers. Our dowdy apartment building would have looked far worse were it not for his exceptional skills. Henry was about my size, even though he was twenty years older. He dressed in the typical Japanese gardener outfit: puttees, khaki knickers, work shirt, and a sweat-stained pith helmet. I recently noticed that he looked like a soldier in the Japanese Imperial Army.

Henry was being relocated to a newly constructed detention camp at Manzanar, which was nestled along the eastern face of the Sierra Nevada Mountains, about two hundred miles north of Los Angeles. Since Pearl Harbor, all Japanese were under suspicion, even those like Henry, who were born here. The best were assumed to be loyal to their homeland, and the worst, top-secret spies. The Federal Government was taking no chances; all Japanese, including U.S. citizens, were being forcibly uprooted and relocated.

Poor Henry didn't belong in a detention camp any more than I did. He was one of the most benign human beings on earth. He would go to extraordinary lengths to avoid killing a snail, and I never saw him squash so much as a tiny spider. All he wanted was to be left alone to trim his hedges and mow his lawns, but he could do nothing about his relocation.

As far as being sympathetic to his homeland, that was nonsense; Henry was more upset about Pearl Harbor than most of the people whose gardens he tended. It was assumed he posed a danger to our country, but, in my opinion, the internment of Henry posed a far greater danger to our apartment house.

A few days before leaving, Henry said to me, "I think you're ready to take over my job. I want you to take my mower and a few other tools. I won't need them where I'm going. Consider it a farewell gift from me."

"I can't accept that," I said. "Let me pay you now, and when you come back, you can repay me and get back your tools."

Henry put an arm around me and said, "You're a good kid; I'll miss you." And then he hugged me as tears began to run down his cheeks. It was a profoundly sad moment, and I was on the verge of tears myself. Poor Henry's world, like so many others in recent weeks, was being turned upside down. The following week I contacted the owners of other properties previously tended by Henry, and suddenly I had a part-time business. Additionally, I was about to earn more money than I could spend.

There is no ill wind that doesn't blow some good. The windfall of my new gardening business proved that. Transparent Materials Company also realized overnight success when they began supplying material to several defense-related factories in our area. My father sold all the material they could get, but getting material became more difficult. Nevertheless, business was good and the Kramarsky-Newman enterprise prospered. After my cousin Kay was graduated from high school, Uncle Nathan purchased a ranch house in Sherman Oaks, and his family moved to the San Fernando Valley. The house had a swimming pool, and we met there many Sunday afternoons to swim and have barbecued dinners.

My father was also in a position to purchase a house; and one on Hamilton Drive, the block west of us, was offered to him. It was a cute bungalow with three bedrooms, which meant I could now have a room of my very own, and the total price was a bargain at eight thousand dollars.

"No," said my father, "I don't trust real estate, and I don't want to own anything." The memory of the Great Depression was still fresh in his mind. "Who can forget those poor owners, leaping off their roofs, because they couldn't pay their mortgages? No, sir, I never want that kind of trouble." So we continued to rent, and I continued to resent my presumed roommate for life.

The Bataan Death March was a low point in the war with Japan. It took place within days of Henry's departure, and I was glad he wasn't around to suffer the widespread racism. What we needed was some positive news to raise our morale. This came a few days later when Lieutenant Colonel James Doolittle led a fleet of sixteen B-25 bombers in a raid on Japan. They took off from an aircraft carrier, flew six hundred miles, and dropped bombs on Tokyo and Nagoya. They didn't cause much actual damage, but it was a terrific boost for U.S. confidence and an embarrassing loss of face for the Japanese.

"Did you hear about Jimmy Doolittle? We bombed Japan! We've got 'em on the run now!"

These were the comments I heard the next day at school. Everyone spoke of the raid, and for the first time in months, we felt hopeful. Nobody realized how far we were from the end of the war, and how much more suffering there would be, but finally we had something to celebrate.

My graduation from Horace Mann was in June, and the graduation committee planned a number of events in celebration of the event. Foremost among these was a prom to be held in the gymnasium. I had a new suit for the graduation ceremony and figured I'd wear it to the prom as well. However, there was one critical problem—I didn't have a date. In fact, I had *never* dated.

"Do you have a date for the prom?" I asked Lenny.

"Yeah," he said, "I'm going with my sister."

"That's cheating," I said. "You can't go with your sister."

"Oh yeah? I'm pretty sure there's no law against it."

"Well, there should be. It's just not done."

I asked the same question of Hobie. "Sure," he said, "I'm going with Roberta."

Roberta was his cousin. Not quite as bad as taking your sister, but that didn't seem quite right either. "Does she have a friend?" I asked.

"Sure does, and she's in our class. Linda Berg, remember her?"

Linda was the cute girl who befriended me on my first day of school over four years ago. She was a lot cuter now, so much so, I couldn't believe she'd actually go out with me.

"Do you think Roberta could ask her for me?"

"Why don't you ask her yourself?"

"I'm shy," I said. But the real reason was my fear of being rejected.

"Don't be a jerk, Peter, call her up." That was not only the voice in my head speaking, but what Hobie said as well. I waited a couple of days, screwed up my courage, and took the plunge.

"Hello, Linda, this is Peter Newman. Do you remember me? We're in the same class."

"Of course I remember you, Peter; I see you every day."

"Linda, I'm calling about the graduation prom, and I wonder if you would go with me. It's okay if you're already going with someone else—I'll understand—or if you've decided not to go—or if you're busy with your family—or if you'd prefer not to go with me—or …"

"Peter, be quiet a minute; you're not giving me a chance to answer."

"Oh, sorry." There was a long pause.

"I'd love to go with you."

I wondered if I heard right? Another long pause. "Did you say okay, Linda? I mean, did I understand you? Did you say you'd go with me?"

"I said yes, Peter; yes I'll go to the prom with you."

"Oh thanks, Linda, thanks a lot. Thanks a million. I'll see you in class. G'bye."

I hung up the phone and said to myself, "What a *nebbish*! What a moron! Did you hear yourself? You are the biggest *shmendrik* in the entire world."

What I later learned is that within moments after hanging up the phone, Linda called Roberta and said, "Peter Newman just called; we're going to the prom together. Isn't that's the best news ever?"

Graduation was in two weeks; just enough time, I figured, to learn how to dance.

"Okay, Mom, I hear you were a pretty fair dancer in your day. Can you help me out?"

Old Jenny Kramarsky, an ancient spirit from the roaring twenties, sprang into action. She turned on the record player, resurrected the basic Fox Trot from the distant past, and began counting. "One, two, three, four; one, two three, four." We lurched around the living room for a while, and within an hour I felt I could fake my way through the prom. "Just feel the music," my mother said, "and you can't go wrong."

Our graduation ceremony was solemn, dignified, and impressive. We marched into the Assembly Hall as the school orchestra played

Pomp and Circumstance, and I felt an overwhelming nostalgia. There were a few speeches, a couple of musical solos, and inspiring words from our Principal. Several in the audience, including my mother and aunt Ethel, shed a few tears. Finally, we received diplomas, and our days at Horace Mann were officially ended. "No more Whore-Ass-Man," shouted Stan Fishbein; always looking for a laugh and always acting like a jerk.

That evening, as planned, I met Linda at the gymnasium entrance. I gave her a gardenia corsage that I bought earlier—my mother's idea. She looked sensational, and I was proud to be with her. Purple and white streamers decorated the large space, and recorded big band music blared from a loud speaker. We found Hobie and Roberta, got some Cokes, and sat at a small table. Some couples were already dancing, including Lenny and his attractive sister. I still thought bringing a sister, or even a cousin, was cheating.

"Well, how about it?" said Hobie. "Let's dance."

I put an arm around Linda, held her right hand, and we began to move slowly around the floor. I thought about my mother's instructions: "Just feel the music and you can't go wrong."

I was counting, one, two, three, four—but only to myself. The Glenn Miller orchestra was playing *Moonlight Serenade*, and I felt every harmonious note.

"Excuse me for mentioning this," said Linda, "but we don't have to be quite so far apart."

"Oh, sorry," I said, "I'm kind of new at this, and I want to do everything properly."

"Well, you're being a bit *too* proper."

I held Linda more tightly and was acutely aware of our bodies pressed together. My God, what a wonderful feeling! I hoped the music would never stop. But it ended when Linda's father came to pick her up at ten o'clock. He said to her, "I'll wait for you outside; don't be long."

"I've got to go now," she said. "I wish I didn't; I've had a wonderful time. Thanks again for asking me." And then she kissed me. Not a pathetic peck on the cheek, not a glancing blow, but a passionate kiss full on the mouth. And then she turned and walked quickly towards the door. I stood there for several minutes trying to figure out what just happened. Hobie tapped me on the shoulder and said, "Hey, Lover, you can close your mouth now."

A few days later the newspapers described the decisive victory our Navy won at the Battle of Midway. It was the turning point in the Pacific War. At the very same time in Europe, as we later learned, the Nazis began gassing Jews at Auschwitz.

CHAPTER FIFTEEN

The Home Front

By the summer of 1942, war dominated the news and much of our lives. Those not actually on the war front were doing their part on the home front. Everyone was involved with the war effort and proud to do what they could to help the boys in uniform. Industrial production was converted to war production overnight. Instead of cars, General Motors built tanks and Ford made bombers. Instead of toasters, appliance manufacturers made weapons; and the construction industry produced everything from Quonset huts to plywood PT boats. The vast number of young men in the armed forces created a labor shortage, and many women, like the famous *Rosie the Riveter*, filled positions formerly held by men. Other employers hired high school students, like, for example, my brother Alan.

"I got a great summer job," he said, "and, with what they're paying me, I can buy a car by the end of the summer."

"Great," said my father. "What's the job?"

"I'm going to be sorting clothes at the Beverly Hills Laundry."

"Not too mentally challenging," I said. "Think you can handle it?"

Ignoring my remark, my father said, "The timing sounds perfect; you'll have money for a car by the time you're old enough to get a driver's license."

The job provided Alan with an unintended bonus. A few weeks after he started work, he began collecting colorful military patches and insignias from servicemen's uniforms.

"Where did these come from?" I asked.

"They're patches that came off uniforms when they were cleaned."

"You mean they just fell off?" I asked skeptically.

"Sure, how do you think I got them?"

The surprising answer was revealed several days later, and the explanation came from a police officer that showed up at our front door. My mother said, "Hello, officer, can I help you?"

"Does an Alan Newman live here?"

"Why yes," said my mother, "he's my son. Is there a problem?"

"Yes, ma'am, I'm afraid there is. Your son has been ripping off patches from servicemen's uniforms and taking them home. You should know that abusing government property is strictly against the law."

"I'm sure there's some mistake," said my mother. "Alan wouldn't do such a thing."

I wondered on what planet my mother had been living the last fifteen years.

"No mistake," answered the officer. "Two co-workers testified that they saw your son steal military patches. I'm sorry, but Alan will have to come down to City Hall with me."

My mother and a frightened looking Alan drove away in the patrol car. My father came home two hours later and asked, "Where is everybody?"

"Well, I'm here, and the rest of our family is in jail."

"What? What do you mean? What's going on?"

I explained what happened. My father looked extremely annoyed and then called the Police Department. He was told the matter was resolved, and the family members were on their way home. When they arrived, my mother looked exhausted, and Alan looked as though he had just been released from Devil's Island.

"What a day!" began my mother. "Alan was ordered to pay back all the money he earned since he began working, and, of course, he was fired from his job. The judge also wanted to throw him in jail overnight; but I said this was his first offense, and he was really a good boy. I had to plead with the judge. Finally, he let us go with just a warning. Let me tell you, altogether I could have lived very nicely without this terrible afternoon."

"Do you have anything to say about this?" my father asked Alan.

"I'm really, really sorry," said Alan. "I had no idea taking a military patch was a federal offense. I mean, who figured that taking such a small patch was such a big deal? I promise I'll never do this again."

"I hope you mean that, Alan, because if anything like this happens again," warned my father, "I'm going to let them lock you up, and maybe even throw away the key."

Clearly, Alan was frightened; I had never seen him so contrite. But I figured that, being who he was, the repentant mood wouldn't last very long.

I spent much of the summer doing my job—mowing lawns and earning more money than I ever dreamed of. My father suggested I buy war bonds, to help the war effort and save for my future. I also purchased a record player and some of my favorite big band music. Being in his new good-boy phase, Alan didn't even complain when I played the same Benny Goodman and Artie Shaw records over and over again.

Directly adjacent to our apartment house was an empty lot, and a few of us decided to use it for a Victory Garden. Since rationing began, growing vegetables was encouraged; so we divided the lot into smaller parcels, and each interested neighbor prepared his plot for planting. The government provided free seeds, and these were available at our local nursery on San Vicente Boulevard, a few blocks away.

Hobie, Lenny, and I visited the nursery and, upon the advice of the owner, we selected a variety of vegetables that, he assured us, would be easy to grow. Maybe easy for him, but for those of us who weren't raised on a farm, it was another story. The only vegetables worth harvesting were the radishes; they grew like weeds. But nobody we knew liked radishes! My mother ended up giving away the entire crop. I had modest success with tomatoes and corn, but the worms ate more produce than we did. The string beans and carrots did okay, but they looked like miniature versions of the real thing. Lenny let a zucchini grow until it was nearly two feet long. When he cut into it, he discovered it was inedible. By the fall, I decided if my family had to survive on what I produced, they wouldn't last a week. What we needed was the advice of somebody like Henry, our former gardener. He would have known exactly what to do. A couple of months after he left Los Angeles I received my first letter from him.

> *Dear Peter, Well, here I am, finally settled at Manzanar. It's a beautiful place, except for the barbed wire that reminds us we cannot leave. The place is crowded, and privacy, I'm afraid, has become a distant memory. No one has actually starved, but there never seems to be enough food. We take turns using the mess hall, and there are long lines at the toilet building as well. I'm not complaining, but I sure miss my life in Los Angeles. How are you? Are you keeping the lawns neat and trimmed? I miss you and all my friends, and I hope I will see you as soon as this terrible war is over. Your good friend, Henry*

Henry's letter made me sad. I understood why the Japanese were sent away, but it seemed unnecessary to isolate people like Henry. After the war ended, the government reported a great irony: not one single incident of treason was ever committed by an American-born Japanese.

The war changed many things, but upsetting to most was the rationing. Not all foods were rationed; just those that were in short supply and, it seemed to me, those you really wanted to eat. Most popular among these were meat, butter, milk, coffee, sugar, and most canned food. Since fresh produce wasn't rationed, you might wonder why anyone would bother with a Victory Garden? The answer: labor and transportation shortages made it difficult to get fresh produce to market. Furthermore, it was the patriotic thing to do. We amateur farmers felt we were doing our part for the war effort, despite our pathetic results.

Just as serious was the rationing of gasoline. Most drivers received three gallons a week, except for doctors, clergymen, and those who could demonstrate extreme hardship. Actually, there was never a shortage of gas, but automobile tire production had ended. The Japanese occupied the countries that produced rubber, so our government rationed gasoline in order to reduce automobile travel. They figured the less people drove, the longer their tires would last. So we had no new cars, no new tires, and very little gas. Fortunately, my father had bought a new Chevrolet in 1940, and that lasted for the duration of the war.

Clothing was also in short supply, and many people got out their sewing machines and made their own. Shoes were rationed, which was a problem for teenagers, like me, whose foot size changed almost monthly. And most women mourned the loss of silk stockings. But all in all, compared to what was going on in the rest of the world, we had little to complain about. We never missed a meal, buses and streetcars took us wherever we wanted to go, and radio shows and movies were all the entertainment we needed. One positive note: after Pearl Harbor, people became uncommonly thoughtful, generous, and kind. We felt united in fighting Fascism, and everyone was dedicated to do whatever was necessary to support the war effort. An important part of that effort was being patient, understanding, and remarkably cordial.

At the beginning of summer vacation, I thought a lot about Linda, but I did not see her the entire summer. After graduation, she traveled East with her family, to visit relatives, and they planned to return to California just before school began. She was often in my mind; and, there was no doubt about it, I missed her. I just couldn't stop thinking about that goodbye kiss at the prom.

Starting high school did not make me particularly anxious. Alan had been there for two years, and he seemed to be doing okay, so, I figured, how difficult could high school be? My only concern was the gym class in which, I was told, boys showered together. I figured if my two pubic hairs didn't show up soon, this could be a real embarrassment. Needless to say, I checked regularly, but so far I remained the hairless wonder.

Two weeks before school began I looked down one morning and was shocked to see the appearance of not two, but six sprouts in the pubic area. I got out my stamp collector's magnifying glass, sat under my study lamp, and gazed with wonder at what had tortured me for the past year. I was sitting there in utter amazement when Alan walked into the room.

"What are you looking for, Sherlock? Has your weenie disappeared?"

"None of your business, smart ass. Just leave me alone."

"Maybe if you fertilize and water it, it'll grow big enough to see."

"Get lost, creep, and stay out of my life."

"You know, if you don't find it, you can always pee through a straw."

That's when I threw a book that missed Alan's head by inches.

"Jeez," he said, "aren't we getting touchy. I can take a hint—I'm going."

After Alan left I checked the armpits. Still as hairless as a baby's ass.

A week later my voice started going it's own way. At times I remained a soprano, but when least expected, I turned into an alto, and occasionally a bass. My voice was completely out of control, and there was nothing I could do about it. I also seemed to be expanding right out of my clothes. Shirts were getting tight, and my pants suddenly revealed two inches of ankle that were not apparent before the metamorphosis began.

"Peter," my mother asked, "are you growing, or is it my imagination? And what's with the funny voice? Are you maturing before our very eyes?"

"It happens to all teen-age kids," said my father. "The kid's growing up. *Mazel tov*, son."

"About time," said Alan.

On the last weekend before school began, Hobie, Stan the Jerk, and I went to the beach. We were sitting on the sand when Hobie said, "Hey, I think that's my cousin Roberta. And she seems to be sitting with your girlfriend, Linda."

"She's not my girlfriend. We just went to the prom together, that's all."

I looked in the direction Hobie was pointing, but the crowd of teenage boys around them made it impossible to see the girls.

"Let's go over and say hello. What do you say?"

"Let's not," I answered. "They seem to be busy."

"What's the problem, Peter?" Stan asked. "You're acting all embarrassed."

"Butt out, the both of you. I just want to spend a quiet day at the beach."

Ten minutes later, Roberta noticed Hobie waving at her, and the girls got up and began to walk towards us. I couldn't believe that was Linda. She was always cute, but in the past three months she had become a stunning young woman. I was speechless.

"Hi, Peter, how've you been?"

"Fine," I answered, and my unpredictable voice went through its three ranges.

"Did you have a nice summer?" she asked.

"It's been okay," I said. "How about you?"

"We were back East visiting relatives. It got boring after a while."

And then there was a long silence, which felt very awkward.

"It looks like you've grown," she said. "You're looking good."

"And you're looking just incredible," I said, as I felt myself blush.

"Thanks. Well, we've got to get going. See you later."

I waved goodbye and could not have felt more inept or depressed. What a *shlemiel*! It seemed clear, from the crowd of boys attracted to her astounding good looks, that during the past three months, Linda had outgrown me.

"Anyone for a swim?" I asked. I figured maybe a wave would drag me under and I'd drown. It seemed like the best solution.

CHAPTER SIXTEEN

Beverly High

"Alan," said my mother, "on the first day of school, I'd like you to take Peter and show him around. You've been there a few semesters, and I'm sure you can be helpful."

I found the suggestion offensive. "I don't need Alan," I said. "Plenty of students show up without older brothers, and they don't have trouble figuring things out."

"Fine with me," said Alan. "It's not like I'm looking for a baby-sitting job."

"I'd feel better if you two went together," insisted my mother.

"How about if I went with Alfie?" I asked.

"If you prefer," said my mother. "I'll talk to Aunt Ethel about that."

On a clear Monday morning in mid-September, as the Battle of Stalingrad began on the Russian front and the Battle of Guadalcanal raged in the Pacific, I went off with my cousin Alfie to begin four years of study at Beverly Hills High School. My mother was right; the experience *was* confusing. The campus was much larger than Horace Mann, and I had no idea where my classes were located. Alfie pointed the way to my first-period class, and then, as he waved goodbye, he promised to meet me for lunch.

The class was Mathematics, which worked out well. I figured I might as well get math out of the way early in the day. Actually, I was good at math; it had a logic I found comforting. When I sat down,

I heard from right behind me, "Well, I guess they'll let anyone in this class." It was the familiar voice of Stan Fishbein, joker, jerk, and sometime friend.

"That's pretty obvious," I said. "They let *you* in."

"Hey, I hear you're good at math, how about helping me with the homework?"

"Why don't we wait to see what this class is about? Maybe you won't need help."

We both knew that was wishful thinking.

Most classes, on this first day, were designed to orient students to the subject matter; and, as a result, most were not very challenging. After math came English, and our teacher, Miss Shepherd, outlined the subjects we would cover: rules of the language, books we would read, and papers we would write. So far so good, I thought.

My final class before lunch period was Physical Education, and our teacher was a former football player named Jimmy MacKinnon. He told our all-boy class to call him "Tank", the name he used professionally when he played center a few years ago for the Chicago Bears. He was about the size of a tank, but actually seemed gentle. Tank had a strange lisp, which I assumed came from having his brains regularly scrambled on Sunday afternoons. Because this was our first meeting, there was no physical activity, and consequently, no communal showering. The moment of pubic truth would come soon enough.

I met Alfie for lunch and he led me to the cafeteria. There was an impressive array of food, and after we made our selection, we chose a table on the patio and began to eat. Then I heard another familiar voice.

"Hi, Peter, fancy meeting you here." It was Linda. She was sitting at the next table with Roberta and about a half dozen older boys, who, I would swear, were practically drooling—and I'm sure it wasn't the food.

"Hi," I answered. Long pause. It was weird, I couldn't think of another thing to say.

"Are you okay?'

"Sure." I answered. "Just a little confused; new school and all that." The "all that" part included my infatuation with Linda and my overwhelming feeling of inferiority to the upperclassmen surrounding her. Next to them, I felt about nine years old. I figured not a one of them ever had a pubic problem.

"I get the feeling you're pretty hot for her," said Alfie. "What's up?"

"Nothing," I said. "We went to the prom last June. She's a nice person."

"Nice *and* knockout good looks," said Alfie. "What a killer combination!"

"Yeah, she's okay," I said. But what I was thinking is that she's extraordinary.

My afternoon classes included Social Studies and Spanish. Social Studies combined history, geography, and civics, and our teacher was a gray-haired individual named Mr. Mitchell. He was knowledgeable, but a bit cranky and somewhat unpleasant. I figured it must have something to do with the social mess the world was in.

The dapper Juan Escobar taught our Spanish class. Señor Escobar, as he wished to be called, came from Venezuela, and I assumed he spoke Spanish considerably better than English, because his accent was as thick as a can of refried beans. He greeted us with, *"Bienvenidos, estudiantes. Como estan ustedes?"* Pretty simple stuff, I thought; we learned those phrases at Horace Mann. Little did I know Señor Escobar was setting us up for more challenging days to come.

When the final bell rang, I walked outside and ran into my brainy friend, Lenny Strauss.

"What do you think?" he asked.

"I think I'll stick it out; what choice do I have? How about you?"

"I like it; I think I'm really going to learn something here."

"Well, that's the whole idea, isn't it?"

When I got home my mother wanted to know every detail about my first day in high school.

"No big deal," I said. "The place seems okay, the kids are nice, and the teachers, well, they're teachers." I assumed that covered the entire subject.

We were invited the next Saturday to my Uncle Nathan's house in the Valley. He and my Aunt Gracie were having a farewell party for my cousin Gary, who had just joined the navy. Since he was about to be drafted, Gary figured he'd rather be a sailor on a spotless ship than a soldier slogging through the muddy fields of some foreign country. He signed up for the duration and was leaving for training camp on Monday morning.

"Hi, Pretzel," he said. "Glad you could make my party."

"Wouldn't have missed it for the world. So what are you going to be doing in the Navy; I mean, besides fighting Nazis and Japs?"

"I've signed up for Radio School; but you know how perverse those guys are. They'll probably make me a cook." Then he laughed at his own joke.

"Are you nervous about all this?"

"Sure," he said. "The world's a pretty dangerous place. But we've got to win the war, and everybody has to do what he can. On the other hand, being a sailor has some advantages. I won't have to decide what to wear every day, what to eat, or when to go to bed. And there shouldn't be any money worries, either. I figure I'll pretty much drift through the next few years."

My Aunt Gracie tried to put on a happy face, but you could see she was anxious and depressed about sending her only son to war. Several times that afternoon she dabbed at her eyes that seemed continually overflowing with tears.

"Oh, Jenny," she said to my mother, "what if something terrible happens to Gary? I don't know how I'd go on living."

"Don't talk that way; nothing's going to happen. Gary is going to be fine. But if anything goes wrong, you've got to stay strong for Nathan and the girls. Just think positive."

The girls my mother referred to were now young women. Shelly was nearly twenty-seven years old, bigger than a house, and still, to no one's surprise, unmarried. She also continued to act conceited, although, as the years went on, she had increasingly less to be conceited about. Kay had just turned twenty and was more attractive and charming than ever. She had become a nurse and was working with returning veterans at a military hospital in the Valley. I often thought that a serviceman coming out of a coma and seeing Kay would probably think he had died and gone to heaven. Kay loved taking care of people, and I figured that the guy who eventually married her would be hitting the jackpot.

As the afternoon came to an end, everybody took turns embracing Gary and wishing him well. I gave him a big hug and said, "If you don't come home all in one piece, I'll never forgive you. I love you; don't forget that."

"I love you, too, Pretzel, and nothing's going to happen to me. I promise."

By the third week of high school I was as comfortable as it was possible for me to be. I knew my way around the campus, I was doing well in my classes, and I made a number of new friends who would become part of my future life. Most students, however, felt more comfortable with former elementary school friends. In many cases cliques were established before they ever reached high school. Beverly Hills had four elementary schools. Horace Mann, where I went, was on the eastern end of the city, and it served those in the lowest middle-class group. A bit further west was Beverly Vista, which catered to the middle of the middle-class. Students who went to Hawthorn and El Rodeo were considered the "rich kids." The heads of those families were business titans or prominent in the entertainment business. The children of movie stars came from those schools, as did many of the stuck-up, arrogant, and condescending students.

I met several rich kids in my classes, and actually became friendly with some. Going to their homes, however, was an intimidating experience. I'll never forget the first time I visited the home of Roger Phelps. Few people in those days had their very own swimming pool.

"You can swim whenever you want?" I asked.

"Sure, who's to stop me?" He probably thought: *Who is this bumpkin?*

And then he showed me the playroom over the garage that featured a large pool table.

"Yes," he said, "I can play pool any time I want." Now he sounded patronizing. Roger's father was a producer at 20th Century Fox, and their library was filled with awards he had received. It also had more books than the Horace Mann school library. I decided I'd never invite Roger to visit me at my apartment; our five rooms together were probably smaller than Roger's living room.

It took some time to adjust to our gym class communal showering. Our physical education teacher, Tank, addressed the situation head on.

"To those of you who are not accustomed to taking communal showers, there's nothing to be self conscious about. We're all built more or less alike." There was some snickering at that notion. "In a couple of years, some of you may serve in the armed forces. Let me assure you, there are no private showering facilities in the Army. So get used to this. On the other hand, let me remind you: always wear clothes outside of gym." Now, some laughter. "Okay, you're all dismissed." The last word came out "dithmithed." Poor Tank really did sound brain damaged.

Our teacher's friendly advice didn't change many minds, but we began to feel we were sharing an uncomfortable situation together. Showering with thirty other teenagers was a real education. As it turned out, I wasn't the only nearly hairless Chihuahua. Some had fewer pubic hairs than I, while others had growths in the pubic region that resembled a jungle out of a science fiction movie. And a few boys had, what appeared to be, modest shrubbery with baby hamsters peeking through. I also saw, for the first time, an uncircumcised penis. I found all this weird and fascinating. Two students had started shaving, a practice I wouldn't begin for another six years. And two more had so much facial fuzz they *should* have started shaving. After the first several days, the sideshow seemed to be over, and everybody stopped staring.

By the end of the year I gave up my lawn mowing business and began selling Christmas trees during the two-week school holiday. The tree lot was on the corner of San Vicente and Wilshire Boulevards, in the midst of the holiday traffic, and business was good. I was also good at selling trees. I quickly learned the differences among pines, firs, and spruce trees; and I was able to expound on the characteristics of each. I was knowledgeable, polite, and wore a constant smile, thus ending up with more tips than any of my co-workers. It was mostly a happy holiday season.

The unhappy part was giving up on Linda. She was now going steadily, if not steady, with Kyle Christensen, star quarterback of the Beverly High football team. Kyle was two years older than Linda, built like a Greek god, handsome as Tyrone Power, and dumb as a post. He was also conceited, pompous, and arrogant. During a moment of envy and uncertainty, I considered going out for football myself, but my parents had other ideas.

"Football is for the *goyem*," said my father. "Have you ever heard of a Jewish football player? I don't think so. An old uncle of mine used to say, 'A Jew belongs in the coffee house'. Do you know what that means? It means a Jew uses his head for intellectual purposes; he doesn't use it as a battering ram, like a dumb *goy*."

"Your father is right," chimed in my mother. "We didn't raise you to play football. If you want to play something, take up the violin."

So I gave up on football, and having run out of hope, I pretty much gave up on girls. As for playing the violin, that was never a possibility.

At the final game of the football season, Beverly was ahead of Santa Monica High by a score of seven to nothing. Moments before the game ended, our star quarterback, Kyle Christensen, was viciously tackled by an opposing linebacker. He was carried off the playing field on a stretcher, and, as it turned out, his leg had a serious compound fracture. At last, the intellectual, violin-playing Jews had something to celebrate—Linda's condescending boyfriend had got his comeuppance. And that wasn't all there was to cheer about. The Japanese gave up at Guadalcanal, and the Germans surrendered at Stalingrad. The good guys were finally beginning to have it their way.

CHAPTER SEVENTEEN

About Sex

When I was twelve years old, I joined the local Boy Scout troop. I was a Cub Scout the previous two years and was eager to continue the scouting experience. Alan was a Boy Scout for two years and attained the lofty classification of Life Scout, which was one notch below Eagle Scout. However, he never reached that ultimate goal, because, true to form, my irrepressible brother violated about half the scouting principles over one memorable weekend. Those principles included Honesty, Helpfulness, Friendliness, Obedience, and Courtesy. What did Alan do? Merely steal a fellow scout's pocketknife, plant it another scout's knapsack, blame someone else for the theft, and then consistently lie about his involvement to everyone who later questioned him. The authorities learned the truth, were unable to ignore this un-scout-like behavior, and Alan was summarily kicked out of the Troop.

When the good Newman brother came along, there was great suspicion and the usual hurdles to clear before being accepted. Within a year I became a First Class scout; and the merit badges piled up as I learned to tie knots, excelled in mapmaking, and became an expert in camping and outdoor survival.

One of my favorite books during this period was the Boy Scout Manual, which was a valuable encyclopedia about everything from treating snakebites to building campfires without using matches. A small section of the Manual covered the subject of Physical Fitness and Health, and it was here I discovered the reference to nocturnal emissions. I had no idea what they were. The short paragraph suggested that a scout should not be unduly concerned, because incidents of this kind were perfectly natural and relatively harmless. However, it failed to describe what the incident was that I shouldn't be unduly concerned about. I got out the dictionary and discovered that "nocturnal" meant nighttime, and "emission" was a discharge. I was still confused, but I figured any nighttime discharge was serious business. I thought of speaking to my parents about this, but I sensed it might be an embarrassing subject. So I visited Hobie to discuss the matter. After all, he was almost a year older than I.

"What's a nocturnal emission?" I asked.

"You're too young to worry about it," he answered, "but it's another name for a wet dream. In a year or two, you'll understand."

"Understand what?" I wanted to know. "Is something going to happen to me?"

"Yeah, but it's nothing bad. So forget about it."

It was now two years later, I was fourteen, and I finally understood what the term meant. I don't remember the dream, but I definitely remember waking up in sticky pajamas. The Boy Scout Manual said, "don't be unduly concerned", so I wasn't. Since the Manual had never let me down, why should I start to worry now?

My next sexual discovery came a couple of weeks later. I discovered you didn't actually have to go to sleep and have a dream to experience this thrilling event. If you touched yourself in just the right way, you could produce, within moments, the same excitement. Actually, it was even better—you were awake. What a discovery! The urges were coming fast and furiously, and I was always up for the challenge. I talked to Stan the Jerk and Hobie about this, because I figured anything that felt so good had to come with a high price.

"You ought to take it easy," said Stan, "that's dangerous stuff. You

133

could grow hair on the palm of your hand, become blind, or even go crazy. You better be careful."

"Where did you hear that nonsense?" asked Hobie. "I thought you were smarter than that. It's people who feel guilty about sex who make up those bullshit stories. If you whacked off every day of your life, it probably wouldn't make any difference; you might even live longer. At the very least, you'd be a happier person."

"Oh yeah," said Stan, "well I heard it's just like ammunition; you got just so many shots, and if you use 'em up when you're a kid, there won't be enough left when you really need them."

"Stan," replied Hobie, "you are so full of it, it's pathetic."

I had no idea who was right or wrong, so I figured I'd follow the path of least resistance, and if hair started sprouting in the wrong place, or if my eyesight grew weak, I'd deal with it then.

During the latter part of my fourteenth year, at about the time I met up with Anita Kornfeld's bare breast in the Fox Wilshire balcony, I became obsessed by sex. I wanted to know everything about women, so I went to the library to consult medical texts. I hoped to find revealing photos, but all I found were impersonal medical diagrams. Of course I regularly pored over the Petty and Vargas pin-up drawings in Esquire magazine, and there were also the Hollywood pin-up photos of prominent movie stars. The most famous of these was the one of Betty Grable in a bathing suit, and that photo hung over my bed for the duration of the war. I wondered how many other young men fantasized about that photo. Probably several billion, I figured.

One Saturday night, while strolling with Lenny along Hollywood Boulevard, we found a magazine store that stocked just about every magazine in print. We discovered, in a far corner, Sun Bathing Association Monthly, a magazine devoted to nudists. It was like striking gold.

"Holy crap," said Lenny, "check this out. She's skiing down the hill wearing nothing but a hat, gloves, and ski boots. Just look at those boobs!"

"Here's a great shot of a volley ball game," I said. "What incredible looking girls. What wouldn't you give to be in a game like that?"

We remained in the store until the owner finally said, "This ain't a library, boys; if ya ain't gonna buy anything, ya better just move on." We considered getting a subscription to Sun Bathing Association Monthly, but neither of us wanted it delivered to our house.

My father asked me to help out at Transparent Materials Company during our weeklong spring vacation. Since Gary went off to war, the company was perpetually short-handed. One of my first assignments was to accompany my father in making deliveries. This included a trip to Luis Herrera's Perfumed Candle Shop located on historic Olvera Street. Luis was one of my father's oldest customers, and entering his shop was always a severe shock to the olfactory system. The syrupy, perfumed aroma was so overwhelming, I imagined that's how a Parisian whorehouse would smell. Luis was a short, congenial man, and his young, attractive daughter, Lola, was his assistant that day. I assumed she was spending her spring vacation the same way I was—in service to the family business.

"Would you like to see my art project for school?" she asked. "I'm making an illustrated map of the ancient tribes of Mexico."

"Go ahead," said my father, "Luis and I have some business to discuss."

Lola led me behind the shop to the apartment where they lived. Once there, she locked the door and said, "You want to do it?"

"Do what?" I asked.

"You know—it."

"No I don't know. What are you talking about?"

Then Lola lifted up her colorful skirt, and I was staring at her completely nude lower body.

"That," she said, pointing to her pubic area.

"Are you crazy? Our fathers are right outside the door." I was suddenly filled with fear and desire, but fear was more powerful. "What's wrong with you, Lola? You want to get us into trouble?"

"The door's locked," she said. "No one will know."

"We can't take that chance." Now I became frightened; Lola seemed genuinely unbalanced.

"Well then," she said calmly, "you want to feel these?"

She dropped her skirt and lifted her blouse. Two gorgeous breasts stared back at me.

"No, Lola, I can't do that. What's going on, don't you own any underwear?"

Ignoring my question, she said, "Well, how about if you just gave them a little kiss?"

"Lola, please lower your blouse. Now don't get me wrong, there's nothing in the world I'd rather do right now than everything you've suggested. I want to do it probably more than you do. I'm absolutely sure I want to do it more than anyone else on earth. But we're going to get into such trouble, we've got to stop this right now."

Lola looked crushed. "Don't you like me?" she asked.

"I'm crazy about you," I lied. I barely knew her, and she really seemed unhinged. In another place, at another time, I wouldn't have cared if Lola were a raging lunatic; I would have leaped on her body from across the room. I was so aroused it was beginning to show. But I was overwhelmed by fear. God only knew what she would do next. What she did next was unlock the door and say, "Okay, but next time I don't want to hear any excuses."

As we drove back to the office, my father asked about Lola's school project.

"We didn't spend too much time on that," I said "We started talking about other things."

"She seems very nice," said my father. "What do you think?"

"Yeah, she's maybe the friendliest girl I've ever met." Boy, was *that* ever putting it mildly!

Towards the end of 1942, Japan continued air raids on Burma, India, and parts of Australia. On the other side of the world the U.S. launched an invasion of North Africa. And on the home front, my mother joined the Red Cross canteen service as a volunteer. She traveled to the docks in San Pedro about twice a week to serve coffee and donuts to our embarking servicemen. My mother wore a uniform of sorts, including a perky hat, and everybody thought she looked great. Alan and I didn't mind her absences, since we were getting accustomed to being on our own. My father, however, had mixed emotions about my mother's work. He resented her being gone in the evening, even though he understood she had no control over a convoy's sailing time.

"It wouldn't be so bad if you worked during the day," he said, "but you're gone so many nights."

"That's when the ships sail. I've already explained that to you."

"Yeah, but I don't like the idea of your being on the road at night. It's not safe". If he were totally honest, my father also would have mentioned that he didn't like all those virile, young servicemen ogling his attractive wife, who seemed more desirable than ever. She was still the most precious thing in his life, and he was jealous of anyone who gave her a second glance.

Some evenings, when Alan and I were visiting friends, my father was forced to cook his own dinner. His sister-in-law, Ethel, often invited him to join her, and my mother encouraged that idea. But my father's opinion of Ethel had not changed in the past several years. He

IT COULD BE WORSE

would rather have dinner at a soup kitchen on Main Street than spend time alone with Ethel.

"Why are you so stubborn?" my mother wanted to know. "Ethel cooks very well, and at least you'd have company."

"That's not the kind of company I want," answered my father. "She annoys me. And being with her gives me high blood pressure and an upset stomach."

Far more to my father's liking was our old family friend, Sylvia Garbo. Sylvia adored both my parents and was especially flirtatious with my father. He called her one evening, and some years later I heard the following story:

"Sylvia? It's Sam. How you doing? The boys are out with friends, and Jenny's down at the docks doing her Red Cross thing. How do you feel about having a bite of dinner with me?"

"Lucky you; my dinner date just called it off, and I'm free as a bird."

"I'll pick you up in twenty minutes. Wear something sexy."

Sam had no idea why he said that. He knew it was provocative, and if it ever got back to Jenny, he'd have some explaining to do. But he felt abandoned by his family and was feeling sorry for himself. He was also angry.

"You look great," Sam said as he opened the car door for his dinner date.

"You don't look so bad yourself," answered Sylvia. "Where are we going?"

"I know a little place at the beach. They have terrific spaghetti and meatballs there."

The place at the beach was romantic, the food was delicious, and the two old friends spent a couple of hours finishing off a bottle of red wine.

"This is just what I needed," said Sam, "a good dinner with a beautiful woman, and pleasant conversation. Thanks, Sylvia."

"No, thank *you*. I've really enjoyed this, and I'm sorry we have to say goodnight."

Sam drove Sylvia to her apartment, opened the car door and helped her out.

"I'd like to ask you up, but I don't trust myself to keep my hands off you."

"I'm flattered," he answered. "Maybe we better say goodnight here."

Sylvia pressed her body against Sam and gave him a kiss he would never forget. Sam didn't retreat from the embrace. He not only returned the kiss with passion, but his hands explored every curve of her sensuous body.

"Are you sure you can't come up," she asked.

"I really want to, but I have to say no."

As he drove home, Sam wondered, what just happened? This is a dangerous game you're playing. Be careful, *boychik*, you don't want to lose what's most precious to you.

It was nearly three in the morning when Jenny returned home. Sam was still awake, his mind filled with sexual images of him and Sylvia.

"What are you still doing up?" asked Jenny.

"Just thinking," answered Sam. "I missed you."

"Me too," said Jenny. There was a long silence while she undressed. Then she stood naked at the foot of the bed and stared at Sam.

"What?" he said.

"Let's make love."

They quietly embraced and made love as though Sam were a serviceman going overseas and Jenny was his sweetheart who feared she would never see her lover again. They fell asleep in each other's arms and remained that way for the rest of the night.

CHAPTER EIGHTEEN

Odd Jobs

When my brother Alan turned seventeen, he bought a 1936 Ford convertible with a rumble seat. The car was navy blue, the top was beige, and it had bright chrome trim. It was a knockout. More than a year earlier our father had taught him the fundamentals of driving. For the next few months, when the family car was available, Alan drove up and down the driveway perfecting the subtle sequence of clutch, gearshift, and accelerator. The day he turned sixteen, Alan appeared at the motor vehicle office, took the written exam and driving test, and went home with a California driver's license. His goal for the next several months was to save enough money to purchase a car. He accomplished that feat in less than a year.

The '36 Ford represented, to my brother, a personal declaration of independence. From that moment on, there was no stopping him. What slowed him down, temporarily, was gas rationing; but within a week he found a service station that sold black market gasoline, and thereafter, had all the gas he needed to go wherever he pleased.

My father remained annoyed that Alan bought a Ford.

"That Henry Ford, that *farshtunken* piece of *drek*," my father said, "is one of the most virulent anti-Semites who ever lived. He's in the same league as Hearst, Lindbergh, and Father Coughlin, and they all support that bigger piece of *drek*, Hitler. How could you buy a Ford? You might just as well have joined the Nazi party."

His words fell on deaf ears; my brother felt no more guilt about owning a Ford than he did about purchasing black market gasoline. His conscience had not gone astray; it simply didn't exist. To support his new possession, Alan got a job at the Douglas Aircraft factory in Santa Monica. It was a low level job on the swing shift, which meant that Alan worked each day from four in the afternoon to midnight. He attended school during daylight hours, so there was little time left to cause trouble. But that didn't stop my enterprising brother. Many nights, after his shift was over, Alan went partying with some of his fellow workers, most of whom were women. Many of them were either sweethearts of, or married to, servicemen who were fighting overseas to keep our country free. Alan also believed in freedom, namely the freedom to entertain these lovely, lonely women. The word around Douglas Aircraft was that Alan Newman was an attractive, desirable, and all-around fun-loving guy.

"It's such easy pickings at Douglas," he would say. "These gals are starved for affection, and fortunately, I've got a lot of affection to give."

"Doesn't it bother you that they have boyfriends or husbands overseas?" Even as I asked the question I already knew the rationalization I was about to hear.

"I'm actually doing them a favor," he said. "I'm keeping the gals happy and passionate, so when their boyfriends come marching home they'll be ready to pick up where they left off."

"What if one of the boyfriends comes marching home and decides to rip off your head?"

"I'll worry about that tomorrow," said Alan laughing.

I also had an after-school job, and it paid well. I worked at McGregor's Modern Foods on Beverly Drive from four to seven every evening. Chef McGregor, as he was known, was one of the first proponents of health food, and his popular restaurant featured many foods that were not rationed. For example, one could order oven-roasted rabbit, fresh fish from the Pacific, and choice cuts of horsemeat. Every entrée came with three vegetables, and one of my jobs was peeling, slicing, and preparing the vegetables for cooking.

An unexpected bonus of the McGregor job was meeting some of the most beautiful young waitresses to ever wear a starched apron. Chef McGregor's hiring sessions were like Hollywood casting calls. He professed to obtain the best-qualified women, for the benefit of his suspicious wife. But the reality was, he invariably ended up with young beauties who were amply endowed and looked fabulous in their gingham uniforms. Actually, any of these women would have looked sensational wearing nothing more than an Idaho potato sack.

Two of the waitresses and the pot washer, a toothless ex-hockey player from Canada, comprised an ice-skating group that met at the Pan Pacific Auditorium on Sunday mornings. A few weeks after I began working, they asked if I cared to join them.

"Do you know how to ice-skate?" asked the young and vivacious Barbara Langheim.

"I used to ice-skate when I was a little kid in Chicago," I answered.

"What are you talking about? You're still a little kid."

"Don't let these youthful looks fool you," I said. "Behind this immature face is quite an experienced young man." I don't know why I said that; I just felt comfortable enough with Barbara to make a silly joke.

"You know," she said, "you're cute; I'd love to take you home."

"I'll have to get my parent's permission," I said.

So began my ice-skating routine on Sunday mornings, as well as a good measure of sexual tension created by the McGregor beauties. One Sunday, Stan the Jerk showed up and saw me waltzing around the rink with the waitresses.

"Jeez, Peter, where did you find those babes? They're gorgeous."

"I work with them at McGregor's."

"Have you banged any of them?" asked the not-too-subtle Stan.

"Actually, I take turns with them. If I'm not mistaken, the blond is up next."

The McGregor job was enjoyable, the money was good, and the beautiful waitresses were an exciting added benefit. But after three months I was so exhausted, I felt I had to make a change. I worked until seven o'clock every evening, rode my bike home, started my homework by eight, and never got to bed before eleven. Then it was up before seven and to school by eight. The work left me no time to relax, or anything else for that matter. The manager of the Pan Pacific saw me ice-skating one Sunday, and signaled for me to stop.

"Hey, kid, you skate pretty well. How would you like to be a guard on the weekends?"

Guards at the Pan Pacific wore bright red sweaters, whistles around their necks, and skated backwards, using the whistle and hand gestures to control unruly skaters. Anyone who enjoyed ice-skating would consider this an absolute dream job. It also paid a better hourly wage than McGregor.

"When do I start?" I asked.

"Is Saturday too soon?"

"I'll be there," I said. "Get the red sweater ready."

Facing the crew at McGregor's was more difficult than I imagined.

"We're going to miss your good work," said the chef, "and the girls will miss you, too."

"You bet we will," said Barbara. "Maybe we'll still see you at the rink."

"You sure will," I said. "But no time for waltzing; I'll be watching out for speeders."

"That might be a good way to get your attention," said Barbara.

"You already have my attention," I said. Little did she know the McGregor girls were part of my continuing sexual fantasy, on and off the ice.

Working weekends was a great relief in many ways. I suddenly had time to see friends, play a little ball, and finally, get enough sleep. But working fewer hours resulted in less money. The solution to my financial problem was solved when I was hired as a cashier in the school cafeteria. A note from my math teacher convinced the cafeteria manager that I was an absolute genius at adding numbers and making change. I worked during the lunch period each day, and my modest pay, together with free lunches, made for a happy life. It was also prestigious work; people treated me with greater respect when they saw me handling money. Go figure. There was no red sweater, but I did wear a special orange and white cap, our school colors. The job also came with some unpleasant pressure. For example, Stan the Jerk said one day, "Hey, Peter, ignore the chocolate cake, I'm a little short of cash today."

"You know I can't do that. You want to get me in trouble? Just put the cake back." Stan wasn't the only one who expected a discount. Several people I hardly knew tried the same stunt. Another unexpected incident arose the day Kyle Christensen, star quarterback and pompous knucklehead came through my line. Kyle was now off crutches, but he still had a pronounced limp as a result of his gridiron misfortune. Linda followed Kyle, and she was deliberating between chocolate pudding and apple cobbler.

"For Christ's sake," said Kyle, "pick one stupid dessert or the other; I haven't got all friggin' day. You're holding up the whole damn line." Trouble in paradise, I thought.

"Hi, Linda," I said. "How's it going?"

"Okay, I guess," she answered. She looked sad and embarrassed by Kyle's outburst.

"Why do you let that rude jerk speak to you that way?"

"Mind your own business, buddy," said Kyle "unless you're looking to lose a few teeth."

"I was talking to Linda," I answered.

"Yes, Kyle, stay out of this," Linda said. "Get a table and I'll meet you there."

Kyle strode off, and Linda paid for them both.

"You don't have to put up with that," I said. "You're pretty and charming, and any guy on earth would show more respect for you than Kyle."

"He's changed a lot since he broke his leg; he's become more irritable and impatient. I think he's afraid he'll never play football again, and that scares him. You know he doesn't have much else. I guess I feel sorry for him."

"Why bother with a guy like that? Everybody knows he's basically a dimwit, he's conceited, and I'd guess he's anti-Semitic as well. I mean, think about it—Christensen?"

"He knows I'm Jewish," answered Linda, "so I don't think you're right about that, but you might be right about the other things."

Just then Kyle appeared and said, "Are we having lunch or what? What's going on between you two? Have you been talking about me?"

"We both find you fascinating, Kyle. We were just saying, is this guy fabulous or what?"

"Listen, twerp, I don't need any sarcasm from a butt-face like you. One more word and I'll wipe that smirk off your face—permanently."

"C'mon now, Kyle, I don't think you mean that." The voice was that of my physical education teacher, Tank; all two hundred pounds of him was standing behind Kyle.

"I didn't know you were there," said Kyle. "We were just messing around."

"Mess around all you want," said Tank, "but if you lay one hand on Newman, you'll answer to me. You graduate the end of this semester, and if it's a fight you want, you'll have your pick of the U.S. Army, Navy, or Marines. But there'll be no fighting among my students. And that goes for you, too, Newman; lay off of Kyle." As he turned away from Kyle, Tank winked at me.

So Kyle Christensen, the thickheaded bully, retreated, just as the Axis Powers were beginning to do. U.S. Forces were recapturing Pacific islands, while on the other side of the world, Allied Forces were invading Italy and bombing Germany.

Back on the home front, Alan continued building planes at Douglas Aircraft in Santa Monica, wooing his pretty co-workers, and burning his candle at both ends. This self-indulgent lifestyle might have continued until his graduation from high school, were it not for Polly Pennington. Polly was one of my brother's co-workers, frequent late-night companion, and sometime lover. Appearing at our door one day, Polly demanded to see Alan.

"I'm sorry," said my mother, "Alan isn't here right now. I'm his mother; can I help you?"

"Well, this is kind of personal," said Polly, "but your son and I have been going out, and I figured we had a special relationship. Now I find he's been dating other girls at Douglas, and I'm upset. Really upset!" She looked agitated and on the verge of tears.

"Why don't you come in and let's talk about this," suggested my mother.

"Alan's a nice guy," said Polly. "Why would he do something like that?"

"You know," said my mother, "Alan is like most young men his age; still exploring and discovering the world around them. I'm sure he didn't mean to hurt you—you seem like such a lovely young woman—but Alan can be a bit self-centered at times. I'm sure that ..."

"I might be pregnant," Polly interrupted. Suddenly the air seemed to have left the room.

"I beg your pardon," said my mother. "Are you sure about this, and about Alan?"

"No, I'm not a hundred percent positive, but it was Alan, for sure."

"Do you have a little time right now?" asked my mother. "Maybe I can help you."

My mother called Sylvia Garbo and asked if she could drive her to Doctor Goldman's office. Within an hour, the three women were discussing the situation with the doctor.

"Well, it looks like a false alarm, Polly. These things happen, you know, but if you *are* carrying a baby, it should make medical history. There are no physical signs of a pregnancy."

"Thank you, Doctor," said my mother, "we're grateful and relieved to hear the news."

Polly said, "I don't know how to thank you, Mrs. Newman. I was desperate and ready to do something really drastic. I wish there was something I could do for you."

"Here's what you can do, Polly. First of all, be more prudent when you're with a man, and until you want to start a family, use protection. And never, ever forget that men will do or say anything to have their way with you—even nice men like Alan."

"I wish *you* had been my mother," said Polly. And then she started to cry. The two women embraced, and Polly continued to cry until there were no tears left. She felt humiliated and disgraced but lucky to have survived the most frightening experience of her young life.

The following morning my mother confronted Alan.

"I had a visit yesterday from your friend, Polly Pennington."

"What was she doing here?"

"She came to tell you she was carrying your child."

"What? What did you say? What do you mean by that?"

"Everything's okay now; she was mistaken. She's not pregnant, but she could have been. She was frightened and desperate, and you're partly to blame. Do you ever think about the consequences of your actions? Do you ever consider the feelings of others? You made a terrible mistake, Alan, and you caused that poor girl a lot of grief."

"I'm sorry," Alan said. "I'm really sorry. I never meant to cause any trouble."

"Well let's be sure it doesn't happen again. The next time you feel like sowing a few oats, remember Polly, and, for Christ's sake, keep your pecker in your pants, where it belongs."

CHAPTER NINETEEN

In The Service

By the end of 1944, General Douglas MacArthur began taking back the Philippine Islands. In Europe, the Russian Army was advancing through Poland, and Allied forces reached Germany. The Axis powers were on the run, and the tide of battle clearly favored the good guys. Is it possible they knew that Alan Newman, the infamous Beverly Hills insurgent, had joined the Army Air Corps and would soon be after them? Finally, after all the tribulations I suffered at the hands of my brother, he would now be the government's problem. Better yet, for the first time in my life, I would have a room of my own. My parents did not share my joy; they worried about their eldest son going off to war, and they were apprehensive.

"Now, be sure to write," said my mother. "We want to know everything you're doing."

"Well, maybe not everything," my father cautiously added, "but the important things."

"Don't worry," said Alan. "I'm going to be fine. But the way things are going, I'm afraid the action will be over by the time I earn my wings." Then he turned to me.

"Well, butthead, guess you'll be happy to see me go. I know I've not always been the best roommate, but then again, neither have you."

"Maybe you're right," I said. "I guess our problems started when I was born, which wasn't exactly my fault. But it was something you never got over. Anyway, take care of yourself; I won't be able to help you with your homework anymore." Then Alan held out his car keys.

"Take care of the Ford, will you, but stay out of trouble. If I come back and find even one small scratch, it'll be your ass—understand?"

"Thanks," I said. And then we embraced and I began to cry.

"What's that all about?" asked my brother.

"What do you think, you numbskull? I'm so happy to get rid of you I can't control myself."

A week later, my cousin Alfie followed my brother's lead and joined the Navy.

"They're going to get me anyway," he said, "so I might as well pick my service."

"Why not the Air Corps, like Alan?" I asked.

"You know as well as I, it's time for us go our separate ways. Anyway, I hear that Gary is having a great time in the Pacific, shooting down Japanese Zeros. Maybe I'll become a gunner's mate, too."

My Aunt Ethel was losing the man of the house, and she seemed even more anxious than my mother. It had been nearly four years since my Uncle Art died, and now Alfie was leaving. In another few years Lynn would be gone, and the prospect of a life alone frightened her.

"Don't worry," said my mother, "We'll always be close and always look out for each other."

The next one to leave home was Hobart Johnson. He made good on his promise, ignored the objections of his family, and joined the Naval Air Corps. Hobie was now sixteen, but he appeared at least two years older, the age he claimed to be on his application. I visited him the night before he left for basic training in Corpus Christi, Texas.

"I'm really going to miss you," I said. "This place won't be the same without you."

"I'll miss you, too, but this is something I've got to do. My folks are really upset. They threatened to blow the whistle, tell them how old I really was; but they know how much this means to me."

"What are you going to do in Corpus Christi?" I asked.

"Learn to fly, for one thing; and a lot of other technical stuff, which should be interesting. Listen, while I'm gone, I'd like you to keep an eye on my cousin Roberta. Will you do that? I don't like the crowd she and her pal Linda are involved with. I know Kyle will be in the service soon, but his buddies are just as bad an influence."

"Sure, I'll do what I can, but what makes you think they'll listen to me? I'm not a football star, you know."

"Yeah, I know; but Roberta respects you, and I suspect Linda has a crush on you."

"Me? Don't be silly. We're just friends; besides she goes for the dumb-ass football type."

"Okay, have it your way; but remember, I told you so."

"Wait a minute—did Roberta say anything about this?"

"She didn't have to. I see how Linda looks at you. I figure you're so unconscious you'd probably be the last to know."

"Write to me, Hobie. Let me know how you're doing. So long, buddy."

"So long, Peter, and keep 'em flying." That was our old model airplane club sendoff.

Within the month, Kyle Christensen was drafted into the Army. He figured he'd wait to see how the draft board felt about his injured leg. The fracture had healed, but Kyle still had a slightly uneven walk. When he went for his induction physical he so exaggerated the limp that he looked like a poor imitation of Boris Karloff in the horror film, *The Mummy*. But he fooled no one and was immediately classified 1-A. Some hero *he* turned out to be! Before he left for basic training, he and Linda spoke about their relationship, and the following is what I later learned.

"Look, Kyle," she began, "things between us haven't been so good lately. Even if you weren't going away, I don't think there would be much of a future for us. I'm beginning to think this relationship is over."

"Are you trying to break up with me?" asked the simple-minded ex-football star.

"Yes, that's exactly what I'm doing."

"You can't do that," said Kyle, becoming suddenly agitated. "I'm the one who says when this is over, not you. I'm going off to war, and now you pull this crazy stunt? What a nerve!"

"Too late, Kyle, it's over. Goodbye and good luck." And then she turned and walked away.

"You ungrateful little bitch," he shouted. "Who the hell do you think you are? You'll be sorry—just wait. You'll come crawling back, and it'll be too late. You'll see."

Linda didn't turn around; she just kept walking. It really *was* over.

The situation at the Transparent Materials Company continued to be in flux. Help was difficult to get and even more difficult to keep. Every young warehouse worker had been drafted, and those that remained were barely able to keep up with the demands of the increasingly successful business. Another notable event was the dramatic personality transformation experienced by my uncle.

Nathan realized that his profligate ways had caused major problems for him, his family, and the business. After all, were it not for his personal financial trouble in Chicago, we probably wouldn't even be in California. He sought a solution and eventually found an answer, but it came attached to another religion. My uncle became a Christian Scientist. He claimed he was still a Jew, but one who followed the dogma of Mary Baker Eddy. Nobody had the faintest idea what he was talking about. Was it an epiphany? Who knew? But suddenly, my uncle became unusually benign and generous—you might say, more Christ-like.

"Sam," he said to my father one day, "considering your contribution to this company, I don't think you've been adequately compensated. After all, you took a big risk, like the rest of us, moving to California and giving up opportunities in Chicago. I won't ever forget that."

My father was completely mystified. What was Nathan talking about? How could he forget that Nathan and Daniel saved Sam after his early business failures? And what did he mean, "giving up opportunities in Chicago"? There *were* no opportunities. There was a terrible depression going on, and Sam was dying a slow death.

"So here's what I propose," continued my uncle. "As you know, I bought out Daniel last year. Now, I'd like to offer you an interest in the business. You can pay it off when you're able—a few years, if necessary. But starting now, you'll share in the profits. What do you think?"

"I'm stunned," said my father. "I think that's a very generous offer."

"One more thing," said Nathan, "I'm going to Chicago next week to pay off my debt to the lenders I stiffed seven years ago. I have the money now, and it's the right thing to do. It's been on my conscience a long time." This revelation was even more bewildering.

"I guess a leopard *can* change his spots," Sam said to his wife. He told her what had happened, and how unpredictably Nathan had acted. "I don't know if Jesus Christ was behind this." he said, "but Christian Science has certainly earned *my* respect."

As the Chicago trip approached, my Aunt Gracie became uneasy about taking her first airplane flight. "Maybe next time," she said. In those days, wives flew for free; so Nathan asked my mother if she wanted to take Gracie's place. "And how!" she said. So the two Kramarsky siblings took their first flight together, and enjoyed every minute of their grand adventure. Nathan took care of business, and he and Jenny visited relatives and friends they had not seen in years.

Meanwhile, life went on as usual for my bachelor father and me. We prepared our own meals and, on two occasions, joined Aunt Ethel for what my father called "worse food than they serve inmates on Alcatraz Island." We received several letters from the two Als, and although short on details, they seemed to be adapting to military life. I also heard from Hobie who loved basic training, and was apparently born to fly. *In another couple of weeks,* he wrote, *we're going out in the Gulf to practice landing on an old aircraft carrier.*

Several weeks after they left home, my brother and cousin, the two Als, completed basic training and returned to Beverly Hills. They looked great, Alan in his Air Corps khakis and Alfie in his navy whites. Both seemed to have lost weight, gained stature, and appeared to have grown from teenagers to men overnight. My parents threw a party for them and invited relatives, friends, and neighbors to join in the celebration. It was a wonderful party and I was proud of them both, not only as relatives, but as two patriotic young men serving our country. For the three days my brother was home, we didn't have a single fight or even a hostile word. I figured he must have learned something about humility from his top sergeant.

"You seem so much more grown up and responsible," I said. "I think being in the service is doing you a lot of good."

"And you aren't as big a pain in the ass as I remember," he answered.

Two months passed without another word from Hobie. I called Roberta and asked if she had heard from her cousin.

"No," she said, "nothing at all. You think it's time to start worrying?"

"I don't think so. He's still in the States and probably busy with his classes."

"Well, if either of us hears anything, let's call the other one."

After another two weeks, I decided to speak with Hobie's father. I walked down the block and from a distance saw Mr. Johnson sitting on his front porch, just like always. He was wearing the same ill-fitting undershirt and appeared unshaven. I waved to him, but he didn't respond. When I got closer I saw that he was crying.

"What's wrong, Mr. Johnson?"

In place of an answer he handed me the telegram he was holding. It was from the War Department, and it began: *The President of the United States regrets to inform you …* I suddenly felt dizzy; this is a joke, I thought, nothing was going to happen to Hobie. He was still in Corpus Christi learning how to fly. This has to be a terrible mistake. I continued to read the telegram: *… that your son Hobart Anthony Johnson was killed as the result of a tragic training accident. We extend to you our deepest sympathies for the loss you have sustained. It was signed by the Secretary of War.*

I gave the telegram back to Mr. Johnson and said, "I am so sorry, Mr. Johnson."

"Come here," he said. We embraced, and he continued to cry. I hugged him and was suddenly crying, too. We remained that way for a long time. "We both loved him," said Mr. Johnson in his Cary Grant voice, "and I know we'll both miss him terribly."

Roberta's parents held a memorial service for Hobie several days later. All of Hobie's relatives were there, as well as a number of former high school classmates. In the entry hall of the house was a photo of Hobie taken the previous summer at the beach. What a great looking guy, I thought. Alongside the photo was an enlarged obituary from last week's Beverly Hills Courier.

AVIATION CADET KILLED IN PLANE CRASH
Navy Aviation Cadet, Hobart Anthony Johnson, age 17
of Beverly Hills, was killed last Saturday in the crash of
an SNJ advanced naval training plane in Corpus Christie,
Texas. Cadet Johnson attended Beverly Hills High School
where he was a member of the junior baseball team. He
was the only son of Mr. and Mrs. Reginald C. Johnson.

Hobie's parents were somber and red-eyed; their only child was gone, and they were devastated. Shlomo Goldwasser, the family rabbi who presided at Hobie's bar mitzvah, gave a heartfelt speech. He began, "Hobart Johnson was a genuine *mensch.*" Within moments, half the group was in tears. Then Roberta's father, Sidney Gold, spoke of his favorite nephew. He recalled some of Hobie's wonderful attributes and a few amusing experiences from his life. Then he asked if anyone else cared to speak.

"Go ahead," said Roberta. "You were probably his best friend."

"I loved Hobie Johnson," I began. "He was one of my oldest and dearest friends. Hobie and I built model airplanes together, and that's when I first discovered his amazing mechanical skills. He had so many admirable qualities; he was bright, even tempered, and, best of all, he had a wonderful sense of humor. He was also one of the sweetest people on earth. Everybody loved him because there was so much about him to love. Hobie lied about his age to join the Navy. He could have stayed in school but chose instead to serve his country. That was typical Hobie. When people speak at services like this, they always say, 'He died too soon; he should have lived longer.' This has never has been more true than today. I will miss Hobie, he was special; and I will never forget him."

Linda approached me. There were tears in her eyes, and she said, "That was beautiful."

"Thanks," I said. "I meant every word; Hobie *was* special."

"So are you," said Linda. There was a long pause, as if she had more to say.

"You know, Kyle and I are not together any more; he's off to the army. I mean, even if he weren't in the army, we wouldn't be together. Anyway, if you ever feel like getting together to see a movie or just talk, give me a call."

"I'd like that," I said. "I *will* call you."

What a bittersweet afternoon it had been. Losing my best friend made me miserable, but reconnecting with Linda gave me hope for a better future. Who would have thought happiness could come out of such a tragedy? Life was so strange and unpredictable.

CHAPTER TWENTY

The Death Of FDR

It took a long time to get over Hobie Johnson's death. Every so often I felt like walking down the street to talk to him or just hang out. Then it would hit me—that's never going to happen again. Hobie's gone. I saw Lenny Strauss and Stan the Jerk Fishbein, and we all realized the Gale Drive foursome had, overnight, become a trio. We all felt the loss deeply.

I wanted to call Linda the day after Hobie's memorial service, but I thought it would be better to wait awhile. I'm not sure why, but I felt there should be a period of mourning. I'm sure Hobie would have disagreed; he probably would have said, "*Don't be such a nebish; call the girl already.*" So I did—but it was two weeks later.

"Hi, Linda, it's me, Peter."

"I recognized your voice," she said, "I was hoping you'd call; it's been a while."

"Yeah, well, I've been busy, and you know, this Hobie thing has really got me down."

"I saw you a couple of times at school, and you looked right through me. You seemed to be in a trance. I'm trying not to take it personally."

"If I didn't recognize you, I *must* have been in a trance. Look, Linda, I'd like to get together, but I want to be sure you and Kyle are really through. Even though he's not one of my favorite people, it doesn't seem right to get involved, now that he's in the army."

"Peter, listen carefully—Kyle and I are history, it's over, finished, kaput. Get it? It probably never should have happened; but it did, and I'm over it, and you should be, too."

"Okay, if you say so. But it's hard for me to forget you two together. It always seemed so wrong; I felt you deserved so much more."

"Yeah, I finally discovered that for myself," she said. "But why are we talking about Kyle? Are you trying to make me feel guilty about dating him? What happened is in the past, and we can't go back and do it differently, so let's drop it. And if you think this has contaminated me, or somehow ruined my reputation, well, let's just forget about getting together. I really don't need this, Peter."

Wow—I guess I deserved that. It felt like we just had our first fight, and we weren't even a couple. Not the best way to start a relationship.

"You're right, Linda, I was being a jerk, and I'm sorry. I do want to see you, and no more Kyle talk—I promise. How about Friday? I'll pick you up at six; we can go to a drive-in for something to eat. Please say yes."

"It's hard for me to say no to you. Friday at six; see you then."

After hanging up I kept going over our conversation in my mind. Could I possibly have been a bigger *shmuck?* But she said yes, and I was eager for Friday to arrive.

At the age of sixteen I was becoming a typical, disgruntled teenager. I now had a car of my own (actually my brother's), I earned enough money to be more or less independent, and I was going through the conventional and painful process of growing wings so I could fly out of the family nest. As a consequence, I became withdrawn and undemonstrative at home; and, according to my father, a real pain in the ass.

"What's going on with you?" asked my mother. "We never talk any more. I don't know where you go or what you do."

"I don't know what to say," I answered. "I go to school, I work, and that's about it."

"Well, where do you go; who do you see; what do you do when you're not here?"

My answer was pretty much a shrug of the shoulders. I could see that both parents were becoming fed up with my aloof behavior, but I really didn't care. Since Alan joined the Air Corps, my parents hovered obsessively over me and my activities. They were treating me like a suspect in a murder trial. It was always, *"Where did you go? Who are you seeing? What time did you get home?"* The only question missing was, *"What did you do with the murder weapon?"* It was getting to be annoying. One evening I was going to the library to meet Lenny Strauss, and my father began the inquisition.

"Where are you off to?"

"The library."

"Why the library?"

"That's where the books are."

"Don't get sarcastic, young man. And don't be rude."

"Well, what's it to *you*? I don't see where this is any of your business."

And then out of nowhere—Whack! My father slapped me across the face. Across the face! In my entire life he had never done anything like that. I was stunned and hurt and angry.

"Don't you *ever* show such disrespect to me again, do you understand?"

I didn't answer; I was in shock, and even if I could speak, I didn't know what to say. The slap in the face got my attention; I thought maybe I *should* try to be nicer to my parents. Even Aunt Ethel got into the act.

"What's bothering you," she asked? "You used to be the good one;

now you're beginning to act like your brother Alan. You always seem depressed. Is something wrong?"

"Just the stress of living at home, I guess. Since Alan left, my parents have gone back to treating me like an infant. I'm sixteen—in two years I could be fighting in the war. They should realize I'm not a baby any more."

When I look back now, I think my parents worried that I *might* be in the war; and I suppose it frightened them to have both their sons facing such deadly danger. On the other hand, the war was going our way, and with a little luck, it might be over before I was drafted. General Macarthur had just recaptured the Philippines, and the Japanese abandoned several smaller islands. On the other side of the world, the Russian Army overran Warsaw, and Allied Forces crossed the Rhine. And then suddenly, our world stopped spinning on its axis. On April 12, 1945, Franklin Roosevelt suddenly died of a cerebral hemorrhage and was succeeded by Vice President, Harry Truman.

The death of Roosevelt was the most traumatic event for America since the attack on Pearl Harbor. Roosevelt had been president for more than twelve years, and he was the Commander-in-Chief since the war began. America without him was almost inconceivable. When the news broke, every radio program was interrupted by the shocking report. Some announcers, who were struggling to cope with the news, broke down in tears during their report. Millions of people adored him, and even his detractors were saddened by his death. According to reports, when told of Roosevelt's death both Winston Churchill and Joseph Stalin were moved to tears. Our country—and much of the world—had no idea what would happen next. We were now sailing through uncharted waters. Roosevelt had said, *"There is nothing to fear but fear itself,"* but throughout the country the level of fear rose sky high.

The following day was a national day of mourning. It was also the day I was supposed to take Linda to dinner. It felt like a re-run of my bar mitzvah. You didn't have to be completely paranoid to recognize that, whenever I had big plans, there was a disaster waiting in the wings, ready to screw me up. That afternoon I called her.

"Linda, it's me."

"Oh hi, Peter, I was just about to call you. Really bad news about FDR, isn't it?"

"Yeah, that's what I'm calling about. I think we have to postpone our date. My parents want me to go to temple with them tonight. There's a memorial service, and I don't see how I can get out of it. I'd much rather see you, but I don't have much choice. Things haven't been all that great at home; and if I don't show up, I'm afraid they'll disown me."

"What bad luck," she answered, "but I understand. Everything is so mixed up right now; it would probably be a depressing evening, even if we could find a place that's open."

"Can we do this when things settle down?"

"I'm counting on it," she said. "Stay in touch."

"I will. You know, I really looked forward to tonight."

"Me too. Good-bye for now."

That evening, for the first time since my canceled bar mitzvah, I set foot in the Olympic Jewish Center. Every unhappy memory came flooding back, including the aroma of boiled cabbage. My greatest fear is that I would run into Mordecai Sokolofski, my old teacher. I was now three years older, eight inches taller, and a bit wiser. But what would I say? How would I act? I went over all the possibilities in my mind and finally decided I would do nothing. I had changed so considerably in the past three years, I figured he might not even recognize me. And if he did, I would pretend we never met before. I would say, "I believe you have the wrong person." Perhaps he would think I was crazy, but so what; at least I wouldn't have to speak to him.

We took our seats near the rear of the auditorium, and Rabbi Leonard Gluckman walked on stage. He welcomed us and began the program with a Hebrew prayer for the dead. If Franklin Roosevelt was looking down on us, I'm sure—like me—he didn't understand a single word. Then the rabbi spoke of our dearly departed president; what a good friend he was to the Jewish people, how strong and wise he was in fighting the war against fascist aggression, and how much he would be missed. The rabbi spoke of the future, and he encouraged us to support Harry Truman.

"Let us help our new president," he began. "Now, more than ever, he needs the encouragement and faith of the American people. He has a monumental job to do, he has enormous shoes to fill, and we must offer whatever help we can. May God bless you all, and may God continue to bless our United States."

The rabbi offered another prayer in Hebrew, a string quartet played two depressing pieces, and everybody got up to go home. And then out of nowhere, as though he had been hiding behind the drapes, Sokolofski sneaked up from behind and tapped me on the shoulder. I turned, recognized my nemesis, and my carefully calculated strategy of "it's really not me" went out the window.

"*Gut shabbes*, Peter. How have you been?" asked my former teacher.

"Fine, thank you," was all I could say.

"I haven't seen you since the aborted bar mitzvah, and I never had the opportunity to tell you how sorry I was about the way things turned out." His accented English sounded even more mangled than before.

"Thank you," I said. "Yes, quite a tragedy." I waited to be struck by lightning for the obvious lie I was telling.

"You should come back for a visit every so often. Jewish faith, you know, is an ongoing process, and there is still much for you to learn. It seems to me you have strayed far from the spiritual world. At least you should try to attend Friday night services."

"Yes," I said. But what I *thought* was, I'd rather be run over by a legion of Egyptian chariots.

My parents were *schmoozing* with neighbors, most of whom were certain the death of Roosevelt was the worst news they ever heard. Almost without exception, they were depressed, pessimistic, and convinced there would be an escalation of anti-Semitism. The most cynical of them were predicting a new American pogrom. They didn't actually rend their garments or beat their breasts, but, as a group, they were pretty miserable. While my parents were talking, I walked out the front entrance; the aroma of cabbage was beginning to make me nauseous. Standing outside was Stan the Jerk.

"I didn't see you in there," he said.

"I was hiding from Sokolofski," I answered.

"Was he there?"

"Yeah, and he found me. And he's still a *putz.*"

The Fishbein and Newman parents came out of temple together, and we all walked home. It had been an emotional and depressing day, and we were exhausted.

A week after Roosevelt's death the Allies liberated Buchenwald, the concentration camp near Weimar, Germany. A week later, the Soviets reached Berlin. Within ten days Adolph Hitler and his mistress, Eva Braun, had committed suicide.

CHAPTER TWENTY-ONE

It's Love

The Allies accepted the unconditional surrender of German forces during the first week of May, and the next day was proclaimed VE Day—VE standing for Victory in Europe. There were massive celebrations throughout Europe, most notably in London, where German bombs had leveled much of the city during the earlier blitz. Americans celebrated as well, from Times Square to Hollywood Boulevard. But unlike the Europeans, Americans were more restrained, realizing the job was only half done. We were still in a brutal war with Japan, and it was impossible to predict when that would end.

Everybody at Beverly High was thrilled with the news, especially those who had relatives in the armed forces and refugee students who still had families in Europe. I saw Linda at school several times, but we were unable to make a date. First of all, going out on weeknights was difficult. There was always homework, there were frequent blackouts, and we both had a nine o'clock curfew. Our parents must have feared that a Japanese spy would pop out of a bush one dark night, hijack us onto a ship heading for Tokyo, and torture us until we revealed how much money our fathers earned. They also must have thought Japanese spies took weekends off, because on Fridays and Saturdays we were allowed to stay out until eleven.

Finally, near the end of May we made a plan to have a quick bite at Simon's drive-in and then go to Hollywood to see the new movie *Anchors Aweigh*. If all else went wrong, I figured we'd at least enjoy a good meal and pleasant movie. As time approached to pick up Linda, I became strangely nervous. The trouble was, I was uncertain about our relationship. I knew Linda liked me, but did she see me as a boyfriend or just a friend? That was an important distinction. My feelings were less equivocal; I was simply infatuated with her. So here I was, building up a fantasy romance without knowing if we would actually hit it off as a couple. But what if it was nothing more than a fantasy? What then? This kind of thinking obsessed me and, simultaneously, depressed me.

"Relax," I said to myself. *"Even if it doesn't work out she'll still be a friend."*

"Who are you kidding?" answered the voice in my head. *"You poor shmuck, if she's never more than a friend, you'll be miserable—and you know it."*

I parked in front of her apartment, walked to the front door, and rang the bell. When the door opened, I nearly fell over. The person in front of me was Linda, but a Linda I had never seen before. She was wearing a black and beige wraparound dress that revealed every curve of her faultless figure. She also wore heels and was lightly made up with faint eye shadow and a delicate red lipstick. Her hair was brushed back and held in place by a silver clip, and there was a single strand of pearls at her throat. Her perfumed aroma made me lightheaded.

"Hello, Peter," she said, and I stood there speechless. "Are you okay?" she asked.

"Yeah, I think so. You look fantastic," I said. "You know, we're only going to a movie."

"Well, I hope you don't mind; I just felt like dressing up a bit."

Now I was really worried. Standing before me was a beautiful young woman who appeared poised, mature, and self-assured. What was *I* doing there? She should be going out with a poised, mature, self-assured young man, someone I could never pretend to be. To say I was intimidated would be putting it mildly. I was overwhelmed and disheartened as I realized she was a woman and I was still an immature teenager. What a mismatched couple! I felt like making a run for it.

"What's wrong?" she asked. "You look upset."

"Do you really think going out is a good idea?" I asked. "We could still call it off, you know. I mean, if you'd rather not, I'd understand."

"What are you talking about? Don't you feel well?"

"Yeah, I'm okay, but, well, you look so sensational, and I feel like such a *schlepper*."

"Now listen, you're talking a bit crazy. I've wanted to go out with you for a long time, and I assumed you wanted to go out with me. Now if you've changed your mind, just say so. But, just so you know, I haven't changed my mind, and I think we ought to give this a try."

We got into the car and headed for Simon's Drive-In on Wilshire Boulevard. I was unable to say anything until the waitress asked for our order.

"I'll have a hamburger and vanilla shake," said Linda.

"Make that two," I said, even though I preferred chocolate. I wanted to appear agreeable. We remained quiet as we waited for our food. Then Linda reached for my hand.

"Here's an idea—why don't we pretend we're just a couple of old friends having a bite to eat and seeing a movie together. I think this dating business has you all anxious and jumpy. Let's just relax and see what happens."

I thought about that for a long time and finally said, "By the way, old buddy, old chum, old pal, where's our food? I'm starving." We both laughed, and suddenly I felt better.

Nobody watching *Anchors Aweigh* could help but be in a good mood. Frank Sinatra and Gene Kelly were two sailors on leave in

Hollywood, and the love interest was Kathryn Grayson. The music and dancing were wonderful, and the love story had a typical Hollywood happy ending. We held hands during the movie, and when Sinatra sang *I Fall in Love Too Easily*, I could swear she squeezed my hand. I cannot remember being any happier than I was at that moment.

We had hot fudge sundaes at C.C. Brown's, and then it was time to go home. We walked to the door and then I had the strangest feeling. I didn't want to say goodnight; I didn't want the evening to end. And I said so.

"Me too," she said, "I had a wonderful time. I hope you're over your nervousness, because I think this was probably a date. And I think it went very well."

Then she leaned close to me, put her arms around my neck, and gave me a kiss goodnight. But this was no thanks-a-lot, had-a-good-time, see-you-later kiss. This was the most passionate experience of my entire life. She looked in my eyes, smiled a half smile, and whispered my name. I was aware again of her perfumed aroma. And then our lips touched, hers slightly parted as were mine. I never felt such soft, full, and sensuous lips. A shiver went through me as if we were standing in a cold draft. She pressed her lips more tightly to mine, and then I suddenly felt her tongue. I thought I might pass out. My thoughts turned to all the great screen kisses I had ever seen; Clark Gable and Vivian Leigh in *Gone With the Wind*, Errol Flynn and Olivia de Haviland in *Robin Hood*, and Humphrey Bogart and Ingrid Bergman in *Casablanca*. This was better than any of those—by a long shot.

After some time we slowly moved away from each other. "Thank you," she said. "I enjoyed that." Was she talking about the evening or the kiss? I couldn't be sure. "Goodnight," she said, and then she was gone. I stood there for a long time, afraid to move. I felt lightheaded and thought I might fall if I tried to move. The dizziness passed after a while, and then I walked to the car and drove home. I had trouble falling asleep; I kept wondering what happened. Was this love? And if not, what was I feeling? I was utterly confused; but when I finally did fall asleep, I'm sure there was a smile on my face.

When I awoke, I thought the previous night might have been a dream. But then my mother came into my room and said, "Your friend Linda is on the phone."

"Hi," I said. "How's it going?"

"Just wanted you to know, I really enjoyed last night. I can't remember when I felt so relaxed and comfortable with anyone."

"Me too," I said. "It was wonderful being with you. Suppose we can do it again?"

"Just say when."

"Next weekend for sure. Better write that down."

"I don't have to; I won't forget. See you at school. Bye now."

I sat there a long time after she hung up. Now I think I knew. I think it was love.

School was out in June, and Linda again traveled with her family to visit relatives back East. She was supposed to return by the end of July, and the several weeks she was gone dragged by. We had dated steadily before school was out, and hardly a day went by without our seeing each other. We often spoke on the phone, but the conversations were generally short. Both my parents seemed to have a mental stopwatch; when my conversations approached ten minutes, one or the other would say, "Time's up, young man. Somebody's probably trying to reach us." My father had the bizarre notion that some radio game show was going to call to inform us that the Newman family had just won an immense cash prize. Of course, that call never came.

I spent the summer working full time at the new and modern automated car wash that just opened on Wilshire Boulevard, a few blocks from home. The Speedy Car Wash was a modern invention in which cars were pulled along by a continuous chain in assembly line fashion. Workers, like me, were stationed along the line performing one specific task or another. For example, I began in the wheel pit and washed only wheels and tires. I must have washed thousands of wheels before I was promoted to washing windows. I washed the left half of windshields and rear windows, as well as the left-side widows. My counterpart on the other side of the car did the same job with the right-side windows. It was grueling work as the assembly line never stopped. And if you couldn't keep up, the half-washed car would be sent back for rewashing, and the car owner was sure to be so annoyed, you could forget about a tip.

I hesitated to complain about the work because the pay was so good. And, as an added bonus, I was developing muscles I never knew I had. In fact, when I looked in the mirror I could hardly believe what I saw. Don't get me wrong; the Charles Atlas look was still a long way off. But I suddenly lost what was left of my baby fat and was now proud to be seen lying along Santa Monica Beach. I also grew another inch that summer. So even though I went home dog-tired each night I continued to count my growing nest egg and admire my new, barely rippling muscles.

As demanding as it was, the car wash job was not the worst job I ever had. That honor belonged to La Cienega Lanes, a bowling alley where I set pins on weekends just before school let out for the summer. Pins were set by hand in those days, and just picking up those chunks of maple nearly did me in. Getting struck by a flying pin was an even greater hazard. Several co-workers ended up on crutches because they failed to pay attention to the moron throwing the ball down the alley as hard as he could. If my parents knew the mortal danger in setting pins, they would never have permitted it. But they didn't bowl and had never set foot in a bowling alley. According to their peculiar value system, bowling was strictly for the *goyem*.

With Linda away that summer I spent more of my free time with Lenny and Stan the Jerk. Lenny was attending summer school at UCLA. Being intellectually gifted, he had permission to take college-level science courses. Stan joined me at the car wash for a while, but after two weeks he'd had it. He complained that no amount of money was worth keeping your hands in soapy water all day and working your ass off. So he quit. The three of us frequently met after dinner and sat around talking about sex, which was Stan's obsession.

"How are you and Linda doing?" he asked.

"Pretty well, but she's out of town, you know."

"Have you ever seen her naked?" Stan asked.

"What kind of question is that? It's none of your damn business," I answered. "Anyway, I respect her and wouldn't do anything she wouldn't want to do."

"Yeah, but what if she *wanted* to get naked?"

"Drop it, Stan. You're being crude and disgusting."

"Okay, but have you ever seen *any* girl naked?"

After thinking it over for a while, I decided to share the bizarre story of Lola Herrera, daughter of the perfumed candle shop owner. Both listeners became wide-eyed.

"What?" exclaimed Stan, "She offered to do it with you and you said *no*? I cannot believe this. You wouldn't even touch her boobs? What's wrong with you? Are you queer or something?"

"Take it easy, Stan, I've already told you, our fathers were standing just outside the door."

"So what. You could have done it quietly."

"But she was acting so *meshuggeneh*. What if she turned out to be a screamer, and she began to scream out of ecstasy or, God forbid, fear or pain? Her father would break down the door and find me with my pants down around my ankles. What then? I'll tell you what—I'd be dead."

"I still say, it would have been worth the risk," said Stan.

Lenny suddenly interrupted, "I think Peter was right. No momentary thrill is worth getting caught with your pants down."

"And how would you know that, you pathetic virgin? Did you read it in some scientific textbook?"

"Oh, lay off," I said. "You know there's more to life than sex."

"Not for me," said Stan, who, as we would later discover, had never even held a girl's hand.

On August 6, 1945, a U.S. Air Corps bomber dropped an atom bomb on Hiroshima, and three days later another atom bomb was dropped on Nagasaki. The bombs virtually destroyed both cities and killed over two hundred thousand people. The devastation was so spectacular, the Japanese feared the total collapse and obliteration of their nation. It also didn't help that the Soviet Union declared war on Japan moments after the second bomb was dropped. Within the week Japan surrendered unconditionally to the Allied Powers, and World War II ended.

I was working at Speedy Car Wash that afternoon. A fellow worker heard the report on a car radio and shouted, "The war is over! The war is over!" Suddenly drivers on Wilshire Boulevard were honking their horns, and people along the street were shaking hands, patting backs, and kissing total strangers. It was a wild circus of activity and we were laughing, crying, and shouting with joy. Speedy Car Wash workers threw their soapy mitts in the air, abandoned half-washed cars, and ran home to share the news with the people closest to them.

I found a note on the door telling me my parents were next door at the Gittelman's apartment. Arnold Gittelman and his wife ran the cleaning shop in the area, and they were hosting a celebration for the entire neighborhood. When I arrived Gittelman was already half-drunk. He handed me a tumbler of scotch whiskey and said, "Have a drink, *boychik*."

"I don't drink," I said.

"What are you talking about? Today everybody drinks; we're celebrating peace, happiness, and the end to a terrible war. *L'chaim!*"

What could I do? I sipped the awful-tasting liquid and looked for my parents. I found them in the kitchen making sandwiches for everybody.

"Peter," they shouted. And then we embraced. My mother was crying, "Soon your brother will be home again; isn't that wonderful?" Wonderful? Not exactly the word I had in mind; no more bedroom to myself, no more use of the Ford, no more peace and quiet. I definitely had mixed emotions. I also had another drink.

I wanted to talk to Linda; I wanted to share this incredibly exciting moment with her. But the phone was in constant use. I also kept getting interrupted by neighbors who wanted to hug and kiss me and tell me how happy they were the war was over. Even Stan the Jerk kissed me on the cheek, and I didn't really mind. Finally, the phone was free and I dialed Linda's number. Mr. Berg answered, "The war is over, congratulations! I'm delighted to speak to you. Who is this?"

"It's me, Mr. Berg—Peter. Is Linda there?"

"Peter," she began, "I'm so happy you called. I tried calling you, but there was no answer."

"I'm not home," I said. I'm at a neighbor's house. It's crazy here."

"I want to see you," she said. "I want to kiss you and I want to celebrate with you."

"I'll be right there, that is, if I can get my legs to work."

"What are you talking about?"

"I've had a couple of drinks, and I'm a bit wobbly. But I'm not giving up. No, sir; don't give up the ship! That's not the American way. Shipmates stand together, fair or stormy weather, we won't give up—we won't give up the ship!"

"Peter, are you all right?"

"Be right there," I said.

Then I went to the stairway, missed the first step, fell down the entire flight, and passed out.

CHAPTER TWENTY-TWO

Holy Matrimony!

The day after VJ Day I awoke in my own bed with a massive headache, upset stomach, and a bruised body that only someone who's fallen down a flight of stairs could appreciate. I was a mess. I wondered what Arnold Gittelman had given me to drink. He said it was Scotch whiskey, but who knows? I reacted as though it were a deadly potion concocted by an evil witch. My mother came into my room and asked, "So, how's the young *shikker* doing today?"

"I don't feel very well," I answered. "How did I get here?"

"Your father and Stan Fishbein carried you here. We thought you broke your neck falling down those stairs. Who knew we were raising a professional stunt man?"

"What did I miss?" I asked.

"Well, World War II ended, and you had two phone calls from Linda."

"I know about the war," I said. "Why do you think I was drinking? What did Linda say?"

"She wondered why you didn't show up. I told her she should be dating a prohibitionist."

"That's not funny," I said. "I'm really sick, you know."

As I got up and walked to the phone I felt nauseous and dizzy.

"Hi Linda," I said. "I'm sorry I didn't make it last night. I drank something that really knocked me out."

"Your mother told me the story. I'm sorry you weren't here; I had a

175

real celebration planned. You missed a great opportunity."

"Want to tell me what I missed?"

"Let's just say, you would have loved it."

"I'm sure you're right. Think we can have a belated celebration?"

"It depends on how long it takes you to sober up."

As it turned out, it took an entire week before I began to feel normal. Although my case of alcohol poisoning was mild, the experience was agonizing. My next drink would be more than a year later. The beginning of my senior year at Beverly High coincided with my seventeenth birthday. It was the first time the world was at peace in over four years, and there was a new spirit throughout the school. Several activities curtailed during the war years were reinstated, and a number of teachers returned to school from the armed forces. Neither Alan nor Alfie were scheduled to come home, as they both had more than a year to serve. But at least they were stationed in the country and, we presumed, safe.

My cousin Gary was discharged in October, having served three years as a Naval gunner's mate and having seen enough action to last a lifetime. He proposed to his girlfriend at the end of that month, and the wedding at my Uncle Nathan's house was scheduled for three weeks after the engagement. I assumed he was making up for lost time. Linda came with me to the wedding, and I was nervous about her meeting my relatives.

"Don't be too judgmental," I said. "Some of my relatives are a bit eccentric, but as far as we know there are no serial killers among them."

"I'm sure they're no worse than any other family," she said. "Including mine."

"Hey, Pretzel," my cousin greeted me with a hug. "It's great to see you." Gary looked handsome in his navy whites, and the beautiful girl beside him had a radiant smile.

"This is Marianne," he said. "Marianne this is my favorite cousin, Peter Newman. Peter and I drove down Route 66 together, neither of us will ever forget it or be the same."

"That's true," I said. "Pleased to meet you, Marianne. And this is Linda Berg, my classmate and best friend." A bit later Linda asked me, "What did you mean 'best friend'?"

"Well, what would *you* say?"

"How about sweetheart, dearest beloved, lover, any of those would do."

"Well, we're not actually, technically, lovers, if you know what I mean."

"If you keep this up, we might never be." And then she winked.

The wedding turned out to be a wonderful celebration; there were great heaps of food, we danced to a small band, and I spoke to friends and relatives I had not seen in a long time. The only thing I didn't do was drink. After the ceremony there were affectionate speeches welcoming Gary home and congratulating the attractive couple. The entire day was joyous and emotional. We all realized the war was over, and it was a comfort to celebrate with peaceful optimism. My Aunt Gracie certainly realized it; she must have cried for about three hours straight.

Towards the end of the party my beautiful cousin Kay said, "Be quiet, everybody, I have an announcement to make. I'd like everyone to know that Tony Franco and I will be married next week at his parent's house in Santa Barbara, and you're all invited." Who was Tony Franco, we all wondered? And then it hit me. Tony was the person Kay had been pushing around in a wheelchair. I assumed he was one of her patients at the veteran's hospital. It turned out I was right on both counts. Tony was Kay's patient, he was a paraplegic, and they had fallen in love over the past few months. What a shocker! My Aunt Gracie suddenly launched a fresh batch of tears. There were congratulations all around, and I asked Gary, "Don't you kind of feel upstaged?"

"Not really," he answered, "I'm just happy for them both. I had an idea this was coming."

What happened next, however, nobody saw coming.

"I, too, have something to announce," began my plump cousin Shelley. Bernie Balachik and I are engaged to be married, and the wedding will take place as soon as my parents recover from the shock of today's activities."

So who was Bernie Balachik? Apparently the soldier who had been standing close to Shelley since the day began. I thought he might be her bodyguard. Bernie was on furlough from his American outpost in Alaska, where he was a Russian translator. He was born in Russia and was the son of an orthodox rabbi. We all assumed that Shelly would remain a spinster forever. Suddenly we discovered she had snagged a lonely soldier who had been living among polar bears for the past three years. Shelly was almost as large as a polar bear, and apparently, Bernie felt comfortable with her generous proportions. I also presumed he had impaired vision. I looked at my parents and they both appeared mystified by the announcements of the past few minutes. Linda asked, "Is this what you meant by eccentric?"

"No," I answered, "this goes way beyond what I had in mind."

I asked Gary again, "*Now* are you beginning to feel upstaged?"

"Yeah, this has gone too far. This was supposed to be *my* special day."

By this time, my Aunt Gracie was stretched out on the couch with an ice pack on her head, and my Uncle Nathan looked like he wanted to run away. He probably feared there would be another announcement coming.

I was most perplexed by Kay's choice of husband. Here was a bright, sexy, and charming young woman who chose to devote her life to caring for someone who would be in a wheelchair forever. Tony seemed pleasant, and he was certainly handsome, but the spinal chord injury caused by a Japanese bullet dramatically changed his life. And if I understood paraplegia, there were unlikely to be children, or even the attempt to have children. I spoke to Kay about this.

"Tony seems like a great guy," I began, "but aren't you complicating your life?"

"It won't be the conventional marriage," she said, "but he's such a terrific person."

"So are you," I reminded her. "As far as I'm concerned, you're still O-Kay."

She gave me a hug and said, "I really wanted to marry you, Peter, but you're too young, and I don't think our parents would approve. Besides, first cousins often have crazy children." Then looking towards Linda, she said, "I also think I'd have some pretty stiff competition."

"How's the paraplegic thing working out," I asked. "I mean sex-wise, if you'll forgive my tactless question."

"It's not a problem," Kay answered. "It's different, but still satisfying. We do things you don't often hear about, and we manage very well, thank you. But why this curiosity about sex? You're too young to be thinking about such things. I hope you haven't taken advantage of that beautiful young girl over there."

"No, but I'm trying to. And as far as sex is concerned, I've been thinking about it ever since I learned to spell the word."

The party continued long into the evening, as did the excitement about the three siblings being married within a period of weeks. I joined my mother who was talking to her brother, our host. He still appeared shaken by the unexpected announcements.

"Congratulations," I said. "I don't think any of your guests expected such excitement."

"Neither did I," my uncle answered. "I never thought my house would be emptied so abruptly. In a few weeks Gracie and I will be alone." He seemed depressed by that thought.

Before leaving the party I bumped into Sylvia Garbo, who was holding hands with a handsome young man.

"Hi, Sylvia," I said. "How've you been?"

"Peter," she cried, "one of my favorite people. I'd like you to meet Gregory Valentino. Greg and I acted together in my last film. Isn't he gorgeous?"

"Pleased to meet you," I said. He certainly was gorgeous I thought, gorgeous enough to be a movie star.

"And I'd like you to meet Linda Berg, my sweetheart," I said. Linda squeezed my hand.

"What a beautiful young girl," said Sylvia. "Do you act, dear?"

"No," answered Linda, "I have a hard enough time with reality."

"Oh, isn't she precious?" said Sylvia. "Now don't say anything, you two, but I have a confession. Greg and I became engaged last night, and we're going to be married next month. And then we're going to Hawaii for our honeymoon. Isn't that marvelous news?"

"What's going on?" I asked. "Did somebody put something in the water? Everybody in the whole world seems to be getting married."

"I know," said Sylvia. "Isn't it wonderful?"

"Have you told my parents?"

"Not yet. I didn't want it to get around. There've been so many announcements already."

"Well, what's one more?" I asked. And then I thought, wait a minute, did I hear right? There was going to be a Garbo-Valentino wedding? Who would believe *that*? I could see the Daily Variety headline: *Garbo & Valentino to Wed!—Sorry, not Greta and Rudolph.*

A couple of minutes later my Uncle Nathan asked for everyone's attention, and then he made the announcement.

"Calm down, everybody; there's another important announcement." By this time the audience had a look of: What could possibly happen next? "Our old friend from Chicago, that wonderful actress you recently enjoyed in *Cannibal Women in the Jungle of Death*, none other than Sylvia Garbo, has just revealed that she and her co-star, Gregory Valentino, are engaged and will be married next month."

There was a fresh round of applause; and my Aunt Gracie was so overcome with emotion she had to be helped to her bed. My cousin Gary said, "Now it's become a three-ring circus."

Throughout this entire episode gorgeous Gregory never said a word. He continued to smile and show off his prominent and amazingly white teeth, but not a word escaped his lips. I wondered if he *could* speak. Then I remembered, in *Cannibal Women in the Jungle of Death* he said a lot of *"unga goomby undama"*. Maybe that's all he knew. My mother was delighted by the news, but my father looked as though he was experiencing mixed emotions.

"Last chance," hollered my Uncle Nathan. "Would anybody else like to reveal their engagement, marriage, or any other relationship of interest?" He was really getting into it now.

There were no further announcements, which meant the party was pretty much over.

On the way home Linda noted, "Quite a love-struck bunch of relatives you've got there."

"Yeah, I guess so. But don't get any funny ideas; we're not all that way."

After a long pause she asked in a more serious voice, "Do you think we'll ever be married? I mean, to each other?"

I didn't know how to answer that. Apparently, Linda had been thinking about this, but the idea of marriage had never entered my mind. How could I possibly know about my future? I was young and reluctant to rush through this phase of my life. Marriage? That was for adults. I figured I wouldn't be one of those for some time. Of course I was crazy about Linda—but marriage?

"I don't know," I finally answered. "That sort of thing is a long way off. But if I were ready to settle down today, I can't imagine anyone else I rather be with."

"Pretty good answer," she said.

CHAPTER TWENTY-THREE

Giving Thanks

By Thanksgiving my life had become a pleasant routine of classes, which I enjoyed; school cafeteria work, which provided spending money; and, of course, Linda, who provided all the affection and excitement I could handle. We never actually make a decision to go steady, but that's the way it worked out. Neither of us saw anyone else, nor did we have any desire to do so.

My brother Alan was coming home for Thanksgiving, and my mother made elaborate plans for the three days he'd be here. The crowning feature of the plan was a dinner for our family, including Aunt Ethel and Cousin Lynn from downstairs, and Alfie, who would be home on leave. Sylvia Garbo and Greg Valentino were also invited, since we were the closest thing to family they had in Los Angeles. Linda chose to be with us, rather than her parents, who would be traveling back East. Altogether, there would be ten of us, and my mother began preparing for the feast several days ahead of the holiday.

My mother was in her glory when she could cook and bake and be a hostess. She was like the old Jenny Kramarsky of twenty years earlier, still attractive, vivacious, and moving with the whirlwind elegance of a graceful dancer. She was also in a festive mood and flirted endlessly with my father. It occurred to me some years earlier that my parents really liked one another. This was in stark contrast to some of my friends' parents. For example, I rarely saw Hobie's parents speak to one another, and even Lenny Strauss's parents seemed aloof and remote, more like roommates than husband and wife.

Currently, my mother's biggest problem was locating a kosher turkey.

"Why does a Thanksgiving turkey have to be kosher?" wondered my father.

"It just has to be," answered my mother.

"That's no answer. Anyway, what does a kosher turkey look like? Does it have *payes* and wear a *yarmulke*? Or does it peck from right to left? Maybe it gobbles in Yiddish."

"That's not funny," said my mother, but she laughed anyway. "If you must know, Mr. Buttinski, the kosher turkey was a special request from Sylvia and Greg."

"What?" asked my father, "Gregory Valentino is Jewish? And kosher?"

"Yes, his real name is Gershon Velvarsky; he changed it when he started acting. It was supposed to be Greg Valentine, but his handwriting was so bad Valentine turned into Valentino."

"*Oy,*" said my father. "Such nonsense. Okay, here's what we do: buy a turkey, I'll do a *borucha*, and we'll tell him it's kosher."

"Tell you what, dear; just stay out of it. I'll handle the turkey."

Alan arrived home the day before Thanksgiving, and my parents gave him a welcome fit for a head of state. There were hugs and kisses and the usual torrent of tears. There was also a special afternoon tea consisting of my mother's homemade pastries and accompanied by endless pronouncements about how badly my brother had been missed. My parents obviously had short memories and little appreciation for the peace and quiet we enjoyed for the past several months. Then my brother greeted me.

"Hey, looks like the little *fortzel* is growing up. Whaddya say Pete; how they hangin'?"

"Same old Alan," I said. "Doesn't the Air Corps have a finishing school?"

"Same old Peter," he answered, "tight-assed as ever."

He moved into his old room, and suddenly the space seemed less than half its size. But I reminded myself; it was just for three days. I decided earlier that I would be as tolerant and accommodating as possible, even if it killed me, which I feared it might. That night, for the first time in many months, we ate dinner as a family.

"Tell us everything," my mother said to Alan. "What's it like being in the Air Corps? Have you learned to fly? Have you made any new friends? What do you do on your time off ...?"

"Take it easy," said my father. "Give the poor guy a chance to answer."

"Well, first of all, a lot has changed since the war ended. Most of us who haven't seen action are disappointed that we might not get overseas. About flying—a couple of months ago they discovered I had a heart murmur. No big deal, but I can never be a pilot. I've applied for parachute school and will probably be transferred to a base in Utah next month. Friends? Yeah, I got a bunch of friends, and they're mostly great guys—a couple of jerks, too—but mostly great guys."

"Have you at least gone up in a plane?" I asked.

"Sure, plenty of times; and every so often a buddy let's me take the controls. It's a helluva thrill, and I'll probably do it again."

And then my father asked the question on most of our minds. "Are you behaving yourself?"

"Why?" asked Alan, "has my name been in the local papers?"

"You know what I mean. Are you staying out of trouble?"

Alan just laughed. "You've got nothing to worry about. There's not enough free time to get into trouble."

The downstairs Newmans joined us after dinner, and we sat around drinking coffee and talking until almost midnight.

Thanksgiving activities began early the next day. By eight o'clock the kitchen was a hub of activity. My mother was preparing the turkey, and Ethel was beginning to make the giblet gravy. My father came into the kitchen, took one look at the kosher bird and said, "Funny, he doesn't look Jewish."

"Unless you're here to help," said my mother, suppressing a laugh, "please leave us alone."

Alan wandered into the kitchen, still in his pajamas, at about eleven o'clock.

"Have I missed breakfast?"

"No, darling," said my mother. "Look on the stove—I made you some *matzo-brei.*"

"Haven't eaten this well since I joined up," said Alan. "Nothing like home cooking." My mother just beamed. "Don't eat too much," she said. "Dinner is at five this afternoon."

I picked up Linda at four thirty, and she looked sensational. "Hope I'm not too dressed up," she said. "Thanksgiving always seems like a formal holiday to me."

"You're perfect," I said.

When we got home Sylvia and Greg had just arrived. My father opened a bottle of schnapps and proposed a toast to the newly married couple, who had returned from their Hawaiian honeymoon three days earlier.

"To our dear friend, Sylvia, and her new husband Greg. May they always be as happy as they are today. *L'Chaim!*"

Alan approached and asked, "Is this the same Linda I first met at Horace Mann? My God, how you've changed—and all for the better."

"Thank you, Alan. What a nice thing to say."

"But what's a beauty like you doing with my dimwitted brother?"

"I don't happen to think he's dimwitted. But your question is kind of dimwitted."

"What a feisty girlfriend you've got, Peter. Well, Linda, if you ever decide to fool around with grown-ups, maybe we can get together."

I couldn't believe what I was hearing. "What do you think you're doing, Alan? You're being rude and obnoxious. Stop it right now!" I was ready to punch him.

"What's going on here?" my mother wanted to know.

"I'm about to clobber my cretin brother," I answered. "He's being his usual disgusting self, and it's disrespectful to Linda. He's acting like a total *shmuck*."

"Now listen, you two, we're having a peaceful Thanksgiving dinner today, and neither of you is going to spoil it. Understand? Now behave yourselves!" My mother then put on a more cheerful face and announced, "Dinner is served."

We took our seats, and I made certain we were at the opposite end of the table from Alan.

"As is our tradition," began my father, "we will each take a moment to speak about those things for which we are thankful today. Let's begin with my dear wife, who created this fine dinner."

"I am thankful that that the terrible war has ended, our family is together, and we are joined by good and loving friends. I'm especially grateful that the Air Corps allowed our son to join us for this traditional celebration." I figured she was the only one grateful for that.

Then my Aunt Ethel said, "I, too, am grateful that my son, Alfie could be with us today; we've really missed having a man around the house. I also want to thank my sister and brother-in-law for hosting this dinner. It's wonderful having such a loving family." Then she began to cry.

Alfie spoke next. "It's great to be home, even temporarily. I'm thankful my family is well, and that we can have a feast like this when many in the world today still have so little."

Sylvia said, "I have so much to be thankful for, I don't know where to begin. Of course, I'm thankful for my new husband; I love this gorgeous guy. He has become my best friend, my lover, and the finest co-star I've ever worked with. I might mention that we're doing a sequel to our last, and—may I add—very successful picture. This one is titled *Return of the Cannibal Women to the Jungle of Death.*" As if on cue, Greg flashed his million-dollar smile. Sylvia continued. "I'm also grateful to have caring friends like Sam and Jenny. You're like family to me and always will be."

Alan said, "I agree with what everybody has said; family, friends, good food, and no more war. Who could ask for anything more?" That was Alan, not an original thought in his head.

"I want to say how grateful I am for our good life," I began. The world is a mess right now, but the war's over, and things will improve. Here, on the home front, we've had a pretty easy time of it. We never suffered any of the fears or problems faced by those overseas. We have a lot to be thankful for; family, friends, and especially this best friend sitting next to me."

"Thanks for that," Linda began. "I'm thankful to you and your family for letting me share this special day with you. I've always admired your good humor and the love you have for one another." *With one major exception,* I thought. "And I'm so pleased to be with you all."

My father asked if anyone else cared to speak, and he looked directly at Gregory Valentino. Greg just shook his head, and now I was absolutely convinced he was unable to say anything other than his famous movie line: *unga goomby undama,* which, translated from Swahili, probably meant: *Why are you looking at me? I've absolutely nothing to say.* Finally it was my father's turn.

"I want to give thanks to all of you for being here. This is what life is all about—family and friends—loved ones sharing good food and good times. I'm thankful the terrible war is over and that the free world has survived. I'm thankful that Hitler and Mussolini and Tojo are gone, and that the world will never again tolerate such wicked dictators. After what we've witnessed the past few years, we now know it definitely could be worse. Finally, I'm grateful for our good health that allows us to enjoy the wonders of life. I love you all and hope we may do this every year."

We were all touched by my father's words, and we gave him a round of applause. My mother rose, walked to the opposite end of the table, and gave my father an adoring kiss. Then we began to eat. Overflowing platters of food were passed back and forth, and conversation came to a near halt as the happy guests concentrated on their food. It was the most delicious Thanksgiving dinner I could remember; everything was cooked to perfection.

"Great dinner," said Sylvia. "Maybe the best you've ever done."

"You know," said my father, "kosher turkeys *do* taste better. Who would have guessed?"

The rest of us were too busy chewing to offer more than, "Right! And how! You betcha!"

After two hours, most guests were stuffed and groaning with delight.

"Hope you don't mind," said my brother Alan, "but Alfie and I are seeing some of our former Cossack buddies tonight. Thought we'd catch up on things."

"Do you need your car?" I asked apprehensively.

"Not tonight, *nudnik*; we're being picked up. But don't leave town, I'll need it tomorrow."

The two cousins got up from the table and said their goodbyes.

Alan approached Linda and said, "No disrespect intended, but keep in mind what I said."

"No disrespect intended to you," I said, "but don't be surprised if I drive your car into the Pacific Ocean." He laughed but looked concerned.

A few minutes later I announced that Linda and I were leaving; I wanted to be alone with her. We said goodbye, and Linda again thanked my parents and complimented my mother's cooking. "If only *my* mother could cook like that," she said. Then my mother gave her a hug and a kiss goodbye.

"You really impressed my family," I said when we were in the car.

"Especially your brother," she said.

"I'm sorry he's such a jerk. He had no right to behave that way."

"Just remember, Peter, you're the Newman I love."

"Can we go to your house?" I asked. "No one home, wink, wink."

"Afraid not, my aunt and uncle from San Francisco are staying with me."

"Well then, where to?"

"How about Angelo Drive?" she asked, and then added, "Wink, wink."

Angelo Drive had become our favorite place to neck, ever since we were rousted out of the Bean Fields. The well-known Bean Fields were south of Pico Boulevard in a former agricultural area. Beans were no longer grown there, because the land had been cleared before the war and was awaiting development. Its obvious advantages to young people were no houses, no streetlights, and no sidewalks for pedestrians. In other words, it was a great place for necking.

One month earlier, Linda and I were parked at the Bean Fields on a cloudy, cold night. It was darker than the inside of a Hasidic

Jew's pocket, as my father used to say—perfect for whatever a romantic couple had in mind. What we had in mind was hugging, kissing, and groping—just short of going all the way, to use the vernacular. Suddenly there was a flashlight shining through the driver's side window, and a police badge stuck up against the fogged-up glass. It was a Beverly Hills cop, and he just about scared us to death. I rolled down the window a few inches.

"What's going on, young man?"

"Nothing much, officer, we're talking."

"Do you always talk with your clothes half off?"

"We were feeling warm, that's all."

"Look, it could be dangerous out here. Go home and talk there. If you get going right now I won't cite you for loitering." Loitering? I never heard it called that.

That embarrassing experience led us to the discovery of Angelo Drive. Angelo Drive was a winding street above the Beverly Hills Hotel. At the very end of the street was a level area on which several houses would be built in the future. The area was large, unlit, private, and had a spectacular view of the city below. Needless to say, we were not there for the view.

I parked near the shrubbery bordering one side, and before the motor shut off, we were in each other's arms. Maybe it was the holiday, maybe it was Linda's parents being out of town, maybe it was the kosher turkey; whatever it was, I had never seen her so passionate. We kissed and fondled and groped and it could not have been more exciting. Within five minutes my shirt was unbuttoned and her bra was on the car floor.

"God, I love you," she said. "Let's do it, let's just do it."

We tried to lie across the bench seat, but the car wasn't wide enough, and the gearshift was in the way. So I shifted into second gear and opened my door so our feet could extend outside. I could not believe this was actually happening. In a moment I was inside her, locked together in the most breathtaking embrace of my life. It was incredible, thrilling, and the most sensual experience I could possibly imagine. I thought I might pass out from sheer ecstasy. We remained in that position for some time, and finally Linda said, "My God, you were sensational." Me? Sensational? It all seemed so natural.

"You were the sensation," I said. "You were just fantastic."

We got dressed, and said nothing more. I drove Linda home and walked her to the door.

"This has been so special," I said. "I've never felt like this before. You've given me the best present ever, and how appropriate it's Thanksgiving. I will be thankful to you forever."

"I love you, Peter, and I suspect I always will." We kissed one last time, and I walked to the car, still in a daze.

CHAPTER TWENTY-FOUR

Practice Makes Perfect

When I got home Alan was still awake. "Quite a gal you got there," he said. "I figured you'd never date, and if you did, it would be Marian the Librarian, or some other sexless old bag."

"I know tomorrow is your last day home," I said, "and I'm trying to avoid fighting with you, but honest to God, Alan, you acted tonight a like a complete and total asshole."

"Why, because I came onto your girlfriend?"

"Because you're inconsiderate and selfish. You're also unpleasant and mean. You have no concern for anyone but yourself, and you're a total embarrassment to this family. You're hopeless, and I'm disgusted with you."

"Hey, I gave you my car to use, didn't I? Doesn't that count for anything?"

"You can take your car, put it in high gear, and shove it. I'm going to sleep."

The events of the evening, from Thanksgiving dinner to my first, serious sexual experience to the upsetting scene with Alan, kept me awake for hours. Talk about mixed emotions. I didn't know whether to be giddy or sad or guilty or glad.

The day after Thanksgiving was a school holiday. I called Linda when I awoke.

"I can't tell you what last night meant to me," I said.

"Me too," she said. "I couldn't stop thinking about us, and how wonderful it was being together."

"When can I see you?" I asked. "Alan leaves late today, and I'll have the car again."

"I'm babysitting next door starting at seven. Why don't you come by at eight or so?"

My mother planned a special farewell lunch for Alan, and she invited my Uncle Nathan and all his recently married children. I had not seen my cousins since Gary's wedding, and I was curious to see if married life had changed them. The first to arrive was my cousin Kay. Alan and I carried Tony Franco in his wheelchair up to our apartment.

"Thanks, guys," he said. "Maybe I can do you a favor some time."

"Forget it, Tony," I said. "You're family now." He smiled and gave me a thumb's up.

"Where's you beautiful girlfriend?" asked Kay. "Are you still together?"

"She's busy today, but we're tighter than ever," I answered. If she only knew!

My Uncle Nathan and Aunt Gracie arrived next along with Shelly and her new husband, Bernie Balachik. Moments later Gary and Marianne showed up.

"Hiya Pretzel," Gary said. "How ya been?"

"That should be my question to you." I answered. "You're the newlyweds. So how's married life, you two?"

"I love it," he said, "and I'm not just saying that for Marianne's sake."

"He's right," said Marianne. "We never imagined everything would be so wonderful."

I walked over to the Balachiks and asked the same question.

"Oh, how nice of you to ask, Peter. We're just delighted to be married, aren't we, dear?"

Bernie looked uncomfortable, and it took him a long time to reply. "Yes, love," was his entire answer. Uh-oh, I thought. It sounded like a wistful plea to be back among the *real* polar bears.

When I spoke to Kay again I asked about her sister. "Is everything okay there?"

"Something's not quite right," she said. "If I had to guess, I'd say they haven't consummated their vows yet, and maybe never will. Shelly may not know how."

Weird, I thought; how could anyone not know how?

To no one's surprise, my mother served turkey sandwiches for lunch—kosher turkey sandwiches, to be exact. Everyone wanted to know about Alan's experiences in the Air Corps, and he regaled them with endless stories of heroic deeds, most of them products of his imagination.

"I had no idea," gasped my Aunt Gracie.

"None of us did," echoed my mother.

Our guests left late in the afternoon, and my mother asked Alan, "Where did those exciting stories come from? You never mentioned any of that to us."

"I figured they wanted to have a few thrills, so I embellished a couple of my adventures."

"Alan, you should be ashamed. You were telling lies to our family."

"It wasn't lying; I just added a few details."

A short time later an Army buddy came by to pick up Alan. It was time to return to camp.

My parents said their goodbyes, and then Alan turned to me and said, "I thought about what you said last night. I wouldn't say you're right, but you're not entirely wrong. And if I was out of line, I'm sorry.

I'll try to do better next time."

I gave him a hug and said, "You're still an asshole, Alan, but you're our asshole. What can we do?" And then he left.

I got to Linda's house at eight o'clock and found a note on the door that said: First door to the right. I knocked and a radiant Linda quickly pulled me inside and gave me a welcoming kiss. "The kid's asleep she said, and let's hope he stays that way. But let's be quiet for awhile."

"You're all I've been thinking about," I said. "I can't get over last night; it was fabulous. And seeing you now, all I want to do is hold you tight and cover you with kisses."

"All in good time," she said. "But let's be sure the kid is sound asleep. And another thing, I've been worried about last night—about using protection."

"I know—it was all so sudden. I didn't expect we'd get carried away. But nothing to worry about; I'm as prepared now as an ex-Boy Scout could possibly be. I've been carrying it around in my wallet for the past two years—just being optimistic, I guess."

"Is it still any good?"

"Actually, when I looked at it this morning it disintegrated before my very eyes. So I figured it was time to replace it." I don't know why we both found that funny, but she said, "Shush, you're going to wake the kid."

We sat on the couch, holding hands, for what seemed forever. Then she got up, turned down the lights, and we both slid down to the floor. In a moment we were half undressed and I was on top of her, our bodies melding into one. Could this possibly be happening, I wondered? It was like the night before, but more intimate, more intense, and even more thrilling. Within several more moments it ended, but the blissful glow remained.

"That was incredible," I said, "even better than before, if that's possible."

"Yes," she said, "but I'm worried; I think doing that here was a mistake. What if the parents came home early and walked in on us? I don't want to be caught that way. Besides, they trust me to watch their kid. If he cried during the last ten minutes, I wouldn't have heard a thing. We can't do this again." I was confused; was she announcing the end to our sex life? Oh, no, I thought, now that I've found Eden, how can she kick me out of the Garden?

"There's always the '36 Ford." I said, with some desperation.

"We'll think about it," she said, "but you better go now. I'd rather no one saw you here." We kissed goodnight and I went home. I still couldn't get over the thrill of the evening, but I couldn't be sure about our future. Had we gone too far too fast? Is that what was bothering her?

"Hey, lover-boy, how was your Thanksgiving?" It was Stan the Jerk. He was walking to class with Lenny Strauss.

"It was good," I said.

"I heard Linda was there."

"She was, but how did you know?"

"Roberta mentioned it. Have you banged her yet?"

"Why would you ask a stupid question like that?"

"Well, you're always with her, she had Thanksgiving dinner with your family, and you're probably as horny as any guy I know."

"Stan, you're being a jerk. Tell me, Lenny, how can you stand being around this guy?"

"Is that a yes, lover-boy?"

"It's whatever you want it to be. See ya later."

I saw Linda that afternoon; we had not spoken since the previous Friday night.

"How's it going?" I greeted her.

"Fine," she said. It felt a bit chilly. "And you?"

"Can't get you out of my mind," I answered. "When can I see you again?"

"You're seeing me right now."

"You know what I mean—together, alone; you know, wink, wink."

"Maybe we should cool it awhile; we're moving awfully fast, don't you think?"

"Well, no, but if that's what *you* think."

"That *is* what I think. But I do want to see you. How about a movie this weekend?"

My fears were confirmed; she wanted to see me, but apparently fully clothed and surrounded by other moviegoers. What would I do with those intense emotions surging through my body? How would I handle the incredible fantasies swirling through my mind for the past few days? What was I to do? I knew the answer before the echo of the questions faded. *You'll survive as you did when you were a pathetic virgin. It won't be as much fun; but like most people your age, you'll have sex alone—by yourself.*

We went to Hollywood on Friday night to see *State Fair*, a Rogers and Hammerstein musical with Jeanne Crain and Dana Andrews. It helped lift my spirits, especially when the two principals found true love, and danced happily into the sunset. Linda was still holding my hand and humming *It Might as Well be Spring* as we walked along Hollywood Boulevard. We stopped for a hamburger and then I asked, "Where to?"

"Do you think we dare visit Angelo Drive?" she asked.

"I dare if you dare—but are you sure?" She nodded.

What can I say? Here I was, seventeen years old, quite possibly oversexed, sitting beside a beautiful young girl. What would anyone else do? Did she ask me to stop when I undid her bra? Did she resist when we stretched out along the seat? Did she protest in any way when I removed her panties? Did she, at any point, say, "Stop"? The answer is no, no, no, and no. So why should I feel guilty? I don't know, but I did. We were quiet a long time, and then she broke the silence.

"You never once said you loved me."

So that was it. Could she possibly think I *didn't* love her; that I was just *using* her?

"Listen to me, Linda; I've loved you since my very first day at Horace Mann, when I felt I didn't have a friend in the world. Suddenly, there you were, talking to me, being compassionate, and offering friendship. Before I ever thought about sex, I thought about that sweet, adorable girl who was so nice to me. I've always loved you, Linda, and I still love you. I do, I really do."

She held me tighter and whispered, "And I love you, Peter, totally, completely, forever."

So with that problem behind us, what was next? The simple answer: unmitigated sex. Anytime, all the time, anywhere and everywhere—we were insatiable. Standing up, lying down, sitting in the car, even in the rumble seat. In the bushes, behind a tree, on the beach, in the bathroom, the closet, even the classroom. We couldn't get enough. We ignored the danger and took foolish risks, as we tempted fate at every encounter. Unbelievably, we never got caught. There were close calls, to be sure. Twice I leapt out her bedroom window with my clothes in my arms, and once I dived into the bushes at La Cienega Park to put my pants back on. But aside from temporarily raising my blood pressure, there was no lasting discomfort.

By the time the Christmas season rolled around we were obliged to take a sexual holiday. Linda went to San Francisco with her parents to spend the holidays with relatives, and I got a job selling Christmas trees at a lot on the corner of Wilshire and Doheny. An out-of-work Hollywood producer ran the lot, and our clientele included several film personalities. I sold trees to Gene Kelly, Joan Crawford, and Jack Benny, among others. It was a wonderful and profitable temporary job, and I was sad to see the holiday, and those generous tips, end.

I tried to interest my parents in having a tree, since I could buy one for cost, which was cheaper than wholesale. I figured my father would find that kind of bargain attractive.

"Isn't it bad enough you're selling those bushes to the *goyem*; do I have to have one, too?"

"That's a pretty old-fashioned idea; lots of people think Christmas trees are decorative."

"Decorative? Do you know anything about Christmas trees? Let me tell you something: the tradition began in Germany, and you know what anti-Semites *they* are. It was during the Middle Ages; fir trees were intended to honor the birth of Christ. Can you imagine? Since the birth of Christ no Jew has had a good night's sleep. And still, you want me to have a Christmas tree? What are you thinking? Hanukkah, that's what we celebrate. Not Christmas! Hanukkah!"

"I know, I know, but why not both? They're both happy holidays."

"One celebrates Christ, and the other celebrates a Jewish victory over anti-Semitic Syrians. Don't you get the difference? *Oy vey*, you know nothing; where have I failed you?"

"Okay, take it easy," I said. "You're beginning to sound like Sokolofski."

I celebrated New Year's Eve with Lenny Strauss and Stan the Jerk. We went to Hollywood Boulevard where the crowds at midnight were nearly as thick as at Times Square in New York. People filled the street and traffic came to a complete stop. There were horns, noisemakers, and confetti; and everybody was thrilled to celebrate our first New Year since the war's end. In fact, the event felt a lot like VJ Day. Many servicemen were in the crowd, and pretty young women were kissing them in gratitude for their service. Stan said to one of the girls, "You know, I may be in civvies, but I was right there on Omaha Beach when it counted." And he was rewarded with a deep and juicy kiss.

"You're terrible," Lenny said. "What a bullshitter!"

"And," continued Stan, "my buddy here was right next to me through it all".

Then the girl said to Lenny, "Okay, big boy, open wide!" Then she planted a terrific kiss on him. I really thought he was going to pass out.

"That-a-boy, Lenny," shouted Stan. "I think you just lost your virginity."

I missed Linda that night; ours would have been a much quieter celebration. But I was comfortable being with old friends, and we had a wonderful time together.

"Happy New Year," I said to them. "Call me crazy, but I love you guys."

"Me too," they answered in unison. Then we all hugged and went home. It was now 1946, and the world was at peace. I was in love, and it seemed that anything was possible.

CHAPTER TWENTY-FIVE

Reality Happens

When I returned to school, I saw Linda for the first time in two weeks.

"How were your holidays?" I asked.

"Not as good as they would have been with *you*. What did you do for New Years?"

"Lenny, Stan, and I went to Hollywood Boulevard to pick up some wild women."

"Any luck?" "Yeah, all three of us are engaged to be married."

"Hey, me too—to some sailor in Oakland. I didn't get his name, but what a body!"

"Think your sailor would mind if you went out with me?"

"Not if your wild woman doesn't mind you dating someone else."

"Well, here's a thought—let's not tell them."

We had a date Friday night and discovered that our sexual hijinks had become more intense, more original, and more exciting than ever. Any configuration a professional contortionist could conjure up, we could duplicate in the front seat of a 1936 Ford convertible, with the top up or down. But our activity was not restricted to the car. Linda's mother had a high level job at Lockheed Aircraft in the Valley, and so neither parent was home before five o'clock. That gave us an opportunity, most school-day afternoons, to continue our wayward ways. I would walk Linda home, we would satisfy our insatiable carnal desires, and we'd be doing homework when one or the other parent walked in.

"Hello, Peter," Mrs. Berg would say. "How nice of you to help Linda with her homework."

I wanted to say, after all she's done for me, this is the least I could do. But instead I said, "It's my pleasure." And indeed it was. Boy, was it!

The thought did occur to us, from time to time, that we were engaged in a forbidden activity. Wild, wonderful sex, especially between unmarried people, was prohibited since the original Book of Genesis. Given that we both knew right from wrong, I suppose you could assume we had no conscience; but that wasn't exactly true. I know I felt a sense of guilt, and I'm sure Linda did, too. Every so often she would say, "You know, we really shouldn't be doing this." But then she'd add, "On the other hand, who are we really hurting?"

We were now in our final semester of high school, and most Beverly High students were planning to go to college. I was taking a college preparatory course and was doing very well—practically straight A grades. But I still had no idea what I wanted to do with my life, or even what my college major might be. I saw an advisor at school and asked his opinion. After reviewing my record he said, "It appears you've had four years of math. I think *that* should be your major."

"I may have taken four years of math," I said, "but I certainly don't want to be a mathematician."

"We'll put you down as a math major anyway," he said, "and that will get you started." That turned out to be a terrible mistake, but I wouldn't know it for another six months.

Lenny had applied, and was readily accepted, at UCLA. He wanted to become either a research biologist or a physician. His grades were so phenomenal he probably could have attended any school in the country, or even the world. But his parents were reluctant to let him go too far from home. "Also," said his father, "it will be cheaper for us if you live at home." Poor Lenny, his parents just couldn't let go.

Stan the Jerk applied to Stanford. His grades were nothing special, but an uncle went to school there and had some influence with the Director of Admissions. Stan was awaiting final word from the school, but it looked good for him.

"How can your folks afford Stanford?" I asked. "That's an expensive school."

"My grandmother left a trust fund for my education," he said.

"You lucky bastard! What are you going to study?"

"I'm thinking about pre-law. I'd like to become an attorney; they make a fortune, you know, and no one screws with an attorney. Everyone's afraid of getting their ass sued off."

"Attorney sounds just right," I said. "Stan the Jerk, Attorney at Law— Asses Sued Off, Our Specialty. How perfect is that? You'll have to beat away clients with a stick."

So that left only me in the higher education quandary. What was I going to study, and where would I go to school? I couldn't very well discuss this with my parents. They were sympathetic, but neither had gone beyond the eighth grade. And no one in our entire family had attended college. To them, higher education was a vast and mysterious world. Their consistent answer to my quandary was always the same: "Do whatever makes you happy." But how could I possibly know what was going to make me happy? Lenny suggested I go to UCLA with him. "It's a good school," he said. "Just give it a try and you'll figure out a career later."

So that's what I did. I applied to UCLA and was accepted within a few weeks. My major? I went with my advisor's suggestion and put down math, but I might just as well have put down Brain Surgery, about which I knew nothing and cared about even less.

Linda's grades were about average, and her parents gave her three choices after graduation; go to City College, get a job, or get married. In other words, she had to get serious about her future.

"What am I going to do?" she asked. "I don't want to go to City College, that's for dummies; and I really don't want a stupid, low level job. Hey, I've got it, why don't you marry me? That would solve everything. Just look at the upside, I mean, we're sexually compatible, and besides, I know how to cook."

"Really tempting," I said, "but what'll we live on, sex three times a day?"

"That's not a bad idea."

"I think I have to do more with my life than operate a cash register in a cafeteria."

We joked about the future, but beneath it all, we were frightened and anxious. Graduating from high school was intimidating; we were being forced to grow up, and that was uncomfortable. I finally decided, what's the rush? I'll think about it tomorrow.

Tomorrow came much sooner than anyone could possibly imagine. Early in April, on a beautiful spring day, Linda passed me a note that said: *Meet me at the flagpole right after your last class. This is really, really important!*

"What's this all about?" I asked.

"I don't know how to say this," she answered.

"Say what?"

"Something's happened, and I'm afraid it's not good."

"Well, tell me, already, what happened?"

"Please, Peter, promise to be calm about this."

"I'm calm, I'm calm!" I was now shouting. "Just tell me what I'm supposed to be calm about!"

"I might be pregnant."

At first I thought I didn't hear right. Then I thought, ha, ha, this is supposed to be a joke. That's it—it's a joke. But it's not a very funny joke. Not funny at all. I leaned against the flagpole; I was beginning to feel dizzy.

"Okay, I guess this isn't a joke. How do you know you're pregnant?"

"My period is more than two weeks late, and I'm *never* late."

"Well, maybe things have changed. You never used to be late, and now you are. Anyway, I don't see how this could this have happened? We always used protection."

"Well, there was that one time when you didn't, and you said you'd pull out in time. Peter, I'm worried. What if I'm pregnant? What'll we do? Oh God! What are we going to do?"

"Okay, calm down. The first thing we've got to do is find out for sure if you're pregnant. We've got to see a doctor. Have you mentioned this to anyone else?"

"Nobody else knows anything."

"Do you know a doctor who deals with this kind of thing?"

"I don't want to see any doctor my parents know. I'll have to find another one. I could speak to Roberta about this. She's my best friend, and she knows about things like this. She's also discreet, and I trust her."

"Okay, speak to Roberta, but don't mention this to anyone else."

"I'll call you later she said. But for now, please tell me everything's going to be okay."

"Everything's going to be fine," I said. But I had all I could do to keep from throwing up.

I walked home in a daze; I simply could not come to terms with that unsettling news. If she really was pregnant, then I was about to be a father. A father! Me—a father? That was impossible; I was still a high school kid. What did I know about being a father? And now I'd have to get married. Married! If I were married, how would I support a family? Working in a school cafeteria? Washing cars? Setting pins in a bowling alley, for God's sake? I felt an anxiety attack coming on. I was practically in a panic. How the hell do I get out of this? If I were Alan, I'd just laugh it off and go on with life. And if I were my father I'd probably say, "Well, I suppose it could be worse." But how could it possibly be any worse? I used to be the good one, the one who followed the rules, the one who avoided trouble. Now here I was breaking the rules—serious rules. This wasn't a jaywalking kind of thing; this was more like murder in the first degree. Oh, God, my life is over! Forget college, forget the future, I'm finished. Nail the lid on the coffin; you're as good as dead, *boychik*.

"Peter, you look terrible," said my mother. "Is something the matter?" I was tempted to tell her she was about to be a grandmother, but I figured that might bring on an instantaneous stroke. So I said, "I'm okay, just a little tired. I'm going to my room to lie down."

I lay there for a long time, going over and over the same thoughts. Wait a minute, I thought, why am I rushing to dire conclusions? She may *not* be pregnant. Why the moaning, why the hand wringing, why are we rending our garments like some old Jew at the Wailing Wall? This whole thing might be one giant mistake! Then the phone rang.

"Hi," she said, "it's me. I just spoke to Roberta, and she offered to take me to a doctor she knows downtown. We're going tomorrow after school. I hope you don't mind, but I think it's better if you don't come along."

"Fine," I said. "I'm not sure I'd be much help anyway. But I want to know what's going on as soon as possible. Would you call me from there?"

"Of course. And, Peter, I know you're upset, and I'm really sorry about that."

"Thanks, but I guess you know, it's something we both did. I'm sorry, too. And remember, no matter how tomorrow turns out, we're going to do the right thing."

To say I had trouble sleeping that night would be the understatement of the century. I stared at the ceiling for hours and continued to wonder what I was going to do. I remembered the old Boy Scout advice: whenever you're in trouble, explore your available options. Okay, I thought, what if Linda got an abortion? That would not be easy; laws forbidding the procedure were very strict. I heard there *were* doctors who would perform the operation, but they were expensive. No one would risk losing his license for less than a few hundred dollars. Where would I get money like that, even if Linda agreed to it? Towards morning I fell asleep and awoke exhausted a couple of hours later.

I wandered around school the next day like a zombie, unable to concentrate on schoolwork. Around four in the afternoon I finally got the call. "Congratulations!" she said. "We made a baby." I nearly threw up again. You would have thought I was the one with morning sickness.

That evening we met to discuss our dilemma. I brought up the subject of abortion, and Linda expressed her reluctance. "It's not exactly a moral issue with me, it's just so scary."

"Well then," I said, "there's no other choice; we have to get married right away. I'm not bringing any little bastard into this world."

I don't know where that came from; it sounded like a line from a bad movie where the hero steps up to face his responsibility. *"Okay, fellas, you got me. I screwed up, but I'm man enough to admit it. I'm ready to own up to it, face the music, and take my medicine. Now do with me what you will."* Apparently, that meant getting married—and fast!

"You don't make marriage sound very romantic," she said. "Couldn't you at least get down on one knee?"

"Sorry, at the moment I'm not feeling very romantic. Here's a plan I've thought about. Next week is Spring Break, and I told my father I'd work that week at Transparent Materials. I think we should go to Las Vegas late one afternoon, get a quickie marriage, and drive back that night."

"How could we possibly do that in one night?"

"It's about two hundred and eighty miles, and we can drive that in about five hours. Allow about an hour for the ceremony and another five hours to get back, and that's eleven hours total. If we leave at, say, four in the afternoon, we should be home by about three in the morning. What do you think?"

"I think we won't have time for a honeymoon."

"Honeymoon! Honeymoon? What in God's name do you think we've been having for the past few months? The problem is, we had the honeymoon *before* the wedding. Our whole relationship has been one big, irresponsible honeymoon. A honeymoon is the least of our problems!"

I was yelling at Linda, but I was really angry with myself. You dumb, stupid *shmendrik*, I thought, if you had used your head instead of your *schlong*, you wouldn't be in this embarrassing fix. You've made a shambles of things, and now it's time to clean up your mess.

Anyway, we now had a plan; but the plan failed to address the bigger problem. What would happen *after* Las Vegas? That's what had me worried. Plenty worried.

CHAPTER TWENTY-SIX

Frustrations Of Sisyphus

Sisyphus was a king in Greek mythology whose indiscretions so offended the other gods, they administered a deserving punishment: Sisyphus was compelled to push a heavy boulder to the top of a hill. But before reaching the top, the boulder would escape, roll back down, and Sisyphus was obliged to start over. It was a futile, frustrating, and endless ordeal with, presumably, no chance of success. That, in a nutshell, describes our excursion to Las Vegas.

The trip began on Thursday afternoon during Spring Break week. I selected Thursday, because my mother would be attending her mah-jongg game at a neighbor's house a block away. We made detailed plans, hoping to avoid any obvious mishaps. The only thing left to do was gas up the Ford, pick up Linda, and drive like hell for five hours. I threw a small bag with a change of clothes into the car and hopped into the driver's seat. But there was a problem; the car wouldn't start. Coming home from work, only twenty minutes before, the car had operated perfectly. Now, it was like a recalcitrant mule; it refused to budge.

What a horrible omen, I thought. I lifted the hood and checked the plug and battery connections, and I double-checked the gas gauge. The engine still wouldn't start. I ran back to the house and called Linda.

"There's a problem: the car won't start."

"Oh, crap," she said—one of her favorite swear words. "Let me think a minute." There was silence on both ends of the line, and finally she said, "Here's an idea; we'll take my mother's car. She's out of town and won't be back until late tonight. I'm sure she won't check the garage until tomorrow morning, and we'll be back by then."

"Great!" I said, "I'll wait for you. Hurry!"

Within ten minutes I saw the pale green '40 Chevrolet sedan round the corner. She slid over, I hopped into the driver's seat, and we sped away. According to our strict schedule, we were now a half hour late.

"That was a close call," I said. "I didn't figure the car would poop out before we ever left home. What rotten luck!"

We headed east and said little until we reached San Bernardino, more than an hour later.

"We better stop here and get some gas," I said. "Care to use the rest room?"

"Never pass up an opportunity," she said. "According to the map there's an awful lot of desert after we leave here."

Indeed, it seemed an endless desert surrounded us. The desert soon became dark, and we saw nothing but the white line down the middle of the two-lane road. Even though it was a black and moonless night, there were a million stars. It all looked so eerie. I tried to maintain a steady speed between sixty and sixty-five miles per hour, which was about as fast as the old Chevy would go before its vibrations became worrisome.

"Care for a sandwich?" asked Linda. "I can offer you tuna fish or peanut butter."

"Not exactly the pre-nuptial dinner I had in mind," I said, "but it's much appreciated."

She also brought a thermos of coffee, which I suspected would come in handy later. We reached Barstow at six-thirty and stopped long enough to eat our sandwiches.

"A bit off schedule," I said, "but we should in Las Vegas before ten o'clock."

My optimism was premature, because an hour or so later, just as we reached the tiny town of Baker, we heard the frightening sound of metal parts clanking together under the old Chevy's hood.

"Damn it," I muttered. "Now what?" I stopped the engine, and the car continued to roll, as if guided by a mystical force, toward the Baker City Auto Repair Shop. The mechanic was preparing to close the place for the night.

"What's the trouble?" he asked.

"Don't know," I answered. "There was this awful clatter of metal, and the motor just stopped. I think you can help us?" Please, God, let him say yes.

"Let's get 'er up on the rack and I'll be able to tell ya more."

Linda and I stood there silently while her mother's car was hoisted on the rack. If her mother knew what was happening, she'd probably hoist me on a rack—the medieval kind—the kind designed for torture. The mechanic prodded and poked around like a doctor and finally said, "Ya threw a rod, but it ain't as bad as it coulda been. No serious damage to the engine."

"Can you fix it now?" I asked. "We're in a terrific hurry to get to Las Vegas."

"I was just shutting down for the night. Haven't even had dinner."

"It would mean so much if you could help us," said Linda. "And I've got some sandwiches you could have—tuna fish or peanut butter, or both."

"That's mighty tempting," he said. "Say, are you two fixin' to be married?"

Linda blushed. "How did you know that?"

"Lucky guess. But young fella, if ya don't mind my sayin', you don't look old enough to be datin' let alone marryin'. Anyway, let's see what I can do for your car."

212

"Thank you," we said in unison. Could this be divine intervention, I wondered? And then I discovered an identifying sign over the small office. Our guardian angel was named Mike Devine, which was really astounding, because an angel is a divine attendant of God. Get it? Mike Devine the divine attendant-mechanic. How weird is that?

The repair work took forever, and it was nearly nine o'clock before it was completed.

"That ought to get ya to Las Vegas" said Mike, "but don't go over sixty. Otherwise I'll be seein' ya on the way back."

"Anything else?" I asked.

"Yeah," he said, "be nice to each other; marriage takes a whole lotta work."

We thanked our angel and paid the bill. We had now spent our entire contingency fund. If anything else went wrong, our plan would fail miserably. We had a hundred miles to go, and I figured we wouldn't reach our destination until eleven o'clock, two hours later than I had originally calculated. Now the plan seemed riskier than ever, but it was too late to turn back.

We arrived in Las Vegas a bit before eleven and headed for the County Clerk's office. But first we stopped at a gas station to use the rest rooms as dressing rooms. I put on a coat and tie, and then applied a modest moustache with an eyebrow pencil Linda gave me. Since facial hair was still years away, I figured I had to do *something* to look older. I stood back to look at my reflection and was reminded of the way I looked years ago, when my father applied burnt cork moustaches at Halloween. I always went out dressed as a hobo, and my father always applied the phony moustache. I wished he were here now, because he would have done a better job. He also would have said, "Hey, relax, it could be worse." Linda came out of her rest room looking sensational. She wore a simple, short white dress, low heels, and a small white hat.

She looked almost old enough to be the mother of a twelve-year-old with a dirty upper lip.

"Can you do something to look older?" she asked. "You're supposed to be eighteen, and you don't even come close."

"What do you want me to do? I've got a baby face. How about if I walk hunched over and pretend I have a slight limp?"

"You could also drool a bit, but I still don't think you'll look eighteen."

"Well, it's too late now. Let's just hope the clerk has lousy eyesight."

We entered the County Clerk's office and I limped, hunched over, to the marriage license window. A tired looking woman handed us some forms, and we spent the next several minutes filling out personal information. When it came to the age question, I wrote eighteen and waited for a punishing bolt of lightning. At the bottom of the form was a place for my signature, which included the following: *I affirm that all information submitted is true.* I quickly signed the form and braced myself again for God's revenge.

We returned the forms to the clerk, who was now looking at the clock, wondering why it wasn't already midnight, their closing time.

"I'll need proof of age," she said sharply.

Without hesitation, I whipped out my phony driver's license, the doctored one I used whenever I needed to get into a nightclub. The clerk stared at it for what seemed forever. That's it, I figured; she knows it's a fake. The jig is up. Just point me towards the jail. Finally, she said, "I have a cousin living in Beverly Hills. Do you know Clementine Gooch?"

"Sorry," I said.

She reviewed Linda's information and never asked a single question. We paid our fee, and five minutes later were issued a license permitting us to marry in the state of Nevada.

"*Mazel tov*," I said. "Let's find a wedding chapel."

The first place we spotted was called Cupid's Little Dream Chapel.

"Well, if it's good enough for Cupid."

"Looks charming," said Linda.

A somber gentleman in a black suit met us in the foyer and said, "May I help you?"

"We want to be married as quickly as possible." I said. "Can you help us?"

"Would you like flowers, photos, organ music, perhaps a small choir?"

"We don't want any of that—we just want what's legally required to be married."

"Have you a witness?"

"No."

"Aha—so we'll have to provide a witness; that's the law, and there's an extra charge."

"Okay, any witness you can dig up is fine with us. But can we just get going?"

The gentleman, who turned out to be a Justice of the Peace, summoned his wife, who would be our witness. She was well-dressed and serious— typical of all professional witnesses, I assumed.

The ceremony was extraordinarily brief and resembled those you've seen dozens of times in old movies. *"Do you, Miss Berg, take this man … "* That sort of thing. I must admit I failed to hear nearly the entire recitation, because I was in a suspended state of disbelief. None of this seemed real; it was all so dreamlike. Well, I figured, sooner or later I'll probably wake up. At some point, I heard a voice saying, "You may now kiss the bride." We kissed, but I still felt detached and bizarre.

"Are you okay?" Linda asked. I noticed she had tears in her eyes.

"Sure," I said, "but you look so sad."

"Well, you look a little dopey," she said. "What a pair. We better get going."

It was now a quarter to twelve; our entire Las Vegas stopover was less than an hour. If we raced home, we'd make it back by five. We wanted to rest, but despite the stress and fatigue, we couldn't stop now. We got back on the road and I pushed the Chevy to its limit.

Suddenly, Linda said, "Pull over." We had been driving for thirty minutes, and there was nothing surrounding us but black desert.

"Why, what's wrong?"

"Nothing's wrong, but we have to take a minute to appreciate what's happened. We're married now, and I want to make love to you, legally, as man and wife. I think we deserve that much. This shouldn't take very long."

I pulled off the road, close to a grove of trees, and turned off the lights. I moved toward the passenger side of the car, and we embraced. Then she straddled me and, face-to-face, we joyfully consummated our recent vows.

"I love you," we both said, nearly in unison.

The Chevy hummed along without incident for the next couple of hours. We didn't speak much, because we were tired and very much in our own thoughts. What have I done, I kept wondering? Was it the right thing to do? I no longer knew. For so many years I was the good one; now I was as bad as my brother, maybe worse. I had knocked up my girlfriend, committed perjury to get a marriage license, and lied to my parents about where I was spending the evening. What was next? Mayhem? Robbery? Murder? Altogether, I wasn't very proud of myself.

We got to Barstow at three in the morning, the time I figured we'd be back home, and we still had a couple more hours of driving. It might just work, I thought—if nothing more goes wrong. What else *could* go wrong, I wondered? But I didn't wonder for long. About twenty minutes beyond Barstow we ran into a wall of fog that suddenly cut our visibility to twenty feet. We were driving through the thickest cloud you could imagine. There were virtually no other cars on the road, but I couldn't be sure when we'd run into one. Our speed dropped to about fifteen miles per hour. At this rate, I figured, we'll never get home.

"I don't know what more we can do," I complained. "We're screwed."

"Don't worry," said Linda, "we're doing everything we can. This is an act of God."

"Some God!" I said. "Whose side is he on, anyway? Say, do you remember when we were in sixth grade? We studied Greek mythology, and there was this guy, Sisyphus, whose punishment was to roll a huge stone uphill. And just as he reached the top of the hill, the stone got away from him and rolled back down the hill. Do you remember that? He kept pushing the stone and the stone kept rolling downhill. Over and over again. Well, that's the way I'm beginning to feel. Every time we get close to things working out, something awful happens, and we end up at the bottom of the hill. Do you think this is my punishment? I gotta tell you, I'm getting pretty damn tired of feeling like that poor *shlemazel*, Sisyphus."

The dense fog continued for about ten miles, and then it cleared as suddenly as it had appeared. I increased our speed to sixty and concentrated on the road's white line. I was so tired I felt my eyes begin to close. Gotta stay awake, I thought. I opened the window a crack, and the cold air helped revive me. Linda was napping next to me, and I would have given anything to curl up beside her. She looked so peaceful and so beautiful. She's my wife, I thought. How incredible!

By four-thirty we passed through Bakersfield, and with luck, I figured we'd make it home in an hour. While traveling through Pomona, I noticed in my rear view mirror the flashing red lights of a police patrol car. Oh no, I thought, the goddam boulder is rolling back down the hill again. I pulled over along the edge of the road, turned off the motor, and rolled down the window.

"Good evening young man," said the officer. "May I see your license and registration?"

"Sure," I answered. I handed him the car's registration and my phony license.

"Do you know why I stopped you?"

"No, sir, I don't. I believe I was driving within the speed limit."

"Yes, you were, but your right rear taillight is out."

"I had no idea," I said, which was one of my few truthful statements that evening.

"I'm going to give you a citation and an order to get it repaired. If you take care of it in the next ten days, there'll be no fine. Okay?"

"Fair enough, officer. I'll get right on it as soon as we get home."

"By the way, who's that next to you?"

"That's my girlfriend, er, I mean, my wife, sir."

"Is she drunk?"

"Oh, no, she's just exhausted. We were just married in Las Vegas."

"You don't look old enough to be married. How old are you, anyway?"

"Just like my license says, eighteen. People say I have a baby face."

"Yes, you do. Well, congratulations, and drive carefully."

I sat there until the patrol car drove away, and then I started to cry. What was I doing? I just lied to a policeman, and I saw my rap sheet grow longer than Pinocchio's nose. I wasn't cut out for a life of crime; I had all this Jewish guilt, and it was increasing exponentially. Here I was, married, a baby on the way, and no source of income. I had no idea how I'd escape this tangled mess. I didn't know if I should drive home or just go off in a totally different direction. So I sat there and cried and continued to feel sorry for myself.

"Why are we stopped?" Linda asked, as she suddenly came to life.

"Just got a warning from a cop," I said. "A rear taillight is burned out."

I started the car, Sisyphus and his wife, pushing that damn boulder uphill again. I suddenly didn't care about the time. Whatever it was, it was. And by the time we reached my house it was past six o'clock. I kissed Linda goodnight, and she drove home. I went in the house, sat down on my bed, and began to get undressed. Just then my father came into my room. "Oh, good," he said, "you're getting dressed. We have to leave here in another half hour."

CHAPTER TWENTY-SEVEN

The Whole Truth

I'll never know how I got through the day. I was virtually asleep on my feet for much of the time, and even when I was awake I had no idea what was going on. The pay I received that day from Transparent Materials Company was like a gift; I did little to earn it. I had now been awake for nearly thirty hours. I wanted to speak to Linda, but I figured she wouldn't be awake until well past noon. I called from the office during my lunch break.

"Hi there," I said, "it's your better half."

"Peter!" she cried, "I miss you terribly. How are you doing?"

"I'm dead tired," I said, "but I had to go to work. Any problem with the car?"

"No, I got it back in the garage a half hour before my folks got up this morning. They know I got home late, but they have no idea how late or what happened. We actually don't talk much."

"At some point we'll have to tell them what's what. This can't be a secret forever."

"I know, but not today."

"No, not today. I'm going home and plan to sleep most of tomorrow. It's Saturday, no work, just sleep. I'll call when I get up. I love you. Bye."

And that's what I did. We left the office at five, I skipped dinner, was asleep by six, and I didn't move until after ten the next morning. When I walked into the kitchen I got a funny look from my mother.

"You've been sleeping a long time," she said. "Is everything all right?"

"Yeah, just catching up, that's all."

"Are you sure that's all?" she asked. What did she mean? What could she possibly know?

"I was tired, so I slept. That's what teenagers do; they sleep a lot. Why the inquisition?"

"I just want to be sure you're all right. That's what mothers do; they ask questions."

My first order of business was getting my brother's car running. I walked down to Hobie's house and saw Mr. Johnson reading the newspaper in his usual chair on the front porch. It was now clear that he never worked; but also, since Hobie's death, he never left the house.

"Hi, Mr. Johnson," I called. "How are you doing?"

"Same as usual," he answered.

"Say, Mr. Johnson, I've got a problem with the Ford. Any chance you could take a look?"

Reggie Johnson was an expert auto mechanic in Bristol, before he emigrated from England. Much of Hobie's genius originated from his father's enthusiasm for all things mechanical. If anyone could help get the Ford running, he was the one.

We walked back to where the car was parked, and the first thing he did was take off the cap on the gas tank. Then he stuck a stick down into the tank. "You're out of gas," he said.

"But the gauge says I have a quarter tank."

"Also," he said, in his Cary Grant voice, "your gas gauge is on the fritz."

Had I consulted Mr. Johnson earlier, we could have avoided a lot of trouble. I walked to the gas station and got enough gas to get the car going. Then I filled the tank and drove to Linda's house.

"I'm so glad to see you," she said. "I can't believe what we did; did it really happen?"

"I'm afraid so. It seems like a dream, but I've got an official document that says we're hitched. Can't argue with that."

"What do we do now?" she asked.

"That's what I'm here to talk about. We've got to tell our parents; the sooner the better."

"I don't think I can do that," she said. "I've been thinking about this. My parents aren't like yours—they won't understand. They'll tell me how disappointed they are, how I've let them down, and that I probably did this to embarrass them. I can't go through that—it's too painful. They've never understood me, and they certainly won't understand this. I can't tell them anything."

"But they love you," I said. "I'm sure they'll understand."

"I know them better than you," she said, "and you're wrong. I'm just not telling them."

"So what'll you do? Wait until you have a baby and shout, 'Surprise!'"

"I don't know. I just don't know."

"Well, I've got to tell my folks. I can't ignore it. I'll do it tomorrow."

Like Linda, I didn't want to tell anybody anything. It was an embarrassment and an admission I had really screwed up. I knew it would be shocking news to my parents; they were conventional people, and they lived a decent, proper life. This would not go down well. I spent a fitful night and when I got up my father had already left for his regular Sunday morning horseshoe game with his old cronies. My mother was in the kitchen when I walked in.

"Good morning, darling, she said. You still don't look too good; what's bothering you?"

"I've something to tell you," I said, "but it's difficult to say."

"You know you can tell me anything." Boy, I hoped she meant that. Well, here goes.

"Linda and I are married," I blurted out.

"You're married?" she asked calmly.

"Yes." There was a very long pause.

"Is she pregnant?"

"I'm afraid so," I said.

She put her arms around me and said, "Oh, my poor baby boy, what have you done?" And then we both began to cry, each releasing giant sobs of anguish and relief and love. We clung to each other for a long time, and then I said, "I'm so sorry, I never meant for this to happen. I was the good one—remember? I don't know what went wrong; I tried to do the right thing, but everything has turned out so badly." I couldn't ever remember feeling so miserable.

"It's all right," she said "We'll figure this out. Don't worry, we'll figure this out."

We remained that way for a long time, and then she asked, "Do her parents know?"

"Nobody else knows. She doesn't want to tell her parents; she feels they wouldn't be sympathetic. They don't exactly have a great relationship."

"Bring her here, dear; we have to talk about this. And for the moment, let's not mention this to your father. There's always enough time to share disturbing news."

I picked up Linda later that day and drove her to our house. She looked distraught but more beautiful than ever. My mother had sent my father on a few errands, and we were alone.

"I'm happy to see you," she said to Linda, and she gave her a big hug. "Please sit down; we have to talk. I know you and Peter are in love; and it's only natural that you want to please one another. When two people feel that way they often express their love in ways that may create other problems. Neither of you is the first, nor will you be the last, to get into this kind of difficulty. I know you are good people and meant no harm to any one. However, you've created a potential new life, and that's the problem that concerns me." *That* was the problem that concerned us all!

"Neither of you is prepared to care for a baby; you're both in high school and still live at home. Where will you live? How will you support a child? How can you continue your education? You have promising futures, but if you're tied down with a baby, it will be difficult to realize those futures. I think you should consider your options, and one of those options is to terminate your pregnancy. This is serious business, but I believe your lives are more important than the embryo that's not yet a human being. If you make that decision, we can handle the details. Even though the procedure is illegal, countless pregnancies are terminated every day. We can find a doctor, but first, you must agree that this is what you want. Think about it and we can discuss it again when you've made a decision. But let's not wait too long; the clock is ticking. Meanwhile, let's keep this to ourselves; there's no need for anyone else to know."

"Mrs. Newman," Linda asked, "is having an abortion wrong; is it considered a sin?"

"Abortion is a serious matter. Some believe it's a sin; but Jewish law says that abortion is not a sin, since the embryo is not yet a human being. For a life to be human it must have a soul; and the soul doesn't enter a body until the first breath of air at birth. So, I can only say that it's a procedure that should be used with great discretion."

"Thank you," said Linda, "Peter and I have a lot to think about."

On the way back to Linda's house, we discussed the situation.

"A part of me wants to have your baby, but I know that's not very realistic. Everything your mother said was true; we have no idea how we'd manage our life with a new baby. Maybe we should solve this immediate problem, and think about having a child another time."

"I agree," I said. Boy, did I agree! I didn't want to be a father; it was the last thing in the world I wanted to be. But I felt the decision should be Linda's. After all, she was the pregnant one. By the time we got to Linda's house we had pretty much agreed to end the pregnancy. Later that night, I told my mother our decision.

"I think you're being sensible," she said.

My mother called my cousin Kay the following morning.

"I need your professional help," she said. "Peter and his girlfriend need to see a doctor at your Veteran's Hospital, someone who can terminate a pregnancy. Can you arrange it? We can pay the doctor directly."

"Of course," answered Kay. "I'll make the arrangements right away. I must say, this is a surprise. Who would have guessed that little rascal was *shtupping* that beautiful young girl? That's some boy you've got there, Jenny!"

"You don't have to tell *me*; I already know it."

I drove Linda to the hospital the following Friday, just after her parents left for work. The entire procedure took less than an hour, and she was home and in bed a short time later. That afternoon, unbeknown to me, my mother came by to sit with Linda and comfort her. She held her hand and said, "You're a brave and courageous girl, and we love you." And then Linda began to cry. "I love you, too. I wish *you* were my mother."

I visited Linda that evening. Mrs. Berg answered the door and said, "Linda seems to be under the weather; she's in bed. Perhaps you'd better come back another time."

"I won't stay long. I just want to say hello."

"Okay, but make it quick."

"Hi," I said. Linda looked so depressed, so exhausted, and yet, so pretty. "How'ya doing?"

"I'll survive. But, I'm so tired, and I'm sad, too. The kid might've become president."

"Yeah, I know. Maybe the greatest president who ever lived. Your mom wants you to rest, so I can't stay long. But I just want you to know, I'm sorry for causing such problems."

"Thanks, but we did this together." Then she closed her eyes and a tear ran down her cheek.

We were back in school Monday morning, and I wondered about events of the last ten days. What just happened? At the beginning of that time we were a conventional high school couple—holding hands, passing silly notes, and making plans for the senior prom. Ten days later we were married, had just aborted our first child, and were wondering how we suddenly became part of the messy adult world. Most teenagers can't wait to grow up, but we had just set a world's record. Maybe I was in love, but that didn't mean I wanted to be married. What I wanted was my previous life, where I could enjoy the good times with a minimum of responsibility. I guess that was it—the responsibility. I wasn't ready for it; I couldn't handle it. But how could I tell that to Linda?

It felt weird seeing one another the next few weeks; I concentrated more on my schoolwork and was anticipating graduation and college life in the fall. However, it was impossible to ignore the elephant in the room—*we were married!* What could I do about that? It was so peculiar; we didn't live together, I didn't earn a living, we weren't even intimate! Then, all of a sudden, the matter was resolved by one of those strange twists of fate.

"What's this?" asked Mrs. Berg of her daughter. She held out a letter from the California Highway Patrol. It said: *Due to your failure to correct the required automotive repairs noted in your recent citation, you are hereby ordered to appear in court and to pay the fine listed below.* "Peter is named on the citation as driver, and it was issued in Pomona at five o'clock in the morning three weeks ago. Why was he driving my car in Pomona at five in the morning? What automotive repairs are they talking about? Someone please tell me—what the hell is going on?"

The burned out taillight, Linda suddenly remembered. Caught red-handed; it's time for the truth; well, maybe not the *whole* truth.

"Better sit down, Mom." How shall I tell her, she wondered. Well, there's always the direct approach. "Peter and I got married—it was a spur-of-the-moment thing."

"You what? You got married? Are you crazy?" Then after a pause, "Or, are you pregnant?"

"No," she answered truthfully, "I'm not pregnant."

"Why would you do such an irresponsible thing? How could you be so stupid? You're too young to be married. Your father will have a stroke when he hears this. Oh God, what next?"

"Calm down, Mom. There's no reason to tell dad. We just did something impetuous; it's not exactly the end of the world."

"Oh no? Well, it's certainly the end of your marriage, that's for sure. We're having this marriage annulled! I've got to speak to Peter's parents."

The two mothers spoke later that day, and my mother said, "Of course you're right; I couldn't agree with you more. Leave it to us; I know an attorney who will file the annulment papers immediately. But I really think it's best if we leave our husbands out of this. It will just upset them terribly."

The papers were filed, and, as the petitioner, I was ordered to appear in court in about seven weeks, soon after graduation. I had never been in court, and the prospect was upsetting. But being back on the road to bachelorhood did much to calm me down. Linda's reaction was more equivocal. "I love the idea of being married to you," she said. "But I guess this is for the best."

So—you might ask—what did I learn from this emotionally wrenching experience? First and most importantly, I recalled my mother's words to my brother Alan over a year earlier: "Keep your pecker in your pants where it belongs." Heeding that advice would have avoided the entire, troublesome mess. Next, solve your problems in proper order. Dealing with the pregnancy should have preceded the rush to matrimony. The trip to Las Vegas needlessly complicated our lives. Finally, I learned that being seventeen is not the same as being a grown up. At that age, as I proved conclusively, one is old enough to get into gigantic, adult-sized predicaments, but it takes a loving mother to pat you on the head, give you a kiss, and make it all better.

CHAPTER TWENTY-EIGHT

Commencement

With the unselfish and loving help of my mother, I escaped a fate that, undoubtedly, would have changed the course of my life. Without her intervention, I have no idea where I'd be today; but it's likely I'd be emulating Sisyphus again. I'd be pushing that damn boulder up the hill and watching it roll back down—for an eternity. With a wife and a kid and no viable skills I wouldn't have had a chance.

With our immediate problems resolved, my relationship with Linda changed dramatically. Most notably, both of us feared further sexual activity. After one serious kiss I would be anxious and worried. One more kiss like that, I would think, and it's a one-way ticket back to Las Vegas and another panic call to Kay. Neither of us wanted to repeat that. And so, even though we enjoyed being together, we suffered sexual frustration and, to some degree, mutual resentment. It was not the carefree life we enjoyed a month ago; and slowly and sadly we began to we began to drift apart.

I had no desire to date anyone else; what would be the point? Linda was everything I ever wanted, and part of me remained in love with her. So I spent more time with my old pals, Lenny Strauss and Stan the Jerk.

"Where've you been?" asked Stan. "We haven't spent any time together in weeks."

"Mostly with Linda," I answered, "but we're kind of cooling it now. I have to concentrate on finals and I've got to find a summer job."

"By this time," said Stan, "you ought to be bangin' her, for sure."

Lenny came to my rescue. "Oh be quiet, Stan; you are so unbelievably crude. Is that all you think about? I'm beginning to think you're the one who needs to get laid."

For the past couple of months Linda and I had discussed our end-of-school activities. The Senior Prom and Grad Night were two of the most eagerly anticipated events of our high school lives, and we wanted to attend them together. These were the events that symbolized our commencement—an end as well as a beginning. They signified the end of our adolescence as well as our carefree and irresponsible lives. They also represented the beginning of our adult lives—attending college and contemplating a serious, lifetime career. As noble as these thoughts may have been, I wasn't ready to end or begin anything. Mostly I felt unprepared to face life. Nevertheless, we were being pushed out of our cozy nest, and all the birds were shouting, "Fly, damn you, fly!"

The Senior Prom was held at the Beverly Hills Hotel on the weekend prior to graduation. It was a formal affair with young women wearing long gowns, high heels, upswept hair, and sporting fragrant corsages. Young men wore dark suits, white shirts, colorful ties, and highly polished shoes. Everyone was scrubbed, scented, and not a hair on any head in the entire room seemed out of place. There was a small dance band on an elevated stage, and the room was decorated with orange and white streamers and colorful lights. The prom committee had done a sensational job, and we entered the enchanted space with wonder and delight.

Linda and I planned to meet her best friend, Roberta and her date, Roger Phelps. Roger was the son of the wealthy 20th Century Fox producer whose large house sat on five acres just north of the hotel. My visit there, when we first met, so intimidated me I didn't invite him to *my* house for over a year. When he finally did meet my folks, he was greatly impressed.

"Are they always like that?" he asked.

"Like what?"

"Well, they seem so interested in everything you do."

"Yeah, they're always hovering like a flock of vultures; it's really annoying."

"No, I mean they seem to care about you; really care about you. Not like my folks."

Roger was born with money, good looks, and a charming personality. What he didn't have and what he sorely missed, however, was a close relationship with his parents. His father was often away, and his mother, a part-time actress, had little time for him. Roger was an only child and often lonely. He was also a genuinely nice guy for whom I felt compassion. Roberta must have felt the same way, since she was so sweet and kind to him. Not surprisingly, Roger was crazy about her.

We sat at a table with two other couples. Lenny Strauss was with Carol Cohen, who was every bit Lenny's intellectual equal, and Stan Fishbein was with Anita Kornfeld. Yes, *that* Anita Kornfeld, the same Anita Kornfeld whose bare breast featured prominently in my first sexual encounter in the balcony of the Fox Wilshire Theater more than two years ago. Anita had grown into an attractive young woman who was strangely fascinated by my coarse friend, Stan the Jerk. Stan had matured in the last year or so and had become socially conscious to the point where even his socks matched. Nevertheless, he could still raise an eyebrow when he would say something like, "That's one Kornfeld I wouldn't mind plowing!"

So there we were, eight Beverly High classmates, sharing a richly decorated table, a memorable evening at the beautiful Beverly Hills Hotel, and a particularly poignant experience. The small band played our favorite standards, and couples danced slowly and closely together, as if they realized that in another week we'd all be traveling down different roads. I felt profoundly sad.

"What's wrong?" Linda wanted to know.

"I'm depressed," I said. "I don't want this to end."

"Graduation is supposed to be a happy time," she said.

"What's so happy about leaving your friends and having to grow up?"

Leaving my friends was only a part of it; I also regretted my separation from Linda, and I worried about my uncertain future at UCLA. There was no shortage of grim anxieties.

Lenny took me aside and asked, "What's going on? You don't seem happy to be here."

"Yeah," chimed in Stan, "you look like you're going to a funeral. Cheer up, buddy, maybe one of us will get laid tonight." That did it; I had to laugh.

"Did you bring your plow?" I asked. And then we all laughed some more.

When the band stopped playing and several couples began to leave, Roger invited us to continue the party at his mansion. "No one home," he said, "except the butler, maid, and cook." We laughed, but it was no joke; the entire staff greeted us when we arrived. The cook had prepared some delicious treats, the maid put some records on the phonograph, and the butler provided swimsuits for those who wanted to take a late night dip. I felt as though we were playing parts in some romantic Hollywood movie.

"Roberta and I are going for a swim," said Roger. "Anybody care to join us?"

"Why not?" said Linda. "C'mon, Peter, let's go."

We changed in the pool house and were soon splashing about in the Phelps's large pool.

After a while, Linda said, "I'm getting cold. Would you mind holding me?"

Me? Mind holding Linda? Our bodies separated by two thin swimsuits? Who would mind that? But wait a minute; was she tempting me or teasing me? Did I have enough self-control? I put my arms around her and every sensuous memory came flooding back. We were alone at the deep end of the pool and, almost involuntarily, my hands began to explore her body beneath the water.

"What's going on?" she asked. And then I kissed her.

"Don't do that if you don't mean it," she said.

"I can't help myself. Please tell me to stop, I don't think I can."

The next thing I knew our suits were sinking to the bottom of the dark pool. We held on to the side of the pool with one hand, and our lower bodies became tightly joined in blissful union.

"Don't make a sound," I warned, "and for God's sake, don't drown."

She giggled, and Roger asked, "Everything all right down there?"

"Couldn't be better," I answered.

After a short while I dived to the bottom of the pool, retrieved our borrowed suits, and exited the pool gracefully. We returned to the pool house, toweled off, and got dressed.

"What just happened? We weren't supposed to do that."

"You're right," I said, "I should have known better. It won't happen again."

Back at the house Lenny and Carol were examining the book collection in the library, and Stan was dancing in the living room with Anita. He had one hand inside the back of her dress and the other resting firmly on her beautiful behind. When we walked in they quickly assumed a more proper position.

"We've got to go," Linda said. "I told my parents I'd be home before sunrise."

We thanked our host, said goodbye to our friends, and I drove Linda straight home.

"Sorry," I said, "for what happened tonight. I have no will power, and I have no excuses."

"Well, I might have done more to preserve my honor," she said. "I feel just as guilty, but I'm probably not as sorry as you. So sue me."

We shared a tender kiss, and said goodnight.

Our graduation ceremony was held exactly one week later on the large terraced lawn of the school. Chairs were set up for families and friends, and several of my relatives came to wish me well. There were stirring speeches, musical interludes, awarding of scholastic medals, and finally the presentation of diplomas. It was a stirring program and classmates and guests alike shed a few tears. I saw my family after the program, and both my parents were still dabbing their eyes.

"Hey, it's a graduation, not a Shakespearian tragedy."

"We're so proud of you," my mother said. "Your father and I never got this far in school."

Kay was there, and so was her brother Gary.

"Nice going, Pretzel," he said, "and welcome to the grown-up world."

Kay said, "I noticed your friend Linda. She's lovelier than ever. Any chance for you two?"

"Who knows?" I answered. "Life is so unpredictable."

I said goodbye to many classmates and had no idea if I'd ever see them again. Others I would see at UCLA. Finally I saw Linda.

"I'm picking you up at six-thirty tonight. It's Grad Night you know. Don't forget."

"Forget? Are you crazy? I've been looking forward to this since I was a freshman."

There were two-hundred-and-fifty students in our graduating class, and nearly two hundred of them showed up for Grad Night. The event was held at Ocean Park, which was an amusement area on Santa Monica Pier. The pier extended several hundred feet into the Pacific Ocean, and contained carnival rides, restaurants, and a dance pavilion with a small band.

We planned to meet our friends at the Italian restaurant at the end of the pier. When we arrived, they already had a table.

"I like to propose a toast to us all," said Stan the Jerk. "We made it! Despite all odds, we made it! Hooray for us! No more Beverly High ever again!"

No more Beverly High, no more security blanket, no more happy memories. I was sinking into a depression again.

After dinner came the carnival rides. We ran to the merry-go-round and chose our favorite horses. Everyone wanted to win the brass ring, but Anita had the only success.

"It's an omen," said Stan. "She really knows how to pick 'em—for example—me."

Next was the Ferris wheel and we were suddenly lifted high above the crowd below and the ocean beyond.

"Wouldn't it be nice to stay up here for a while?" said Linda. "Great view, plenty of privacy, just the two of us."

I suddenly thought that the Ferris wheel was a perfect metaphor for my recent life—round and round, up and down, but not really getting anywhere. "Yeah, just the escape I'm looking for."

"Come on, Peter," Linda said, "we're going on the roller coaster. We've got to do something to get you out of this dark mood."

It didn't work. After the ride, in addition to the dark mood, I now had an upset stomach.

"I'm sorry to be such a pain," I said. "This is supposed to be a happy occasion, and I'm screwing it up for everybody. Maybe I should just jump over the rail and drown myself."

"I've a better idea," said Linda. "Let's go dancing."

We held each other tightly, and soon the worries began to fade away. Let tomorrow take care of itself, I thought, this is what I need right now. I kissed Linda and said, "Thanks, you always know just what to do." And that was the last time I would see her for a few months. She spent the entire summer back East.

So those were the highlights of my graduation night—enjoying the company of old friends and suffering anxieties about my future. But there was little time to wallow in my unhappiness; I was beginning my new summer job Monday morning at the RKO Studios in Hollywood. I was hired to be a lowly messenger, but it was an exciting opportunity to see movies being made. I had recently experienced a lifetime of reality; I was now ready for some good old-fashioned Hollywood fantasy.

CHAPTER TWENTY-NINE

Summer Interlude

In the summer of 1946, it would have been easier to break into Fort Knox than to get into a movie studio. Studio police guarded entrances around the clock, and those having no business there were routinely denied access. Sightseers never even made it to the front gate.

It was also nearly impossible to get a job there, even a job as lowly as a messenger; and believe me—no job was lower than a messenger. So how did I get the job? The same way most people in Hollywood got *their* jobs—nepotism. My father did business with an RKO purchasing agent, and the agent got me an interview. The interview was grueling; one would have thought I was being interviewed to replace Orson Welles in *Citizen Kane*. But the interviewer liked my enthusiasm, approved of my tidy appearance, and probably saw in me a budding sycophant.

"Report to Charlie Dingle at the Messenger Office," he said, "and good luck to you."

Why would I need good luck, I wondered? And where *was* the Messenger Office? I entered the vast main lot, got directions from a studio policeman, and was soon on my way to the Messenger Office. I became lost two more times, but eventually found the place.

"Where the hell you been, Newman?" asked my new boss. "I expected you half an hour ago." Charlie Dingle was a crusty old bird in his sixties who had worked in every phase of the movie business since silent film days. Despite a deficit of hair and a surplus of wrinkles he was still a handsome man. Dingle had seen it all, done it all, and was finally ending his career as head of the busy Messenger Office.

"Sorry, sir, I've never been on the lot before, and it's a bit confusing."

"Well, you better learn your way around; it's your job to find people wherever they are." Wherever they were could have been in any of two-dozen sound stages, a dozen office buildings, several shops, garages, a commissary, and an elaborate network of streets within the several acres of RKO property at Gower and Melrose. A veteran messenger, Robert Mitchum's sister Anne, suggested I take one of the studio bicycles and immediately tour the entire lot. "You're not going to last long if you don't know where to find people," she said.

I pedaled around the lot several times, and within days, the place became as familiar to me as my Gale Drive neighborhood. Most deliveries consisted of scripts, scheduling data, studio business, and personal communications. Messengers were warned that all communications were strictly confidential, and any breach of that confidentiality would result in immediate termination. "So don't go snoopin'," warned Charlie Dingle. "Most of this stuff ain't so interestin' anyway."

On my first day I delivered scoring changes to the music department, personal messages to the producer's building, drawings to the construction shop, scripts to and from the writer's building, and menus from the print shop to the commissary. The entire lot was alive with activity, and I found my new job fascinating. On my second day I delivered a message to a sound stage where a movie was currently being shot. I waited until the red light went off, signaling the end of shooting, and then I entered. A guard immediately asked what I was doing there.

"I have a message for Mr. Capra," I announced in my most official tone.

"He's right over there," directed the guard. He pointed to a short, unassuming man dressed in rumpled clothes. Could this possibly be the same Frank Capra who won directing Oscars for *It Happened One Night* and *Mr. Deeds Goes to Town*? And the man who gave me personal nightmares with *Lost Horizon*? Who would believe this *nebbishy* guy was Frank Capra?

"Message for you, sir," I said handing over the envelope. He thanked me, and then sat down to read the message. That's when I noticed the actor James Stewart standing nearby. What a great looking guy! He was standing on a bridge that was completely covered with fake snow, but the bridge was built on the floor of the sound stage. This was the scene where his character, George Bailey, contemplates suicide by leaping off the bridge into the river below, but there was no river. The film was called *It's a Wonderful Life.* Two days later I returned to that stage to deliver a message to a sound technician. It was one of the hottest days of the summer, but snow machines above the stage were grinding away. There was poor, suicidal George Bailey standing on the bridge and fake snow was coming down like it was the middle of February in St. Paul, Minnesota. Ah, the magic of Hollywood in action!

My mother, who was an ardent movie fan since the twenties, wanted to know everything I did and what I saw. She seemed more excited about my job than I.

"It's a job," I said. "Maybe the people are more interesting, but it's work."

"What? Pedaling around the lot, watching movie stars act? You call that work?"

That summer at RKO was particularly rich with interesting projects. One of the most exciting being filmed was *Sinbad the Sailor* with Douglas Fairbanks, Jr. On that sound stage, a large part of a sailing ship was built on springs so it could simulate the action of the sea. On the director's command large fans and fire hoses were turned on, and hundreds of gallons of water were driven over the bow as the ship plowed through one simulated storm after another. And there was Douglas Fairbanks, leaping around, sword in hand, like a storybook hero. I was absolutely enthralled.

On an adjacent stage Cary Grant was starring with Shirley Temple in the *Bachelor and the Bobby Soxer*. Shirley Temple was that great child star of the thirties who sang and tap-danced her way through some of the most memorable movies I'd ever seen. She was about my age and as cute as ever. A week later I delivered a message to Cary Grant. I went to the stage where his film was being shot, walked through the big soundproof door, and announced, "Message for Cary Grant!" A stagehand pointed to his dressing area, and I knocked on the door. "It's open," I heard a voice say. The voice sounded like Reggie Johnson, Hobie's father.

"Message for you, Mr. Grant"

"Thank you, young man. Do you mind waiting, this may require a reply."

"No problem at all, sir."

He read the message and began to write his response. "This may take a few minutes."

"Take all the time you need; I'm not going anywhere." I was kind of hoping he'd write a short story or maybe even a novel. Just being in his dressing room was such a thrill. I couldn't wait to tell my mother or Stan or even Lenny, who wasn't particularly impressed by movie stars. And I'd certainly mention this in my next letter to Linda.

"That ought to do it," he said as he handed me the written note. "By the way, you're new here, aren't you?"

"I started a couple of weeks ago," I answered.

"So, do you intend to go into show business, like the others?"

"Me? Oh no, I'm going to UCLA in September. But I'm not sure what I'll study. I put down math as a major, but I don't think that's for me.

Recently I thought I'd like to get away, become an adventurer and travel the world like Richard Halliburton. Do you know who he is?"

"Certainly do. Several years ago, before his tragic death, I met Richard. Fascinating guy, wonderful storyteller, and handsome as a leading man. You could do a lot worse than emulate Richard Halliburton."

I don't know why I told Cary Grant about my longing to get away, or about Halliburton; I hadn't mentioned that to anyone else. Lately, I'd been thinking that disappearing for a while might be my best move. And seeing the world had been a dream of mine for years. But why did I think Cary Grant would care about that? I felt like a total *shmendrik* and tried to change the subject.

"I've got to ask you, Mr. Grant, were you born in Bristol?"

"How did you know that?"

"My best friend's father was born in Bristol, and your accents are identical.

"What's his name?"

"Reginald Johnson. Wait 'til he hears this; he won't believe it. Well, I better get to work." "Yes, me too. By the way, young man, what's your name?"

"Peter, sir, Peter Newman. Nice talking to you, Mr. Grant."

"Same here, Peter. Hope to see you again."

In fact, we did see each other several times again. We even had lunch together once. While in the studio commissary one day I heard someone call my name. It was Cary Grant who said, "If you don't have a better offer, why don't you have lunch with me?"

We sat together and spoke about the film he was shooting, and then he asked, "How's the adventure business coming along? Any plans yet?"

"Nothing definite," I answered. "Actually, I'm still wondering if it's the right thing to do."

"Well here's something to think about" he said. "People don't usually regret the things they do nearly as much as the things they don't do. So, sometimes it pays to take a chance on your dreams; and, who knows, this may be one of those times."

I wouldn't say that Cary Grant and I became best friends, but we enjoyed a pleasant relationship. He seemed to like me, and I thought he was the nicest guy I ever met.

On a sunny Tuesday morning in July my mother and I went downtown for a final hearing on the annulment of my marriage. It was a day I had dreaded for more than two months, and I was still terrified as we entered the County Court building. The presiding judge, the Honorable Charles Allen Gifford looked as though he hadn't cracked a smile in about twenty years. When my case was called he spent several minutes shuffling through a file of papers, and then he looked at me with steely eyes.

"Mr. Newman," he began, "you don't look a day over fifteen. How did you convince anyone in the County Clerk's office you were eighteen years old?"

"That's just what I told them, sir."

"You told them you were eighteen, even though you weren't?"

"Yes, sir."

"Do you realize you committed perjury?"

"I know it wasn't right to lie, Your Honor, but we wanted to be married."

"Regardless of the reason, you perjured yourself before a County employee. Whether it's in Nevada, California, or Shanghai, China, it's still perjury. Do you know the penalty for perjury, Mr. Newman? Have you any idea what serious trouble you're in?"

Now I was really frightened. Judge Gifford looked like the worst kind of kangaroo court judge out of an old western movie. I'd be lucky to avoid the gallows.

"I meant no harm, sir, and nobody was really hurt."

But the old sadist wasn't quite through with me.

"You know, Mr. Newman, I could put you in jail for what you've done. You could end up working in a jute factory all day, sleeping on a hard cot at night, and eating watered-down soup three times a day. What do you think about that?"

What could I say? I felt like an abused character out of a Dickens novel. And what *was* a jute factory, anyway? The court was silent for a long time, and I noticed my mother was ready to throw herself onto the courtroom floor and plead for mercy. Would this nightmare ever end?

"Here's what I'm going to do," began the judge. "I'm going to grant your annulment and, because you've no previous record, refrain from punishing you for perjuring yourself. Now, you should understand what an annulment means. Your marriage is voided; from a legal standpoint, it never happened. I should also mention that if you ever appear in my court again, things will not go as well for you. So let this be a warning. You may go now."

"Thank you, Your Honor. I appreciate your kindness."

"And so do I," added my mother. But the judge was already reviewing his next case.

I'll never know how much of the court appearance my mother told my father, but he seemed particularly kind to me for the next several days. That night I wrote a letter to Linda informing her we were no longer married. I tried to express regret, but I was so clearly thrilled to be liberated, the words sounded hollow. A week later I received her response.

I have such mixed emotions about the news. I knew it was coming, but I'm so disappointed. I always wanted for us to be married, and we were, but it was for such a short time. Will it ever happen again? I can only hope. All my love always, Linda.

I began to feel guilty again. Our responses to the annulment could not have differed more.

I continued to enjoy my job at RKO, as each day brought new revelations. One day, while delivering a message to the model shop I noticed, standing inconspicuously in the corner, the original model of the most famous ape in cinema history, King Kong. There he was, no more than three feet high, but perfect in every detail. How did they get those shots of him holding a terrified Fay Wray? Again, it had to be the magic of Hollywood. I also discovered the recording studio, where background music was coordinated with a film's action. I spent countless hours watching film projected above the stage as the conductor led the impressive symphony orchestra.

As a messenger, I had complete access to all parts of the studio, but guards constantly challenged me as I loitered here and there. Anne Mitchum, my fellow messenger, advised me to always carry an envelope inscribed with the name, Moishe Pipik. When confronted, you would say you were looking for Mr. Pipik. The name sounded professional, but obscure, and nobody ever knew where to find him. Nobody even knew what department he worked for. Was he a writer, director, producer? Who cared? He didn't exist. And how do you expect me to know, anyway? I'm just a messenger.

All the messengers were bright and interesting, but Anne was my favorite. And, apparently, I was hers. She was three years older than I, attractive, and she had a million stories about the movie industry. Her brother, Robert Mitchum, had gotten her the job and often came by to say hello. He was a wild one, Anne said, but as his films became more successful, the studio warned him to behave more appropriately. Anne was a shameless flirt and I seemed to be her main target.

"Hey, Peter," she would say, "when are you going to ask me out?

Have you any idea what you're missing?"

I really liked Anne; she was great fun to be with. But my recent misadventures made me reluctant. Besides, I was still connected, more loosely now, but still connected to Linda.

"I'd love to go out with you," I'd say, "but I have a girlfriend who's back East, and anyway, I'm always broke."

"Tell you what—we won't tell your girlfriend, and how about if I pay? Or we could go to my place, smoke a little dope, see what develops; it wouldn't cost you a thing."

"Just my reputation," I'd say, "and probably my virginity." Then we'd both laugh. I thought about Anne for the rest of the summer, as I vacillated between guilt and arousal.

The summer ended and so did my job at RKO. Charlie Dingle and the messengers gave me a small going-away party, and for the final time, Anne propositioned me. Within a week I'd be a full-time student at UCLA. I needed time to prepare for my classes, buy books, and learn my way around campus. I also saw Linda a couple of times. It was not the same as before, but I wasn't sure what it was. Things will just work out, I figured—or maybe they won't.

I began to think about Richard Halliburton more frequently, and I started to contemplate life as an adventurer. How wonderful it would be to stand on the deck of a ship, see nothing but horizon in all directions, and head for some exotic port. "You could do a lot worse than emulate Halliburton," Cary Grant had said. Who was I to say he didn't know what he was talking about? And then I wondered—how *does* one get a job on a ship?

CHAPTER THIRTY

Ave Et Vale

UCLA was everything I feared it would be—difficult, impersonal, and not very interesting. It was like going to high school all over again, except it was much larger, farther from home, and not nearly as much fun. My high school geometry teacher, Miss Lindsey, advised that one should go to a college far enough away from home so that you couldn't easily come home on weekends. She would have clearly disapproved of my attending UCLA, where I was not only home on weekends, but on every other night of the week as well. So I was in college by day and treated like a little kid each night, and I was not very happy.

Another irritation coincided with the start of college life. My brother Alan was discharged from the Army Air Corps. Suddenly my lifelong, annoying roommate was back in my life, and just as suddenly, I was without the use of a car. So there went my privacy, my freedom of movement, and my motorized love nest. I was back to using the family Chevrolet, but only when available, and that wasn't often. Alan seemed to have no plans for the rest of his life; he was often home or hanging out with old friends. After a few days my father brought up the subject of his future.

"Have you thought about what you're going to do now, maybe go to school or get a job?"

"Not yet," answered Alan. "I just want to ease back into civilian life; there's no hurry."

"At some point you have to decide what you want to do," suggested my father.

"For the last couple of years," said Alan, "everything's been decided for me; what I did, what I wore, what I ate, and when I went to sleep and got up in the morning. I want the next decision—what I do with my life—to be mine. And I don't want to be rushed. Is that too much to ask?"

"Take your time," said my father. "I suppose it could be worse."

So Alan took his time, a couple of months, in fact, at which point nearly all his discharge pay was spent. And then he decided to go to the Sawyer School of Business in Westwood to study accounting. That turned out well for me, because I could drive with him and then walk from Sawyer to the UCLA campus in about five minutes.

My friend, Lenny Strauss, also attended UCLA and often rode to school with us. In exchange for that favor, Lenny tutored me in calculus. In every math class I ever took I never received less than an A. But for whatever reason, calculus became my Waterloo; I just didn't get it. A major problem was my teacher, Dr. Melkenstein, who was a chubby little refugee from Austria. Melkenstein had an accent thicker than week-old goulash. He made my old Hebrew teacher, Sokolofski, sound, by comparison, like the great actor, John Barrymore. Not only was Melkenstein incomprehensible, but when you asked for clarification, like Sokolofski, he became abusive.

"Vas you tink I mean, dummkopf?" he would say.

The textbook was little help. Page one of the introduction read: *We shall not attempt to give a definition of calculus. It is not merely a collection of theorems and formulas; in its principles are found powerful methods for applying mathematical reasoning to natural phenomena, particularly those where varying magnitudes are encountered.* I was defeated from the first words on page one.

Lenny used to do calculus problems in high school, for the fun of it, as others might do crossword puzzles. He was the perfect teacher. When he realized I didn't get it, he devised ways for me to correctly solve problems, even when I had no idea what the answers meant. After the first week, the idea of my being a math major became the most far-fetched, unrealistic fantasy. Happily, my other classes were easier, so flunking out of school was never a real possibility.

Despite earlier objections, Linda ended up at City College, the school for dummies, as she put it. Our schedules were such that we rarely saw one another during the week and sometimes not even on weekends. We still cared deeply for one another, but clearly, our relationship was changing. I think we feared the consequences of further, unrestrained sexual relations. We had been scared straight back to a state of virginity, and neither of us could be trusted to exercise restraint. Furthermore, once having tasted the fruits of paradise, it was difficult to settle for a diet of fish heads and rice. So we stayed in touch and spoke often, but we were definitely growing apart.

By the time the holiday season arrived I had pretty much made up my mind to leave school. I realized that abandoning UCLA after only one semester was an admission of failure; but if I continued, I knew I'd remain disinterested and depressed. I just couldn't face that. The question now was: what would I do? If I told my parents I was dropping out of school to become an adventurer, they would probably have me committed to an asylum. *"What kind of meshuggeneh idea is that?"* they would ask. And what could I say? I had no answer. So I remained quiet about my plans and continued researching how one actually got a maritime job.

Stan the Jerk came home from Stanford for the Christmas holiday. We had not been together for a few months, and because he rarely answered my letters, I knew little about his recent life. We got together with Lenny and enjoyed a wonderful evening that helped lift my spirits. Who would have guessed these old buddies could have such an effect on me?

"I gotta know," began Stan, "have you gotten laid yet?"

"Same old Stan," I said. "Remember our last conversation on the same subject? Well, nothing's changed; it's still none of your business."

"I get the feeling Stan wants to tell us something," said Lenny.

"Always the smart one," said Stan. "You can see right through me. Yes, boys, I've got big news. I lost my virginity in Palo Alto, and I'm damn proud of it. Wanna know the details?"

"No!" we both said in unison.

"Aw, c'mon, you're going to love this. It's a great story. She's a classmate, a babe, really built, definitely not a dog."

"Sounds like true love," said Lenny. "Is she retarded?"

"You guys are terrible. No, she's not retarded. And she thinks I'm a great lover."

"Gotta be retarded then. Everybody knows you're a lousy lover."

And that's how the evening went; high school banter, tasteless jokes, and a lot of genuine affection among old friends.

"How about you, Peter? What's going on?" I thought it was time to come clean.

"Unfortunately," I said, "things aren't going very well. Linda and I are moving in different directions; my brother's home again, and he's still a pain in the ass; and I can't stand UCLA. I'm thinking of dropping out of school and getting a job as a merchant seaman."

"What? Dropping out of school? Merchant seaman? What the hell are you talking about?"

"Like I told you, nothing in my life is working; I'm not interested in my studies, I'm depressed, bored with my routine, and I just want to get away. Sorry to say, fellas, I'm at an all-time low. What I really need is a new perspective. It may sound crazy to you, but that's how I feel."

"Well, yeah, crazy is about right," said Stan. "Isn't there another option?"

"Not one that interests me."

"Have you told your folks?" asked Lenny.

"Not yet, so don't say anything. I figured I'd finish the semester and then tell them, maybe a few days before they pull up the gangway behind me."

"Poor *shmuck*," said Stan, "I figured you had it made; wonderful parents, great girlfriend, smart, charming, and now you tell us you're all fucked up. Jeez, what's next?"

"I'm really sorry," said Lenny. "I knew you were depressed about calculus, but I had no idea you were so unhappy about everything else. Now that I think about it, maybe your plan's not so dumb. Sail off to, let's say, India, find a spiritual guide, and work it out. Why not?"

Revealing my plan suddenly made it more real. Now the question was: could I do it?"

Just before Christmas I received a package with an RKO return address. I unwrapped it and discovered it was a rare first edition of *The Royal Road to Romance*, Richard Halliburton's most famous work, published in 1925. Inside the cover was a handwritten note that said: *Follow Your Dream!* It was signed, *Kindest Personal Regards, Cary Grant*. I felt like crying. What a sweet and thoughtful present; and how perfectly timed. I was no longer uncertain; I now knew exactly what I would do.

Linda and I planned to spend New Year's Eve together at the Beverly Wilshire Hotel. As the date approached, I didn't particularly care if we went out or not. However, others were involved and I didn't want to be a total wet blanket, so I went along. It turned out to be a happy reunion with Roger and Roberta, Stan the Jerk and Anita Kornfeld, and Lenny Strauss who brought Carol Cohen. Roger and

Roberta were attending USC, as was Anita, and Carol was home from Sarah Lawrence. We were last together as a group on Grad Night, and the first thirty minutes was non-stop chattering as we caught up with the latest personal news. We drank champagne, ate a wonderful dinner, and danced, as the orchestra played continuous sweet music. Just before twelve-o-clock, waiters passed out funny hats, noisemakers, and confetti; and at the stroke of midnight the room erupted. The orchestra played *Auld Lang Syne*, and we threw confetti, tooted our horns, and kissed one another to welcome in the New Year. It was a wonderful celebration. It was also poignant; I had no idea when—or if—we would ever be together again.

Shortly after midnight Linda wanted to leave the party. We walked into the hotel foyer and she said, "I have a surprise for you." She held out a key. "Fourth floor, room 416."

"What's going on?" I wanted to know.

"Let's go upstairs, and I'll tell you."

When I saw the elegant room I said, "We can't afford this."

"Too late—I've already paid for it."

"But why?"

"Because I found out you're running off to sea, and I don't know if we'll ever be together again. Besides, I love you."

What could I say? I was overwhelmed with emotion. "I love you, too," I said. "But I thought we agreed not to do this any more. Anyway, I have no pajamas."

"Silly boy, you won't need pajamas; and I think, under the circumstances, we can indulge ourselves just this once. To put your mind at ease, I have a brand new diaphragm, and I'm dying to try it out."

We made love that night, and it was as exciting as the very first time. After a while she asked, "Now what's this silly business about becoming a sailor?"

"I was going to tell you," I said, "but apparently one of my indiscreet friends got to you first. I want to get away and see more of the world. Things aren't going well, and I'm not very happy."

"You seem pretty happy now."

"Of course, but I can't spend my life in bed with you; though it's not a bad second choice. I need to get away and figure out what to do with my life. You know, I've always admired Richard Halliburton, and I want to travel, as he did. I want to see foreign ports and historic monuments. I want to see the Eiffel Tower, the Parthenon in Athens, the Taj Mahal. I think this is the time of life to do that."

"I have the feeling I'll never see you again, and that makes me sad. I can't imagine a life without you." And then, very softly, she began to cry. After a long pause she said, "I'm sorry; I didn't mean to do that. I don't want to make you feel guilty. How long will you be gone?"

"I don't know. But I do know this this: I *will* see you again."

My next unpleasant task was telling my parents. It was something I didn't look forward to.

Everyone was home on New Year's Day and I figured it was now or never.

"I have something to tell you," I began, and I saw a worried look cross my mother's face. "It's not bad news," I said, "but it involves a big change in my life."

"So, tell us, already," said my father.

"I'm dropping out of UCLA, and I plan to get a job working on a merchant ship."

I might just as well have said, "I'm growing a new pair of wings and plan to fly off to the planet Mars." I never saw such looks of consternation. There was a long period of silence while the words penetrated the consciousness of each family member.

"Okay," said my father, "let's not get excited; we'll figure this out."

"What do you mean, let's not get excited?" said my mother. "It's too late, I'm already excited. What kind of *cockamamie* nonsense is this? You need an education, not an ocean cruise. I never heard of such a thing."

"It's not a cruise ship, Mom; I'll be working on a merchant ship."

"Sailing off with a bunch of hooligans, and drunkards? Is that any place for a nice Jewish boy? What are you trying to do, push us into an early grave?"

"I think it's a great idea," said my brother Alan. "I think I'll go along."

"No, Alan, you're not coming with me. You're part of the reason I want to get away from here. I need to be alone; I need time to sort things out. What I don't need is more stress. Think about it; I'm unhappy at school, I've no clue about my future, I need some time off."

I could see that nothing would be settled on New Year's Day. I had dropped a bomb, and we all needed time for the smoke to clear. School would be over in a month; and between now and then, I figured they'd get used to the idea. Less than two weeks later my father was heard to say, "You know, I've given this some thought and here's my decision— it could be worse."

The month passed quickly. I arranged for a leave of absence from UCLA, though I doubted I'd ever return. My grades for the semester were all Bs except for calculus, which was a C minus. Imagine that, a low average grade in a subject I didn't understand, and to this day, know absolutely nothing about. I also visited the Seafarer's Union Hall in San Pedro and inquired about joining the union and getting work. Currently, jobs were scarce in the Southern California ports, but the dispatcher suggested I go to Galveston, where there was a severe shortage of seamen.

So that's what I decided to do. I bought a one-way ticket on the

Sunset Limited, and the whole family drove me to Union Station downtown.

"Don't forget to write," said my mother. "We want to know that you're well."

"And be careful," advised my father. "We love you and want you to be safe."

"Of course," I said. "I'll write, be careful, and probably be home before you miss me."

But I was suddenly uneasy. What the hell was I doing? I was leaving the people who loved me to be with an unknown crew about whom I knew nothing. Would they be drunkards, pirates, or simple-minded misfits? Who knew? I was jumping off into the great unknown. And for what—to become an adventurer? What kind of harebrained scheme was that? Smart Jewish kids became doctors, attorneys, or violinists— not adventurers. Did you ever hear of a Jewish Marco Polo? I doubt it. And if you ran into a Jewish Lewis and Clark, you could bet they were a comedy team on their way to the Catskills. It occurred to me that running off to sea was more than a little risky. But wasn't all of life a risk? Wise men had declared for centuries that a life without risk was not a life worth living. Were they right about that? I figured I'd find out for myself.

"Not too late to have me join you," said Alan.

"I'm afraid it is," I said. "But, stay out of trouble and stay in school. We'll always need an accountant in the family." And then we kissed and hugged for the last time. My mother was sad. She couldn't understand why her baby boy wasn't happy, why he had to go gallivanting around the world searching for adventure.

I suddenly thought of the Roman, Catullus. He was the ancient poet who coined the term *Ave et Vale*—Hail and Farewell. As he visited the grave of his brother in Troy, Catullus wrote about the sorrow of separation from loved ones. *Ave et Vale, Hail and Farewell for an eternity. That at last I may give you this final gift in death, to speak in vain to silent ashes, since fortune has borne you away from me. Accept my gift of sadness; accept it flowing with brotherly tears. Ave, I greet you, and Vale, I bid you a sad goodbye. Hail and Farewell.*

I boarded my train and waved goodbye from the platform. My adolescence was at an end, and my adulthood was about to begin. I would be gone more than nine months, and when I returned I would be a young man. Not all my problems would be solved, but I would have the experience and maturity to establish a new and productive life. Most importantly, those I loved and those who loved me would still be there, standing on the sidelines, cheering me on.

9670

Printed in the United States
204750BV00002B/205-222/P

9 780595 4978